Llyfrgelloedd Caerdydd
www.caerdydd.gov.uk/llyfrgelloedd
Cardiff Libraries
www.cardiff.gov.uk/libraries

Christobel Kent was born in London and educated at Cambridge. She has lived variously in Essex, London and Italy. Her childhood included several years spent on a Thames sailing barge in Maldon, Essex with her father, stepmother, three siblings and four step-siblings. She now lives in both Cambridge and Florence with her husband and five children.

in
deep
water

Christobel Kent

SPHERE

SPHERE

First published in Great Britain in 2022 by Sphere

1 3 5 7 9 10 8 6 4 2

A CIP catalogue record for this book is available from the British Library.

Hardback ISBN 978-0-7515-7661-0
Trade Paperback ISBN 978-0-7515-7662-7

Typeset in Bembo by Palimpsest Book Productions Ltd., Falkirk, Stirlingshire

Printed and bound in Great Britain by Clays Ltd, Elcograf S.p.A.

Papers used by Sphere are from well-managed forests
and other responsible sources.

Sphere
An imprint of
Little, Brown Book Group
Carmelite House
50 Victoria Embankment
London
EC4Y 0DZ

An Hachette UK Company
www.hachette.co.uk

www.littlebrown.co.uk

For my mother Angela Kent née Argent,
May 13th 1924 – March 30th 1977

Prologue

Heather

At a certain point she thought, *the next thing that happens is, he kills me.*

She'd watched him play his set, the headphones on, one arm raised, she'd gazed. Across the dancing heads, he'd looked back at her.

His smell: sweat and dope. His voice. *It's your first time, isn't it?* Your first time was supposed to be magical, was that right?

The lights off the pier. The music still going on, the moving shadows, the grind and rattle of the stones under the waves, the stones that were under her back. And then his thing white in the darkness, she hadn't even seen one before and it wouldn't go in *I've never I've never* and the words were in her head, she didn't say them because he knew already.

He knew she'd never done it before. And she beat at it with her hands, her knee, and then he hit her. She could taste vomit and blood. He was whispering something, in her ear. She couldn't hear. She couldn't hear.

He was holding her by the throat.

'This is going to hurt,' he said.

Chapter One

Sukie

You can forget your comfort zone. She'd heard someone say that, or had she seen it online? *If you want to find someone, you have to push things.*

It was online dating. She'd done it before, fifteen, twenty, God, could it even be thirty dates?

Some of them awful, Sukie could say that now. Nobody's fault: say that quickly.

Sukie Alexander, whose mother thought she was still a virgin at almost thirty. Twenty-seven was almost thirty.

But it was a numbers game, you couldn't take it personally. The girls from work went on and on about how many bastards were out there, how it worked in a man's favour, how it was all about shagging, Sukie had listened patiently, she'd waited to explain. *The landscape's changing,* she'd tried to tell them that. *You have to do your research, there are sites for that.* For a quick fuck, although she wouldn't maybe put it that way. As a matter of fact Sukie didn't know if she'd ever said that actual word out loud, but she'd thought it. There are sites for people who just want sex, maybe with a different person every night, advertised like that. Down they went, up they came again, dishevelled and dauntless, battered and bruised, ready for another go.

And then there were sites for people who want a relationship: who want marriage, children, cohabitation, whatever. That was the dividing line and although there would be a few who crossed it, ended up in the wrong place – it was in everyone's interest to make sure they were talking to the right market. Right? It was evolving. It was turning into something good: you couldn't always do things the old way.

Was she beautiful? Looking at herself in the mirror and seeing herself fresh-faced with an anxious smile, a bit on the plump side. Some might say pretty. Beautiful? That was a question Sukie shied away from but then most sensible people do, because most sensible people know, *it's not all about that. It's really not.*

He said that. Jake said that.

And there he was now, standing there in this chilly un-familiar place with his hands in his pockets, he was looking a little away from her, his jaw was moving a little. He was worried about her. Worried *for* her. Of course he was.

You can't go on looking for ever, you can't go on waiting for perfect to come along. You have to get real.

And then when you do – maybe you do have to forget your comfort zone.

The airport wasn't comfortable and that was for sure: dirty and cold, a draught from somewhere that wasn't air conditioning, and the landing strip that sat through the big grubby window beyond the luggage carousel looked bleak.

The carousel was hardly moving now and the whole place looked neglected, a half-built hangar, some bungalows up against a wire fence. But this island wasn't their final destination, Heather reminded herself. Jake was taking her home. To his home.

The carousel had emptied out now, a dusty backpack had been the only thing on it for ten minutes, and the other passengers had collected theirs and gone. Jake had his bag, it was resting against his leg. And his hand was on her shoulder.

Departure seemed like days ago and the big bright UK airport they'd flown out of seemed almost cosy from where Sukie was standing now and shivering, yawning and stiff after three cramped hours in an aeroplane. The sparkling floors in the duty-free – shots of Baileys on a cocktail cabinet and girls holding out perfume sticks, seven different food outlets, the men with pints in a dark bar, at five in the morning. Not the kind of place you were supposed to feel nostalgic for, not when you'd just started on your holiday, just the two of you.

It had been sweet of him to check it in for her and leave her to sit with her latte, but Sukie had felt the jitters set up before he'd even got out of sight and wished she might have gone with him. A woman leaning against the wall in the coffee bar had looked at her from over Jake's shoulder, a look that said to Sukie, what do you think you're doing with *him*? Unsettling her. Sukie had to admit, Jake was good-looking, in a dark sort of way, and the way he wore his clothes – maybe people did think he was out of her league. But then the woman had turned and gone and maybe it had been all Sukie's imagination.

Sukie had been thinking of her mother. Sitting with her latte, thinking about the look her mother would have given her, if she'd been in the airport, passing through and had seen them together.

And she might have been: Sukie's parents did a lot of travelling, since they'd retired. 'You can't take it with you,' her mother would say, at drinks parties, her father looking the other way, mildly. They'd gone to Bermuda last Christmas, and Sukie had stayed at home in her flat, which had suited her fine. She wished she'd known, that was all.

'They didn't *tell* you?' That had been Joey, from work, kind and shocked, and Sukie feeling the need to defend them, or defend herself, had said, 'Oh, of course they did. Don't be silly. I'd forgotten.' But she hadn't. They hadn't.

Her mother had been packing when Sukie had called to ask what time she should come, Christmas Eve or would they rather Christmas Day? And her mother had made an impatient noise. 'Talk to your father.'

Sukie had been born when her mother was twenty-six. 'I gave her the best years of my life,' Sukie had often heard her say, with a sigh, although Sukie, at twenty-seven, did always think but didn't ever feel able to say, that there might be better years.

So she'd been relieved, when they got through the sparkling brightly lit duty-free without coming across Marsha
trying on nail varnishes or getting a free makeover while
Sukie's father – for some reason she'd never had the same
anxiety about what to call her father, he played so little
part in either of their lives, just there, on the edge of things,
vague and dim and loitering, *my father* – looked at the single
malts. And guilty, and longing: Sukie loved her mother.
There wasn't really another word for it. Yearned for her,
which was how Sukie experienced love, the need for something that was missing.

There was no chance of seeing Marsha in an airport like
this, cold and dusty with three rows of plastic seating bolted
to the floor and a creaking carousel; Sukie was glad her
mother hadn't really been listening when she'd told her
on the phone, the words sounding odd and jumbled and
rushed, that she was going on a little break. If she'd said
it was to Greece, with a man she hardly knew, Marsha
would have been all ears, she'd have begun to rattle off an
interrogation – *you've known him a month?* – which was
why, although it was on the tip of Sukie's tongue to tell
her, she hadn't.

Funny thing was, in some part of her, Sukie knew, she'd
said yes when Jake had asked her to come because Marsha
would have been impressed. She could even hear Marsha's
voice in her head as she hesitated, even as Jake looked away,
already disappointed, *go on*. Go for it for once, get stuck in,
seize life with both hands. Carpe diem. Marsha said that a
lot.

7

Someone spoke.

It was Jake, and he was smiling, protective, looking into her face, and she felt a flood of something, gratitude, and the image of her mother, a painted head on a golf ball, rolled away, into the dusty corner of the airport.

'Sorry?' she said.

'I said, all right, little one?'

'Yes,' she said, squeezing his arm against her. *Little one*, she thought, grateful. I'm his little one.

Coming in to land they'd flown low over a beach and skimmed the roof of a squat hotel, a drained swimming pool beside a link fence, and there they were. He'd given her the window seat, he had insisted, and Sukie hadn't liked to go into how scared she was of flying at that point, it seemed both too late and too early.

'The island, you might – well no, I don't suppose you'd have heard of it. It's pretty wild. Off grid.' Hesitant. 'I want to know if you like it.' And in that moment so much had hung on Sukie's answer, and she knew it.

What would he have said, if she'd said no? Would his face have fallen?

Would she never have seen him again?

She had taken a deep breath. 'So romantic,' she said. 'Let's go. Let's do it.'

So they're doing it. They're going. They're here.

And how being beside the window made it worse: he so wanted to do everything for her, to make it all perfect. She'd taken the seat and surreptitiously pulled down the

8

blind and closed her eyes. She had slept, on and off: at one point she opened her eyes and he wasn't there, for a wild moment she'd thought, he's gone. Mid-air: he's gone. But there he was at the other end of the aisle, talking to a stewardess. The next time Sukie woke it was because he was leaning over her to pull up the little blind so he could see out, she could feel him warm and heavy, his shoulder against her breast as she pulled back to give him room, and they were landing.

They weren't going to sleep together on this holiday. It had been his suggestion and she had felt everything relax when he did, because almost immediately after she'd said yes it had begun to worry her. 'We won't' – hesitating, looking into her eyes until he had been sure she understood. 'Not until you're ready,' he said. Smiling. 'I'm too old these days to rush into anything.'

Forty-something – she'd have quite liked a look at his passport, it occurred to her, to know what the *something* was – wasn't too old. Marsha would have laughed at the idea.

There was a whine and a jerk now, the carousel gave a little jolt and another bag appeared at the top of the conveyor belt and Jake was pulling away from her, saying, 'Is that it?' But someone had stepped in between them and she couldn't see where he was pointing and he was moving, had broken into a little jog along the conveyor belt after the bag. She craned her neck to look after him. Sat back. At least he understood – about the sex. About waiting. Most men didn't. She shifted, thinking of those evenings.

And now her bag just wouldn't appear and it was the end of the season and it was colder than she'd thought it would be, the wind was blowing through the big airport doors that you could see beyond customs from the carousel if you turned the other way because the airport was so small, so flimsy, a concourse made out of a shoebox. A mangy pigeon had found its way in, through security, right into the baggage arrivals, pecking round an overflowing bin.

And Sukie was cold and tired, and she was worried about work because she'd had to shift a big edit over to Anastasia just like that. At the drop of a hat. And someone else had picked the bag up that Jake had thought was hers, and was walking off with it and it didn't look anything like her one, anyway.

But then Jake had turned and was walking back towards her, both hands spread as if to say, I tried, as if to say, sorry. And then he was in front of her and he said, softly, 'Sorry, darling.' And he held her face between his hands and kissed her, and she felt her eyes flutter closed.

Day One, Wednesday (earlier): Heather

Heather watched her mother go, lifted a hand to wave.

Mum was flying back to Scotland, wittering and anxious at the departure gate, reaching to clasp Heather's hand, her one and only child. Dad died two years ago and Mum was still turning around on the spot like an animal, looking for something that wasn't there any more, something she'd misplaced, not sure if she'd left her shopping on the bus or her husband, last seen in a pine box heading through the hessian curtains at the crematorium.

They'd moved – he and Mum – to Scotland not long before: it all came out of the blue. Well, only out of the blue if you didn't know the relationship between cigarette smoking and lung cancer. He knew it, Mum knew it, they all knew it. They'd tried, he'd tried. And then there he would be again, at the end of the garden, coughing in a haze of blue smoke. And then it was too late.

Heather missed her dad. There were things she wished she'd told him, though it didn't occur to her to tell them to her mother instead. *Bye, Mum,* she mouthed as her mother turned her head one last time from the far side of the barriers, through Plexiglas, stricken. *See you soon.*

And Mum was gone, through a grey door. She'd be all right.

And then Heather turned, and a couple was in her way, young woman, older man, dark-haired, walking across her path to a coffee bar and she didn't know which of her senses triggered it but the world – the wide glass of the windows, the ranked aeroplanes on their stands beyond, the strip lighting, the moving crowd – all spun around her. Dizzy, she stepped back, not knowing what had done it.

Oh, no. No. No.

The lights, the voices, the airport sounds seemed to come from far away, through a fog. She heard a roar in her ears like the sea crashing on stones, long ago, while someone held her down in the dark.

And when the world settled, the girl – the plump, pretty, anxious young woman in her floppy cardigan – was sipping her coffee, alone on a barstool and the man, the man – was walking away, towards a sign that said Check-In.

And setting down her coffee on the ledge – as if she knew what she was doing, as if she had planned all this – Heather pushed herself away from the wall, and followed him.

Chapter Two

A month ago: Sukie

The first time Sukie had seen him, as she peered round the door and there he was, that smile had been there. If she closed her eyes she could remember every detail of their first date and always would, she thought. It had been in a lovely old-fashioned pub, with booths, somewhere in the city. Victorian glass enclosing them, red velvet banquettes. He said in the messages that he worked nearby. His name was Jake Littlejohn, he was a graphic designer but he'd done all sorts, the music business. He'd lived. He was planning to start his own company. He told her about that later.

She knew there were people who said they knew already when the person was right, from the profile, from some detail or look or the books on the shelves in the background, but Sukie hadn't really had a special feeling, not then. It was when she saw him, that shy look from the table where he waited, that things began to look hopeful.

She asked for white wine and he bought her the small size. Most of them bought a double. When Sukie had told Joey that, she had frowned and said, 'Maybe they're just generous?' And Anastasia, still jaded after one of her nights out, had rolled her eyes. Maybe they were. Jake had got himself fizzy water. Sometimes, watching dates swallow one drink after another, Sukie had the horrible feeling that it was her, that they needed to get drunk just to sit at a table with her, so the fizzy water was a good sign.

Her mother would sigh, she knew that. *Let your hair down.* Pouring herself the third gin, slipping her feet out of high heels and averting her eyes from her hopeless daughter.

And Jake had been as nervous as she was. Turning a cardboard coaster over and over in his fingers at the table: his hands weren't like the rest of him, somehow. They were rough, the fingertips were discoloured. She had to blink away from her examination of them when he'd leaned forward and said, 'I love that.' Nodding.

He was nodding at her necklace, a tiny locket, old gold, that she had bought for herself. It was clever of him, Sukie thought, because she had learned to dress very quietly and carefully for dates, because if she wore something new or brave or bright she would only feel self-conscious, would worry people would get the wrong impression, and so she was wearing a dark knitted dress that covered everything and the locket was the only bit of her outfit she loved. She thought he might reach out and touch it and she could feel herself beginning to blush, but he didn't.

He read her mind. 'I hate this internet dating thing.' Sukie had almost been able to see tears in his eyes.

'How did you – get up the courage, then?' she said, watching his nervous fingers on the table top. 'You know. The internet dating.'

'Oh . . .' She remembered the hesitation, deciding whether to trust her. Then Jake had smiled. 'It was this – a friend of mine,' he said, with that frown she was beginning to love. 'He shoved me into it.'

'I'd like to meet your friends,' she'd said then, impulsively, and for a second had wondered if she'd said the wrong thing – too soon, too soon, because he stopped, the frown was there.

And then he'd said, 'You will.'

Day One, Wednesday: Heather

He was gone. *They* were gone, into the queue that snaked and looped back on itself, people shuffling towards the machines that would x-ray their bags.

She'd thought she'd lost him, coming round a corner, running into a queue for newspapers and some disabled seating and the illuminated check-in sign at the far end of the walkway. Thought they'd both lost him, and it had almost been a relief, deciding, he's just going to have her bag and run, he's just a thief, now, that's all he's become, thief, or conman. Heather thinking, she's safe anyway, that girl, woman, whoever she was, but whoever she was she had no clue, did she? What he was, what she was in for. You could see it in her face.

And then she'd seen him. Down to her left, sitting – not giving a shit – in the disabled area, bent over the bag and rummaging in it. There was an empty seat beside him.

So close Heather could feel the heat of his body, his thigh against hers. He didn't even look up. Whirring, her brain absorbed details, random. The dirt under his nails, scurf on the flattened crown of his hair. A luggage tag, face down, and all the time her heart hammered in her chest like a piston.

She made herself stay in her seat when he stood, eyes on the bag that hung, at knee level, in front of her. Count: one, two, three – and then she followed. When he got to check-in she took a seat, watching his back as he advanced in the queue. When he turned around there she would be.

You didn't always know. Heather had already learned that, of course. You didn't know how it would take you, when those chemicals flooded your body, they took you in their own direction, tumbling you in a roaring flood or turning you to stone. Heather could have run at him claws out, screaming, *it's you you fucking you fucking you fucking* or she could have lowered her head to hide herself, sitting like any other passenger in transit, absorbed in her phone. Typing over and over, *you fucking rapist*. But she'd done neither.

Something in her brain had clicked over, turned all the alarms off. He had edged forwards, leaned to charm the woman behind the counter, while behind him Heather had got out her phone, she'd polished the lens on her phone's camera, and waited for him to turn. Over the check-in woman's bowed head there was his destination. Their destination.

Now she had to let them go. She had to stand and watch as they held their barcodes to the barrier and it closed behind them with a big red cross barring her way.

There was an old fashion shoot she'd found, oh, years back, rootling through archives — that was her job, after all, the real world somewhere out there that no longer felt real — a sixties shoot of a model in a Perspex bubble like a toy, hands and feet spread and braced, fingertips against the glass, and that was all Heather could think of to explain how she felt, watching them walk ahead of her to the gates. She had become invisible. She could scream and shout from inside the bubble, and no one would hear.

'Madam?' She had reached the front of the queue and the woman behind the ticket desk had a foreign accent. The couple that had been haggling in front of her for what seemed like hours had disappeared.

And Heather was almost surprised to hear her own voice, answering. She cleared her throat. 'I'd like a ticket for that flight, please.' Realised she was talking nonsense, realised she could hardly tell what *did* make sense. 'The seven forty-five flight to Skiathos?' she said smoothly, looking up at the digital display over the woman's head, that read, six fifty-two.

Skiathos. It rang a bell, dimly. A gang from college, a boy

who had wanted them to all go with him to the Greek islands.

And Heather fumbled in her bag for her purse, the woman was talking but she couldn't hear, it didn't matter, she extracted her credit card. She raised her head, holding out the card, saying, 'Surely it can't be full, at this time of year,' and feeling herself smile pleasantly and sounding almost like a normal human being.

And in the same moment as she realised she didn't have her passport on her Heather heard the woman repeat, incredulous, 'I'm sorry, madam, but that gate has closed.'

In her bubble, Heather didn't blink. Her hand holding the credit card stayed where it was, steady. 'No, no,' she said, lowering it to the counter between them and giving it a little push. 'Sorry, I didn't make myself clear. I meant the next flight.'

The woman held her gaze, and Heather saw her wonder for a fraction of a second, then – what business was it of hers, after all – look down at her screen.

'I'm afraid there's nothing till tomorrow morning, madam,' she said.

A man stroking a girl's cheek, Heather saw it again as if a flashbulb had gone off, turning light to dark and back again.

Heather said something. She didn't know what she was saying, but the woman behind the ticket desk must have because she nodded, and smiled.

Her fingers flew across the keyboard, and a printer whirred, disgorging paper.

Chapter Three

Day One, Wednesday: Sukie

The carousel had finally stopped. A new flight was on its signage.

Jake had been pacing, angry. She supposed as he'd checked it in he felt responsible and when he turned back to her she said, smiling, 'It's fine, honestly. It's only a few days, I'll manage.'

'I'll talk to them.' Jake leaned down and kissed her, softly, and Sukie felt the bristle on his cheek with a small shiver of excitement, and she smelled the faint tang of his breath.

It was one of the things you had to get used to, she thought, watching him go over to the information desk, seeing him tap on it with his finger, still cross. Sukie pulled her cardigan round herself, wishing she'd brought a warmer coat than the mac she had over her arm. When you were close to someone, physically up close: the way they smelled. You couldn't expect that to come naturally. It was one of the things too, about how respectful he'd always been: after going out together for just over a month, sitting next to him on the flight had been the closest they'd been. And even then he'd been considerate, shifting his elbow from the armrest.

When he'd said he was planning a trip back home, and then – hesitating – 'I wonder . . .' with that clear-eyed look from under his dark eyebrows. 'I wonder if you'd like to come with me?' Sukie had thought, somewhere in the countryside, the Cotswolds. A weekend, a pub.

They had gone out west by the river, the pub had had horse brasses on the wall and smelled of roast dinners. As they had walked there side by side on the towpath when his hand had brushed against hers he'd made a shy, apologetic sound. They were on their second drink, in the window of the pub, when he started talking about where he'd been born.

Sukie could see, puzzled by his laughing expression when she said, 'Where, exactly?', that there was more to it. 'Greece,' he said, waiting for her astonishment. 'My parents had a house there, just a little place, two bedrooms, though.' Hesitating again, glancing up at her: had he changed his mind? 'I'm thinking of starting a business . . .' And then he'd dropped her hand.

'No,' he'd said. As nervous as her, and as shy. 'No – it's too much, too quick. I'm sorry.'

'Tell me about it,' she'd said. *Greece*, she thought, in wonder.

And sipping the warm white wine she'd listened to him talk about the sea and the light and the farmer of an olive grove who might supply him, the old olive press that might be brought back into service, and all the time wondering what Marsha would say, Marsha who sighed every time she looked at Sukie, and who'd told one of her friends, at a New Year's drinks party, that Sukie was a virgin and Sukie had been right behind her, thinking, *I'm not*, and even when her mother had turned around, Marsha had only sighed.

Sukie had held her breath just for a second before she said it. 'Yes. Yes, I'd love to.' And seeing his eyes widen, seeing his delight, had drained her glass and after only a second's hesitation, come *on*, kissed him. Kissed him on the lips, there in the pub. She had sat back, flushed, and then she had seen him smile.

Now her head ached, tight with tiredness. Getting up at four in the morning was enough to kill anyone's buzz: Joey had said that to Sukie when they'd gone for that last drink, their warm gaggle of women reduced to just her and Joey. Joey the scruffy one, the dozy one, the laid-back untidy perpetual kid although she, like Sukie, was edging towards thirty. Joey who was always one step behind everyone else.

They all worked together, revolving in and out of each other's orbits in the big glass building. She and Joey were in editorial although Joey should have been somewhere else, doing something that required less attention, she was always on the verge of being let go for some egregious oversight. Not so Sukie, who was valued for her stern scrupulousness with manuscripts, her cool courtesy, her strictness. One author, drunk at a party, had called her schoolmistressy, with a leer.

It was since Jake. Since she'd brought him into their conversation, not even a month ago, things had changed in their group. The girls – women, all clever, good at their jobs, all on the same wavelength Sukie always thought, and all single – had seemed to retreat. Jane in Rights had raised her eyebrows and said nothing, seeming offended, hurt almost, and started on her list of dates gone wrong. *Does he hold hands?* Anastasia the serial dater had been snide. *I bet you've stopped watching* Bake Off *and* Countdown. Only Joey had been oblivious, pleased for her.

But it had been down to dozy Joey to say, that last time, with a curious glance, 'Already? After, what's it been, a month? That's brave.' And then, seeing her face, had leaned in and squeezed her shoulder. 'Greece in November, though. Lovely. Just get some sleep on the plane, that's my tip.'

Which she had not done.

Sukie didn't know if she'd told them he was older than her – well, she did, and she hadn't – but a few years was nothing. Ten, fifteen, whatever. She wondered what her mother *would* say, if she confided. She might have had advice, sympathy – no. Sukie shelved that thought. Too late now, anyway. She looked down at her phone wondering if Joey might have texted, but there was nothing.

Oh, hang on. A missed call. Marsha: Sukie didn't know why her mother would be calling except she had a sixth sense for something Sukie didn't want to tell her, and always had had. Sukie's periods starting, for example. Two missed calls.

She'd have left a message if it was important: Sukie told herself it would just be gossip about someone she didn't know. But still she frowned down at the notification.

Now Jake was walking back towards her, smiling, holding her gaze across the great draughty concourse. Obedient,

Sukie watched him come, waiting, grateful: she could of course have gone to talk to the woman herself. She'd been about to do it, feeling in her handbag for the baggage sticker, when Jake had taken over, his hand on her arm, his voice soft. 'I speak some Greek, you see,' he said, although she could have sworn that, in the end, they were talking English at the information desk.

He put his arm round her, lightly.

'It's sorted,' he said. 'Now, can we start our holiday, please?'

Day One, Wednesday: Joey

On Sukie's desk the phone rang, loud, and Joey, dreaming out of the window at the grey London skyline, jumped, turned and stared at it.

It rang, on and on: from the next cubicle she could see Anastasia raise herself to look over the partition, first her annoyed eyebrows, then her eyes, enquiring.

Turning her back on Anastasia, Joey picked up the phone.

'Susan Alexander's phone,' she said, equably.

'Who's that?' The voice – it was a woman – was sharp and cross.

'Um . . .' And who are *you*? thought Joey, who was never annoyed, and never rude, but sometimes perplexed by people. 'This is Joanna Morris, I work with Su— Susan.' It must be an author. They could be extremely – *off*. How many comfortable conversations had she and Sukie had, pitying poor authors, losing their social skills one by one, working in their pyjamas. Joey tried to think what Sukie had been working on before she left. 'I'm sorry, may I ask—'

The woman didn't let her finish. 'Where's Sukie?'

'She's on leave,' said Joey, alarmed now. 'Look, perhaps I can help? May I ask who's—'

'Marsha Alexander,' said the woman impatiently. 'I'm her mother.'

'Oh,' said Joey, in a different voice. There was a silence, during which Marsha Alexander seemed to be reflecting, with difficulty, on something.

'I think . . .' Marsha Alexander sounded just grumpy now; she sounded almost apologetic. 'I think Sukie must have mentioned you,' she said. 'Joanna – ah – I think she did.'

'Joey,' said Joey, not at all convinced. 'No one calls me Joanna.'

'Oh.' Disappointment, now. 'Oh. So Joey's not – you're not a – boy, then. Boyfriend.'

'I'm not,' said Joey. Every time Sukie mentioned her mother, Joey had found herself getting stiff with – not anger, because that wasn't something Joey went in for – but upset. Disbelief. And she felt that stiffening now. Her own mother was a hugger and a lavisher of compliments, always begging Joey to come home for the weekend, when she would feed her till she almost burst, would drive her back to the station at the end of it and sit in the car waving till she'd disappeared.

Sukie's mother was not, it seemed safe to say, that type. Sukie's mother obviously spent their conversations listening for the mention of a man's name, any man. What Joey couldn't work out was, why she was on the phone now.

24

'Sorry,' Joey said, before she could stop herself. She felt a creep of unease. 'Look, Mrs Alexander, is there something I can do?'

'I've tried to get her on the phone,' said Marsha Alexander, and Joey wondered if the irritability was disguising something else. 'There's just some message about her not being available.' Outrage? Alarm?

Joey said, concerned now, 'Is there something wrong?' Sukie. 'Has something happened?' Sukie had no brothers and sisters, she knew that. 'Is it – is anyone ill?'

'Oh, for heaven's sake,' said Marsha Alexander. 'No, no one's ill, I just want to talk to my daughter.'

A silence, in deference, thought Joey, to the improbability of that statement. And Sukie's mother sighed. 'Look, Joanna. A – an old friend of mine, of ours, she telephoned me to say she'd seen Sukie at the airport, with a man. A – a boyfriend. I merely wanted to ask Sukie – to – catch up . . .'

Huh, thought Joey. She'd heard about all Marsha and her friends, always off in search of winter sun. 'Yes,' she said mildly. 'Sukie went on holiday yesterday with – Jake. He's called Jake Littlejohn.' She took a deep breath: this was Sukie's mother, after all. But as the words came out it sounded all wrong. It didn't sound like Sukie. It wasn't right, somehow. 'She met him online, they've gone off for a few days to the place where he grew up. In Greece. I mean he's not Greek,' *as if that mattered, shut up Joey*, but she stumbled on. 'His parents were English, he—'

'Yes,' said Marsha Alexander, sounding stiff and cross, as if wrestling with emotions unfamiliar to her. 'That's what

25

Julia – my friend – said. They were going to Greece. What – do you remember the name of the island?'

'Um . . .' Joey thought. 'Kyros?' she said.

Marsha didn't ask how she remembered: Joey wasn't sure herself, except when Sukie had told her she'd thought, instantly and not knowing why, *Don't go. Don't go.* And now looking back it seemed to her Sukie had given her a kind of look, asking to be stopped, and Joey had done nothing.

'Oh,' said Marsha Alexander, with a new tone in her voice. 'That place.'

'Do you know it?' asked Joey.

'Yes,' said Marsha Alexander stiffly. 'It was quite – notorious. Thirty,' she cleared her throat, 'forty years ago, perhaps.' A pause. 'Before my time, obviously.'

'Notorious?' Joey didn't understand. 'What for?'

'Oh,' Marsha became vague suddenly, 'you know. Bohemians. Poetry and . . . and all that kind of thing. Expat community. Then it all fell apart, of course.'

The glass towers on the skyline shimmered, blue-grey, and Joey just had time to imagine an island, far from here, far from towers and grey skies and sandwich bars and rush-hour crowds and to repeat it, *he grew up there*, when abruptly a helicopter materialised from between clouds, filling the air with noise.

'He what?'

'He grew up there,' said Joey, and there was a silence as the helicopter receded, a black dragonfly, across the river.

Joey said, 'Are you worried about her, Mrs Alexander?'

'Call me Marsha,' said Sukie's mother.

Chapter Four

Day One, Wednesday (evening): Heather

'Is everything OK?' said Kit. Heather made an effort to smile.

She'd tried to cancel, but Kit had, unusually, put up a fight. He'd booked the table weeks ago, and remembering that, she'd given in.

'Is it your mum?' Kit said. 'I thought she was a lot better this time. We had a few chats even, about your dad.' The restaurant was small and noisy, steamy from the open kitchen at the back and a lot of clattering.

'She did seem better,' said Heather. 'Just – when we were saying goodbye, you know.' She stopped, because the girl was there filling their glasses again.

It wasn't a fancy place, but it was warm. Heather had felt cold since this morning. Shivery with lack of sleep, and sort of – stunned. She didn't have to use the ticket. Had she just – gone mad? Started imagining things? 'I'm just tired. It was an early start.'

'Heather.' He leaned over the table. 'Don't worry, I'm not going to go down on one knee.' She jerked upright, pink with sudden distress. His uneasy jokes. 'Please, Kit . . .' *Not now. Not today.*

He looked at her steadily. 'If you don't want to be here,' he said, calm – Kit was always calm – 'we can go back . . .' but there was no point in finishing the sentence as neither of them had a place of their own to go back to. And as if from far off Heather knew, watching him: there'd come a time when they would be saying goodbye to each other, saying things like, *it just wasn't going anywhere.*

'Did something happen at the airport?' he said then, jolting her.

'You talked to her?' Heather said, lifting her glass again. 'To Mum?' Sidestepping the question, feeling everything hurry, hurry inside her.

It wasn't like she could tell him what had happened. She'd followed someone. A stranger, a chance encounter. On a feeling. It wouldn't have been the first time she'd been wrong.

It was an airport. People did that, wondered if they'd remembered to pack something crucial, had to go through their stuff to find it. All sorts of things happened in airports, they were weird places, faces you half knew passing, turning back into strangers, people free of their moorings, anxious, excited, carrying a little version of home in their suitcase. Make-up and teabags and never enough jumpers.

Her phone buzzed and she picked it up: nothing. A work message. She flipped it away in an agitation, knowing Kit would hate her for staring at a screen while she was in a restaurant with him but she couldn't stop, she didn't want to look up, she went on closing windows one after another and there was the picture. And she might as well have been in another world, back at the airport. Him.

'Heather?' She stared at him then, glazed; lowered the phone to her lap, hand over it.

If Kit had seen her, had wandered into the departures thinking he'd surprise her, already imagining the look on her face, and there she was, only what was she doing, he'd have thought, what the *fuck*? What's she doing *now*? Had the woman at the ticket desk thought that? As far as they were concerned she was just another traveller, passing through, just another customer, making enquiries as to ticket availability, destinations.

It glowed, in her lap.

At what point might Kit have intervened? Or would he have thought, *Better off out of here.*

The first two glasses had made things feel better. Heather could feel the third taking her in a different direction, somewhere less safe. But now she felt unsteady: she got up, leaned briefly on the table. 'Just a quick . . .' She didn't finish but turned and walked into the tiny cramped ladies' at the back of the restaurant.

Splashing water on her face she stopped and looked at herself. She was pale, and her hair was untidy, frizzed and damp now too. Her eyes were black, expressionless. I can cancel, she thought, yes. I'll do it now, and fumbled for her phone – but it wasn't in her pocket and she hurried back in, panicking now on top of everything else. For a blank moment she couldn't remember when she'd last seen it, she'd got up from the table, unbalanced—

And there it still was, on the table, or at least Kit had it in his hand, moving it out of the way because the food was arriving. He handed it to her with an expression she couldn't work out.

Heather sat. She'd looked forward to this for days, cosy seating and candles and steak and chips, but now she just stared at the food.

Kit leaned over and took one of her chips, and started up where they'd left off, so abruptly it took her a minute to realise he was talking about Mum, and everything softened, the light, the proportions of the room, the voices, murmuring.

'She said you must like me,' he said. She smiled, focusing.

'*She* likes you,' she said. 'But why's that, then? What makes her think I like you?' And in that moment she did, she liked him a lot, preparing to be pleased, wanting to hear what Mum thought.

He reached for another chip. 'Because she said I was the first boyfriend you'd told her about,' he said, easily. Heather's glass seemed to be empty again and she refilled it. 'She said you never mentioned any other boyfriends.'

'Other boyfriends,' she said, attempting a laugh. She couldn't imagine this conversation, Mum and Kit talking about her.

'Well, Sam, then,' said Kit. The room around them seemed too hot, suddenly. *Don't*, Heather told herself, in a moment of clarity. Not now. Don't get up and walk off; she could even hear the sound the chair would make if she did, the people in the tiny space turning to stare.

Sam, her ex. Kit had told her about his, a girl at school, one before her at college, someone she vaguely knew herself and could see hadn't been right for him. Too posh.

'Oh, *him*,' she said, her hand going out to the glass. They were staring, they were watching. 'Never mind bloody ancient history,' she said, trying to sound careless. 'I've been dreaming about steak all week.' He was still watching her. 'Shall we have some more wine?'

Chapter Five

Day One, Wednesday: Sukie

They sat outside a fly-blown bar on the harbour-front as the sun dipped, waiting for the ferry, drinking Greek coffee. The coffee was sweet and sludgy and good: Sukie sipped it tentatively, but Jake drained his cup straight away and was sitting forward now with his elbows on his knees, jiggling with impatience. Two or three pigeons were scratching round their feet in the dust and crumbs.

There'd been a couple of battered white taxis idling outside the airport but Jake had already told her it was only walking distance to the ferry so they came around the white cars and on towards the sea, that gleamed in sunshine at the end of the darkening road. Just beyond the runway they passed a succession of cheap-looking shut-up clubs, their neon signage dead and their windows shuttered, a hotel, a scattering of houses and a half-built villa complex that cast long strange shadows in the evening light.

And then the harbour-front appeared, and the chairs and tables of the couple of bars that were open, out of a dozen or so. There was a concrete dock and beyond it a low block of a building with a high fence around it and a little queue outside, a couple of men smoking, one large family — or maybe two small ones — with their belongings in big nylon laundry bags. The building was closed up, but the queue looked like it had nowhere else to be. On the side was a sign in several languages including English: Immigration.

Jake had paused as they came past it and a youngish man had come up to him from the queue; they'd exchanged words, friendly. Sukie had stood there waiting until he shook hands and turned back to her.

She waited until now, at the café table, to ask.

'Who was that?' she asked.

'He wanted money,' said Jake, sipping his coffee. 'They all do.'

'Is it — are they refugees?' she said.

'Yes,' said Jake. 'It's a new thing. Well, since a few years ago. From Syria, via Turkey.'

'What did you say to him?'

He tilted his head on one side, pushing his coffee away. 'You don't understand Greek, then?' he said, and she coloured. He patted her hand on the table. 'I'm joking,' he said.

There was a pause and she said, 'So what did you say?'

'I said, when I made my millions he could come and

work for me.' Jake leaned back and stretched. He shoved
back his chair.

'Your millions,' she said smiling. Jake had said he was
going to import olive oil, and she didn't think there was
much money in that. He leaned over the table to her quickly,
and took up her hand, threading his fingers through hers.
There was roughness at his palm.

'You didn't come for the riches, then?' he said. She felt
herself flush, awkward.

'Could he pick the olives?' She looked around. The blue
hills the far side of the bay looked completely barren. Jake
patted her hand.

'It's annoying,' he said, 'about your bag. But it'll turn up.
She said they'd get it to us, though. I left my name, our
numbers, and everything.'

And he stood up, restless. 'The boat won't be here for an
hour,' he said. 'Shall we go and find you something to wear?'
He rested a hand gently on her shoulder, those rough fingers
by her cheek. 'You're going to freeze to death.'

The last of the light was leaving the quay and the handful
of shops were closing up but one of them had rough blue
linen tunics hanging outside, knee-length, with hoods and
tassels. There were wire trays of shells on the pavement,
pink and white all tumbled together, and gleaming mother-
of pearl in the low light, and a short pouchy-faced brawny
woman was beginning to carry them inside. She eyed them
suspiciously but Jake began talking to her in Greek and
reluctantly she set down the tray she was carrying and gave
Sukie a little push inside.

There was a curtained cubicle at the end of a crowded, musty space, stacks of ancient-looking boxed toys, flags and ornaments. A shelf of hairy brown and cream sweaters sat along one wall and Sukie pointed, miming being cold, rubbing her arms, and the woman pulled a couple down. Jake stood in the doorway.

The curtain around the cubicle was skimpy, and emerging breathless with the struggle of getting inside the too-narrow tunic, and her thighs exposed, her knickers that had half pulled themselves down, she heard Jake's voice and a bright white light flickered on in the shop beyond the cubicle. Hurriedly she tried to tug the tunic down, feeling the light on her, and for a second she caught a glimpse of Jake's face through the curtain, watching her, appraising. She turned away quickly, before he could see that she'd seen his look.

'Coming out?' he said. She said something in reply, she didn't even know what, hearing her voice high and childish as she concentrated on tugging her clothes back on, and then she was pulling the curtains apart and stepping out.

'These'll do,' she said, smiling, smiling, holding the tunic out and a sweater that she hadn't even tried on but had to be warm. She felt hot just holding it against her.

Trying her Greek on the wary black-browed shopkeeper, *please* and *thank you*, for a second – stupidly, because who was he, her father? – she thought Jake would offer to pay for the stuff but he took a step away, instead, waiting discreetly in the door. Beyond him she could see the lights of a boat moving, coming in to dock. The woman softened just fractionally, taking down paper to wrap the things in. Sukie tried to thank her again but Jake interrupted them. 'We need to hurry,' he said. 'We'll miss the boat.' Handing over the paper bag, the woman asked him something in Greek; he replied curtly and she seemed to stiffen.

'Come on, then,' said Jake.

The sun was going down when they got back to the dock, a golden line on the horizon. The ferry was there, waiting.

Day One, Wednesday (evening): Heather

She knew it was the wine, that and Kit's bewildered look as she kissed him goodnight, and her key refusing to go into the lock and the mess that had reappeared in the sitting room when she did get back in. Jay and her boyfriend were on the settee eating takeaway and watching *Game of Thrones* on her laptop, Gill was talking on her mobile in her bedroom, complaining about someone. It was cold. 'Hey,' said Heather, and Jay looked up from the screen, blankly, and mumbled something.

It was shit happening, forces aligning: a woollen throw had fallen off the back of the sofa as she passed and Heather resisted kicking it. She leaned and picked it up and put it back. 'Night,' she murmured but they didn't hear, or at least didn't answer. She set her alarm for three.

Tucked up in bed, Joey had her phone in her hands, but she wasn't sure what to do.

It had been Sukie's mother; Joey had always had the impression she barely knew her daughter existed. Was she just – jealous? Because Sukie was off on a glamorous holiday? Not that. It had been the way she'd said, when she heard the name of the island, '*That* place?' Bohemians and poets weren't dangerous, were they?

'Marsha,' Joey said, trying to contain her impatience. 'Do you want me to get her to call you?'

'Oh,' and Marsha had sounded miserable, suddenly, forlorn, as if she knew she'd blown it. 'Well . . .' hesitating, 'perhaps it's difficult, being abroad, signal or something,' brightening, uncovering a rare moment of self-awareness. 'And if it's all going well, the last thing she needs is to phone her *mother*.' She cleared her throat. 'You might just tell her I . . . hope she's having a lovely time.'

And now Joey looked at the phone. She couldn't remember how long it had been since Sukie had last had a holiday. This had been her chance – her chance with a guy, her chance to escape from her nosy mother. Winter sunshine.

Something simple then. Something bright and encouraging. Not a warning, not passing on her mother's opinions, because this island, forty years had gone by, it had to be just a pretty tourist destination these days. Joey wasn't going to mention any of that. But there was nothing wrong with checking in with her best friend, was there?

Just in case.

Chapter Six

Day Two, Thursday: Heather

Blinking in the security queue, Heather couldn't quite believe she had managed it, had got here. She could have abandoned the whole thing more than once: clambering out of bed in the dark, almost forgetting her phone, waiting on the wet deserted street for an Uber that didn't appear and didn't appear. Last night, even, when she'd had to scramble to find her passport to check in. But the white car had rounded the corner in the dark, tyres hissing in the rain, just as she was about to give up, and she'd got the train with four minutes to spare, and here she was.

Walking past the coffee bar where she'd stood and watched them twenty-four hours before, Heather had felt her heart rate go up again, and it stayed up.

What the fuck, Heather? She could hear Kit's voice. Now,

as the security queue shuffled onwards under the bright, headache-inducing strip lights, she got out her phone.

There'd been a moment last night when his vague enquiries about her mum and the airport had turned to something else. The way he'd looked at her when she'd come back from the ladies'.

Her finger hovered over the message she'd begun in the Uber. *You remember I said something about getting away for a bit?* Of course, Kit had thought she'd meant with him. Something tightened inside her, uncomfortable. If you were with someone you shouldn't be feeling guilty all the time. She knew that. Heather the relationship expert, Heather who, as far as Kit knew, had had only one boyfriend: Sam her childhood sweetheart.

Just a long weekend, maybe four days. Clear my head, it's been a full-on couple of weeks.

She stared at the words. Behind her someone grumbled and looking up she saw the queue had moved, there was the list of things she couldn't take on board. Knives, scissors, liquids. *Remove your laptop from your bag, take off your coat.*

Would she have turned around and gone home if he'd gone straight to the check-in desk with the bag the woman had given him? With one of her strange headaches, perhaps, the kind she got when she'd seen something, that took her back?

It wasn't even a question of being reminded, because the memory, if she searched for it, wasn't there, at least not in the part of her that was brightly lit, where events had sharp outlines and stayed where they were put.

Birthday cakes. Watching *The Searchers* on the sofa with Dad. A girl in a long apron standing with her back to the camera. It had been the film that had got her interested enough to make film archive her job. She hadn't thought about that movie for a long time.

But she'd sat down next to him.

Heather hadn't been a nervous kid. She'd been bold, too bold if anything, too mouthy, too certain. She didn't know if she'd say, if she had a daughter of her own, you'll get yourself into trouble like that. Thinking you know best. Heather didn't plan on having any kids, so it wasn't going to come up.

He hadn't looked up. Heather didn't know what he'd been doing because by then he was doing it – a nylon roll bag – back up, tugging the zip around the corner of something inside. When he stood up again and the tag on the bag had flipped back at her knee, she had stared down at it. A woman's name, and if she blinked now she could see it again.

'Madam?' Heather was jerked back to the present: the security officer was directing her to load her bags and her coat on to the conveyor belt. Obediently she passed through the electronic scanner and for a moment she imagined the machine seeing inside her head, seeing the dark spot where that memory should be, that spot soft and black as mildew, blooming in a corner.

A soft beeping went off and she raised her arms as the

female security officer patted her down, then, walking on, retrieved her bag.

Who gave their bag to their boyfriend to check in? He must have done it on his ticket. Being nice. He wasn't being nice. She'd glimpsed something silky between his fingers and heard his breathing.

Was it? Was it? Was it him or was she completely fucking nuts? She'd sat beside him, next to him, it had been as if she could hear his heart beat, she could see right through him. Yes, it was him.

Heather's bag was light. Jeans, sweatshirt, jumper, two pairs of warm socks, underwear. The next flight back wasn't for three days, and Christ knew what in between – she couldn't think about that, about the fact that she had barely an idea of where she was going or what she was going to do when she got there. Greece was a long way away. She saw the whole mad plan as being of a piece with the empty space the scanner might have seen in her head, it was like stepping into darkness, she might never come out of it again. *Next thing that happens is, he kills me.*

It's just a little holiday. She could go, fail to find him, come back. Just a little holiday. Greece in November.

Who had the guy been, who'd gone to Greece from college? Needy guy. How long ago was college? Christ, ten years. She'd been a mess, at college, five years after – after. Mum had tried to persuade her to stay in Brighton but she'd gone as far away as someone would have her, Durham, not far enough but quiet enough, middle-aged enough. She hadn't wanted London or Manchester, no rave city. Just thinking about it − her and the other fuck-ups trying to get their lives together. She thought it had worked.

In her bag she had her passport and her debit card and fifteen euros left over from a trip to Paris with Kit nine months ago: it had been a short weekend instead of a long one, three meals in restaurants, two gallery visits, careful quiet sex in a hotel and a bit of hand-holding. And it was then, remembering that − as she walked away from security with her bag light over her shoulder and her passport ready and no one to worry about but herself, no hand to reject or accept − the cold, tight feeling her gut had been clenched around since she climbed out of bed turned into something else. Heather walked faster.

Day Two, Thursday: Sukie

When she woke, Sukie knew straight away she wasn't in her warm soft bed in her tiny flat with the noises of south London through the window. Her little nest, with her night light in the corner and her heaped pillows. It was very dark, and cold, and it smelled musty; the only thing that was the same was, she was alone.

It took her a few seconds to remember where she was and what she was doing there, because one thing it didn't feel like, was being on holiday. She lay still, and listened to the wind. It had blown steadily all night, giving her a head-ache. Something had rattled monotonously somewhere, and she had felt so cold under the thin covers she had begun hallucinating about hot-water bottles, and baths, until she'd crept out of the bed and found her cardigan, in the unfamiliar dark, on a chair.

She'd packed a nice nightdress – it was silk and lace and she'd never worn it – but it was in her bag. The only reason she'd hesitated when Jake offered to check her bag in was the silk slip thing she'd bought, in a hurry, handing over her credit card and looking away: what if someone opened the bag, what if he saw it? But there was no reason for that to happen. And besides, a silk nightdress didn't mean anything. It meant you wanted to look nice.

The taxi had been waiting to meet them off the ferry, engine running in the dark, the gleam of a cigarette behind the wheel. The driver had seemed to expect them, Jake had climbed in and spoken to him in Greek. And then the driver had leaned back over the seat, reaching with a hand that looked seamed and dirty in the yellow light. 'Please to meet you. So this is the lady, Mr Jake?'

Was he leering? She couldn't tell. She didn't want to be prejudiced.

And Jake had spoken in Greek again; it sounded a rough, hard sort of language in their mouths to Sukie, who was tired, who longed for something familiar. She wondered about hot-water bottles even then but had flushed in the dark as she imagined even asking. And the inside of the taxi was warm, even if it did smell of garlic and cigarettes.

He'd taken them up a rough piece of bumpy road to the house, dropping them at the foot of a path in the dark. There was no street lighting but the sky had cleared, there had been stars, a bit of moon, a path that seemed mostly rubble and was steep. More than once she had to reach out to grab Jake, who had stood still each time and waited for her to regain her balance. Then it had levelled out, was more like old smooth paving, weeds here and there black in the light of the moon. They got to a kind of crossroads, a little house, a fig tree losing its leaves.

'Here we are,' Jake had whispered, and had led her inside. The smell of the fig gave way to a smell of paraffin, something she hadn't smelled in years, not since camping with the Guides and cooking on little stoves, burning herself and being told off, first by the guide leader then by . . . Marsha.

Where was he? In the bed now Sukie sat up, pulling the thin cover round her. There was a battered anglepoise beside the bed but when she flicked the switch nothing happened, and she remembered. When they got in last night Jake had lit a hurricane lamp and she'd said, 'Is there no electricity?' Hearing her voice high and stupid and panicky, hearing him laugh. 'There's a generator,' he'd said. She'd seen a big spider scuttle away across the floor.

And then he'd said, hearing her panic maybe, 'There are two bedrooms, like I told you.' Touching her arm, one second, then two, then he'd stepped back, watching her.

He'd told her there'd been one girl before her. A long-term girlfriend, they'd grown apart, her name had been Sabine, she had been German. She'd been demanding, he'd hinted – what had he said? 'She was . . . she wanted more than I could give her.' And something in the way he avoided

44

her eye – she'd understood. Straight away. And had put out her hand to him.

She wished he'd introduced her to some friends. She'd have liked to ask about Sabine.

Poor Jake. She listened now but couldn't hear anything, not breathing, not snoring – and swung her legs out of bed. On the floor beside it was the big paper bag with the tunic and the jumper: they'd seemed a shocking price, in the end, and Sukie had worried briefly about whether her pay would go in in time to cover it.

Jake hadn't asked how much she earned: some of the dates had. It was a question that shocked her. And she hadn't asked *him*, of course.

She took out the tunic, hastily tugged off the T-shirt she'd been sleeping in and pulled it over her head. The fabric was coarse and rough but she immediately felt better. Or at least warmer.

'Jake?' No answer. She tiptoed to the door, that opened on to a dim cluttered space, a kitchen with hob along the far wall, a chimney breast. It smelled cold and smoky, and light filtered around the edges of shuttered windows. Blue wooden shutters against whitewash: she opened the window and pushed them back and the light flooded in suddenly.

The sun was up, fast scudding cloud defined a horizon, a blustery day. Cold wind: she couldn't see the sea from here. Below her was the fig tree with half the leaves blown off, a small wooden terrace and along the wall she saw another pair of shutters, closed. She closed the window, and retreated inside.

There was no sign of him. No note. She pondered that. He'd left her to get some sleep. He'd left her, because he trusted her. And it had the advantage that she could look around without being observed. For the first time that morning Sukie felt herself relax, just a bit. Maybe she could – do some tidying up. There was another shuttered window and she opened that one, too. It looked over the big fig, and another, bigger house mostly obscured by it, on the other side of the crossroads she remembered from last night.

There was a fireplace but no wood; on the mantelpiece there was a curious elongated wooden sculpture that looked like . . . that had her averting her eyes. The place was dusty, unloved: Sukie found a cloth, stiff and dry, in the sink, she soaked it and squeezed it out and quickly, guiltily, ran it over the work surfaces, the hob – that was gas, at least. There was a light coating of dust on everything.

Once she could call what she was doing cleaning – setting bottles straight along the back of the work surface, scrubbing inside some mugs, wiping down surfaces – Sukie relaxed a bit more. Not snooping. Did it start to look clean? She wasn't sure. Looking for a tea towel she pulled drawers open and found dried-out wooden spoons, dust – and then something else.

It was a transparent folder of yellowing plastic full of photocopied pages. She lifted it out. It seemed to be instructions – for tenants, holidaymakers? Or maybe just friends of the family. She wondered who else Jake had brought here. Some photographs fell out and she picked them up quickly, just glancing at them – bleached out holiday snaps was what she took them for, beach pictures – and put them back in the folder. Carefully she took out the notes.

Compared with the kind of thing you got in an Airbnb, the notes in the folder looked amateur, and they were at least ten years old, maybe more from the note added later, in faded blue biro, *The World Wide Web hasn't arrived in Kyros yet. Right on: enjoy, guys.* Faded photographs of a walk down to the harbour, some kind of trees in pink blossom, a little hand-drawn map of the village, tiny cartoon heads. Names: Iannis. Sky, Ingrid, Leon. Nat and Betsy. Julian and Peggy, crossed through, and in another hand, David. She turned the map, puzzling over it, who was where. The place had seemed abandoned, last night.

Going back into the bedroom she'd slept in with the folder, Sukie opened the shutters. The bedroom was plain and empty, a room that hadn't been done yet – or was in the process of being dismantled or sold off, piece by piece. A pale square on one wall where something must have been taken down; a little wooden table but no chair. Jake was an only child like her, no one but him to keep the place in order after his parents had died.

A car accident: it must have been brutal. A shock. But after the way the taxi driver had thrown the car around last night . . . Looking down at herself Sukie realised she had got dust on her new tunic from the window. She rooted through her carry-on bag for her travel wash and found she'd stuffed in a spare pair of knickers, a toothbrush, a phone charger but no plug. On the wooden table beside the bed her phone was completely dead. *The World Wide Web hasn't reached us yet.*

She didn't know how long it was since she'd last heard it called that. She wondered what the parents had been like. Digital detox: she brightened at the thought. Except that she couldn't call anyone to tell them and for a second she wished she'd brought Joey along too, why not? Well, a few reasons why not.

The view from her bedroom was a holiday view, at least. A white wall, a bit of sky, some bougainvillea turning rusty. A village street, cobbled, whitewashed, weeds growing through the stones. Pretty, but so quiet. Almost . . . dead, and she had a sudden feeling then, that rose up in her before she could stop it, that she shouldn't have come here. That she hardly knew—

Stop it.

'Jake?' she said again, but still nothing. A door opposite her was ajar and going to it she pushed tentatively: the room was dim, a double bed with a rumpled cover, and his backpack open on it, but no Jake. The room smelled strange, fusty: she crossed to the window and opened it quickly. Turning, she saw that clothes were spilling out of his backpack and leaning down she sniffed. That was where the smell came from, she realised, a sour, animal smell which bothered her. Who packed dirty clothes for a holiday? She held her breath.

Poor Jake: no woman to tell him. She breathed out again. She could wash them for him, when she got the dust off her new tunic. Looking down, Sukie was beginning to be fond of it, it covered everything, it was warm and dry and smelled of some herb like lavender but not quite. Gingerly she pulled at one of the T-shirts stuffed in the bag, it emerged crumpled. Boxers were underneath it, could she wash his— She stopped. Glimpsed something. She let the boxers fall back to cover what she'd seen, which was a packet of condoms. And what else? Something else, the silver corner of a laptop, then a box spilling its contents, she wasn't quite sure what –

Pulling back abruptly she heard something, downstairs. Footsteps.

She ran, stumbling, pulling the shutters closed again. He would know. He wouldn't like it – who *would* like someone going through their things? It was wrong of her, very wrong.

Clattering on the stairs – she knew where the staircase was, they'd come in that way last night, through a kind of cellar where she'd dimly discerned the shapes of things – half a bicycle, something that might have been a chest freezer – she called out again. 'Jake?' Condoms. Even though . . . Best to be prepared. Wasn't that right? Even though they'd agreed. 'Jake?'

There was no one. But it wasn't completely dark: the door was open and as she moved into the space – it was a freezer, and there was a washing machine too but they both had their electrical cables coiled on top of them – she heard voices, outside. At the door sat a plastic bag. She could see the end of a loaf of bread in it. The voices murmured: through the door she could make out a pair of legs in jeans beyond the fig tree, someone was standing there talking.

She heard an old man's creaky voice, speaking American-accented English.

She remembered the little hand-drawn map, the little rough squares dotted around the village, each with their little household, crossed out one by one. Nat and Betsy, hanging on: it must be them.

'Jake?' she said for a third time, feeling strangely giddy. And then he was there, in the door, holding out his hand.

Chapter Seven

Day Two, Thursday: Joey

The office was quiet as it often was towards the end of the week, and as well as Sukie's neatly abandoned cubicle – the photograph of her and her dog, the pink plastic water bottle, the hand gel – Anastasia's position was empty too. She'd had a date herself, the night before, and told them she was taking the day off, told everyone who would listen.

Joey had had to send a message. Sukie would know her mother had called, her phone would tell her, and Joey was just putting her mind at rest.

Yesterday Anastasia had been so sure that this one was going to be a three-day fiesta, for the simple fact that it was just about sex. She'd managed to be evil about Sukie, while she bragged. They were meeting after dinner, her and the guy. 'He said,' said Anastasia, 'eat first.' Examining Joey for a reaction. 'Like, this isn't about fine dining or coffee, this is about one thing and one thing only. Not like three days with the Virgin Princess,' she said. 'Three days of yoga and crosswords? Not my idea of a man, if that's what he's after.'

Joey stared at her work screen, the words blurring. It made her feel ill, if she was honest; why hadn't she thought, sooner? Sukie on a dating app. She'd practically encouraged her. Joey checked her messages again: she'd sent it yesterday, it had been read, but there had been no reply. How hard would it have been just to say, *I'm fine, stop worrying?*

Joey thought of her friend's round pink and white face: always earnest, always understanding. Sukie never took offence, she was so reasonable, she always saw someone else's point of view. A little peacemaker.

Her thoughts shifted to Marsha, in whose shadow kind, considerate Sukie had been formed. As selfish, narcissistic, vain as Joey had always imagined her: yes. But.

The woman was fussing about nothing. Was she? A woman who'd gone away for Christmas without telling her only child? Well, almost.

Joey had to tell herself to stop thinking about Marsha Alexander and focus on the facts. She'd tried googling Kyros, Littlejohn, but had only found some articles online from an ancient publication, a Susannah Littlejohn writing about bringing up children in a Greek paradise, before she'd fallen asleep.

She had woken in the night. Anastasia's parting shot: 'You want to get it on with her yourself, is that it? Maybe that would work for the yoga and crossword guy, a bit of girl on girl,' and their little gang falling apart with the words.

A Greek paradise. Well.

It wouldn't do any harm, though. To . . . have a look. She had Sukie's password and everything. His profile might still be up, that in itself—

Pressing her lips together at the thought, at the idea of Anastasia walking in and catching her at it, Joey pushed herself back in her chair, flustered. But then again. Sukie was her friend.

She stood up slowly and crossed to Sukie's desk, and turned the monitor towards her.

Day Two, Thursday: Heather

The plane was not much more than half full. Heather, with an empty seat between her and a woman hunched over the little window, was in the aisle. On a plane, a train, even in the cinema she'd perch on the edge of an aisle seat, she liked to be able to see the exits. Kit had asked her once, curious, had she ever been in a fire, and she hadn't known what he was talking about or why he would ask that question, until afterwards. So he'd noticed it. He always gave her the outside seat.

Kit. She could still see his face, flushed with the heat of the restaurant, staring at her as she picked up her phone, trying to work her out. She shifted in her seat, uncomfortable.

A guy. There'd been a guy at college, everyone said he'd been there years trying to finish a thesis, a sad chubby guy, who'd tried to get people together to come out here. What had his name been? She couldn't remember. Not her kind of guy. Something about him: involuntarily she heard herself make a sound, uncomfortable. Poor bloke.

The trip that hadn't happened, in the end. Every summer there was something. Thailand, Uruguay, the south of France; someone had an idea or a contact and a gang would coalesce, off they'd all go, except Heather would always have a reason not to.

She got out her phone, for the hundredth time. These days you could use the internet on some aeroplanes, but not this one. She'd done her googling as she waited to board, as she shuffled ahead in the queue, as they tutted behind her and a man ran his suitcase deliberately into her Achilles tendon.

A couple of pictures, and that was it, and one of them was a photograph of a luggage label. She'd had to take the picture quickly – obviously. People were wise to it these days. Heather had seen a fight start on the Tube when some hipster kid had photographed a guy's shoes and not been too clever about it. Heather hadn't had a chance to focus, because she was concentrating on not letting him become aware of her, as he moved past.

It hadn't been his bag, it had been hers, the girlfriend's. Heather had seen pink, she'd seen silk and lace. And sitting next to him, if her brain hadn't been sure, her body had.

All men weren't potential rapists. It was a mantra she'd had to go over and over in her head or she wouldn't have been able to *live*. There was her dad, a bloody angel, after all. All men weren't rapists. But plenty were.

She hadn't run screaming at him, in a crowded airport. She'd watched, she'd waited, she'd memorised. She'd taken pictures.

The luggage label had said SUSAN/SUKIE ALEXANDER.

Mum had marvelled at it, when she'd tracked down some old schoolfriend of Dad's for her, but you just needed to know where to look. Heather couldn't do her job without knowing that stuff. There'd been five or six Susan Alexanders on Facebook and Instagram, the one that looked like the girl in the airport hadn't posted anything or logged in on either, in almost a year. As a last resort – because who bothered, honestly – she tried LinkedIn. There was one Sukie.

And the girl's picture looked right. Sukie Alexander, Assistant Editor. She'd sent a request.

Cabin crew ten minutes to landing. Everything speeded up, suddenly, the trolleys withdrew, the crew lowered themselves into the jump seats and through the window, past the head of her sleeping neighbour, Heather saw the blue horizon tilt as the plane began to turn.

Day Two, Thursday: Sukie

'Breakfast,' said Jake, peering at Sukie. He was holding a paper bag, in the door to the basement room. She must have been staring because he said, 'Well, do you want to eat it down here?' and laughed. She turned for the stairs.

Jake was behind her, taking his time. Glancing back, she saw he was on his phone.

She took bread, feta cheese, olives, a pot of strange brownish jam and a jar of coffee out of the bag. There must be a shop. Civilisation. The bread was hard, it felt at least three days old. As Sukie poked a finger into it, considering, she remembered that her own phone was completely dead.

'The electricity—' Sukie began, standing over the food, but then she felt his hand on her hip. He was behind her at the breakfast bar and his face was in her hair. She held herself very still, although her instinct was to pull away. She could smell – something. Cigarettes? 'The electricity, is it – it . . .'

He stepped back.

'Gosh, yes, sorry,' he said, walking to the window and opening it, his back to her. 'The generator. And leaving you all alone like that without instructions.'

'Do you smoke?' she said then, without thinking. Because she knew he didn't, he'd said so in his profile. It would be like asking him if he was a liar.

'What are you, my mother?' he said, without looking round. *Oh*, she thought, *oh*. And there was something in his voice that constricted her throat. She stood very still and then he did turn.

He smiled. 'I'll go down to the town and ask the guy to come and sort it out,' he said, and moved off. He sat down on the sofa, frowning down at his mobile. She watched him, not sure what just happened.

In silence she toasted some bread in a frying pan, and boiled water for two mugs of coffee, then brought them both over with the jam.

'Talking to friends?' she asked, sitting beside him.

'What?' he said, and put the phone aside in a quick movement.

'I mean,' she said, 'you must have a lot of catching up to do whenever you come back?'

He shrugged, smiling. 'A bit. Most of my old friends have long gone.' He leaned his head back on the sofa, a funny look in his eyes, and Sukie wondered, a second, her idea of what his childhood must have been like – sun, sea, laughter – gone fuzzy. Then he straightened. 'Most of my . . . friends left. Children of expats. Well, left or, well, whatever.'

'Moved to the mainland?'

He gave her a curious look, shrugged. 'The locals did as well,' he said. 'Anyone with initiative. It's beautiful out here, all right, but there's not much work.' His hand was resting on the phone and he saw her looking. 'That was business,' he said. 'Just a little bit of business.'

'I see,' she said, and he heard her hesitation and sighed. 'Arranging for samples to be shipped back.' He pinched her cheek, gently. 'Enough information for you, miss?'

She tried to smile but his fingers were still on her cheek and he relaxed, let his hand drop. 'How've you still got charge?' she said. 'On the phone?'

'Oh, sorry, darling,' he said, 'I didn't think. I asked them to do it in the shop.'

'Maybe I can go later,' she said, taking a bite of the bread. It was very hard, and the jam – peach, maybe – was sharp but very good. 'You should import this stuff.'

'You're an expert now, are you?' he said indulgently and she said, deflated, 'Well, I thought I was here to help.'

'Don't worry,' he said, and a smile hovered. 'You will.'

She looked at him, uncertain. 'What was it like?' Her fingers were sticky. 'Growing up here?' He leaned back, looking up at the ceiling.

'Tell me about your childhood?' he said.

'Sorry,' Sukie said. 'I . . . it just must have been so different to – to mine.' She didn't want to tell him about her childhood: it was quite possible, in fact, that Jake thought her parents were dead. She may even have given him that impression herself. The last thing she'd wanted was Marsha, *saying* things.

He hesitated, just fractionally, and leaned back, considering her. 'It was wonderful,' he said. 'Idyllic. Can you even imagine? The freedom. There were only a handful of us kids up here, a little village school, and all this . . .' He gestured and she thought of the rocky hillside, the wide empty sea – and then of her own childhood. Her uniform – she'd loved her uniform. Laying it out every night, keeping it clean, a little beret with a button on it, school tie, pleated wool skirt, everyone the same. She'd loved school. She could imagine Jake laughing fondly, when she told him.

'I'd heard . . .' What had she heard? She'd googled, briefly, a couple of pictures. 'There was – a sort of community?'

Jake laid his head back on the sofa. 'Well, sort of.' He

frowned. 'Artists, poets came here, they'd stay a bit, bring their kids, move on. A lot of amazing influences.'

'Yes,' said Sukie, cheering up.

Jake was still talking, arm stretched along the sofa back. Sukie took a bite, the toast was getting cold: it tasted dusty and scorched. 'The locals didn't want to live up here because there'd been an earthquake that partially destroyed the old town.'

'An earthquake?' Sukie set down the toast carefully. 'Is it still . . .' She looked around, registering a crack above the fireplace, the wonky window frame.

'Well an earthquake zone's always an earthquake zone,' said Jake, turning to smile at her. 'But it meant it was all very cheap.' He shrugged ruefully. 'Artists, writers are always broke, aren't they?'

'Well,' said Sukie, taking the question seriously, thinking of a fat red-faced author who'd laid his hand on her knee and asked her if she wanted to sit in his Aston Martin, 'some are,' but Jake had moved on.

'I was born here, in this house, in 1979. Home birth.' Something in his face glinting as he watched her.

'Wow,' said Sukie faintly: he made it all sound like an adventure but the idea filled her with horror. What if . . . what if . . . She thought of the bumpy, half-made road, the lack of medical facilities, however many years back. 'Your mother must have been very brave.'

'Her?' Jake sounded disbelieving, getting to his feet. 'Yes, well. Anyway.'

'So you came – went – to England, how old were you?'

Standing over her, Jake cocked his head and with the gesture Sukie was aware of treading on unsafe ground, asking too many questions.

Could she go home now, if she wanted to? The question popped into her head out of nowhere. *No,* she told herself. *No. No.* Think what that would look like. And you want to be here. You do. This is your chance.

'Thirteen?' He was offhand, but watching her. 'Something like that. My mother's parents were loaded, they paid for me to go to boarding school. Then I was back for holidays.' He pulled out the chair, sat down, took a bite of the toast, then smiled.

'I'm quite normal really, honest,' he said, chewing. 'The children of old hippies are often the straightest people in the world.'

Sukie wasn't sure if that was true. He was looking at her sideways: maybe it was a joke.

'There are some people around here that you still know, though, right?' she said. 'Some old hippies?' Smiling.

Jake frowned. 'I heard you talking to people across the way,' she explained, uncertain. 'Just then.' And he stopped chewing, wiped his mouth. 'Oh, Nat and Betsy, yes. They're just like – standard American suburbia, transplanted, he's even got cases of Jim Beam in his cellar. We used to—' He stopped, grinned. 'We weren't always good children.'

She jumped in. 'Are you in touch with any of the kids from back then?'

He shrugged, vague. 'Oh, not really, we mostly, we went

our separate ways, you know? Grew up, moved on.' He looked rueful. 'I'm not much of a Facebook person.'

'Nor me.' She smiled, uneasy. She had never been a natural on social media but she *did* like seeing old friends from school; the best thing about going home was getting together with a few of them for a drink.

'Anyway, Nat and Betsy, sure,' said Jake. 'But most of the people from back then have gone. There's the odd one.' He stood as he said it and in that moment the sun came from behind a scudding cloud and the light flooded the room and he was walking quickly to the window.

She came over and stood beside him, at a little distance. 'You do want me here,' she said in a quiet voice, before she could stop herself. 'You're not regretting it? It's your special place, after all. I'm sorry if . . . I mean, I'd understand if . . .' and for a second she wasn't sure if she was really asking for permission to go, to walk away, get on a boat and leave.

'Let's go for a walk,' he said.

What would they all say? If she ran home? Marsha would winkle it out of her. Joey wouldn't be able to meet her eye. As for the others, as for starting the search all over again, getting the app back up and beginning to scroll through names, pictures . . .

'I'll take you down to the sea.' He smiled, easy, holding out his hand. She searched his face. *Calm down*, it said to her. They'd talked about all this. It was natural to have second thoughts, to be nervous – and besides, he was shy too. He understood.

She took his hand.

Day Two, Thursday: Joey

If anyone asked, Joey could just say, an author called and I needed to check Sukie's email to see if something had come through. But the office hummed along quietly, nothing to see here. The wide London sky was thick with cloud through the windows that ran the width of the big building.

When she got up Joey had checked the weather for Greece – well, Athens – on her phone. Sunshine and sixteen degrees.

She'd managed to access the dating site as Sukie – *Welcome back*, it said, *didn't work out?* as it offered to set her profile up again. There was no profile that she could find for him, either, no trace at all. Disappeared: she supposed it was what happened, if you got serious about someone. She'd glimpsed Jake's, of course, before Sukie had even met him herself, but it hadn't been more than a glimpse.

Sukie had been so methodical, so careful, so sure she had a system, and her faith in human nature was one of the many things Joey loved about her. Anyway, she'd always shown Joey guys she liked the look of, obediently.

Had there been something a bit different with Jake Littlejohn? Had Sukie held out her hand a bit too quickly for her phone as Joey held it in her hand and scrutinised his profile, had she been on the alert, possessive, or protective?

Joey frowned. Just one last thing, she thought. She opened Sukie's email programme and went to their correspondence.

You got in touch by email first, at least if you were careful you did. If Joey knew anything, she knew if they asked for your mobile number straight off, they were trying it on. So it was good, this little bunch of emails. It showed they were both alike, both cautious, both afraid of being damaged.

Joey pondered, putting it together, the bits of the story she had. She wished she could have looked a bit longer at that profile of his. It wouldn't do any harm to have a look at what they'd said to each other.

Glancing quickly around the quiet office to make sure no one could see, Joey began to read.

Chapter Eight

Day Two, Thursday: Heather

'Heather?'

It was Mum, and she sounded anxious. There was a bar, squeezed into a corner of the airport by the doors, and Heather was there waiting for her coffee – wondering what the fuck she thought she was going to do next – when her phone rang.

'Heather, love. Where are you?'

'Mum? What's up?' Heather took the thick china cup from the watchful bar girl and carried it, wobbling, to a metal table, phone under her ear, bag over her shoulder. There was a draught: it was colder than she had thought it would be. She sat, feeling tired and hungry and now anxious, because Mum was anxious. She took a sip of the coffee: it had sugar in it and she put the cup back down. She got up again and went back to the bar, gesturing for one of the pastries that sat in a glass display case. Apologetic. The girl seemed to register her this time, head tilted as she took the cash, watching her.

And that was another thing: she'd need more cash. Not much contactless cashless anything in evidence.

Mum was insistent, though, a terrier. 'Where?'

'I'm off on a mini break,' said Heather, registering Mum's disbelieving silence, 'Just a few days.'

Now she heard the hesitation: Mum hadn't really phoned to ask where she was.

'Mum?'

'Who's Sam?' said Mum.

'Sam,' Heather repeated, feeling a prickle across her scalp, lifting the cup to her lips without thinking, tasting the sugar. Think. 'Mum,' feeling sick with guilt as she said it.

Mum was stubborn. 'Your first boyfriend? I think I would have remembered, hen. I always wished you *would* tell me.'

Heather cleared her throat: it felt tight. 'Well, he was none of your business, was he. It was a long time ago.' Another one of Mum's silences.

'I see,' she said at last, sceptical.

'You and Kit have a nice long chat about me, did you?'

'He's worried about you, Heather, love. Your dad and me, we . . . Maybe your Kit's right.'

'Right about what?' She felt unreasonably angry. 'He's not my Kit.'

'That's the problem, isn't it?' said Mum. 'He said he doesn't feel like he's ever going to get to really know you. He sounded very sad. He asked me about . . . about this Sam, because he thought that might give him a clue.' Her voice faltered.

'Don't get upset, Mum,' said Heather automatically. *Sam Sam Sam Sam*, going on and on in the back of her head as she said it.

'You don't know how unusual it is,' Mum blurted out. 'To get someone who loves you that much, like Kit does, like your dad and me. I look around at the world today and I—'

'I'm sorry I never told you about Sam,' said Heather, her head aching. 'But it was – nothing. Sam. Just . . .' she searched for something to say, 'just holding hands behind the playing field. And I love Kit. Really I do.'

And then Mum sighed, a long sigh that meant she gave up. Then asking about Mum's own journey back to Scotland, and the boiler that she'd thought might be on the blink, Heather managed to say goodbye without getting back to the subject.

She took her cup back to the bar. As the girl turned away with it Heather said, 'Excuse me . . .' What the hell. She got out her phone and showed her the picture. It was the last one she'd taken, it popped right up.

'This man,' she said, and the girl pulled back warily, her mouth set in a line. Heather persisted. 'Have you seen him? He flew here yesterday?' The girl shrugged, squinting down at the screen, and abruptly it went blank.

'Shit,' said Heather, but the girl was already reaching for something behind the bar, a cable, a plug, deftly she plugged the phone in and set it down. Then took down a USB plug in a plastic case and laid it beside the charging phone, her hand out, pointing at a ten euro note protruding from the purse in Heather's hand. 'No I—' but then Heather got it. 'Sure.'

She paid for the plug from her dwindling store of cash, and rested her elbows on the counter. 'So,' she said, 'you saw him.' The girl shrugged. Back on the concourse something was happening, two men in overalls, one carrying a bag strapped around with tape, heading for the desk.

'He had a girl with him.' She turned to look out, at the taxi rank. From here you'd have been able to see comings and goings, the bar was positioned beside the exit. 'You were working yesterday?'

'Yes,' said the girl. It was the first English word she'd used, but at least she'd understood the question. 'Did they get a taxi?' Slowly the bar-girl shook her head. 'They walk,' she said, then shrugged. 'If *is* him,' pointing at the phone, still refusing to come back to life. 'I don't know. Maybe is him.' And then she pointed, beyond the taxis. Following her finger Heather saw a dusty, cracked road and low buildings to either side of it blurring in the pale morning, towards the blue of a horizon. 'Port this way.' The bar girl mimed waves. 'For the ferryboat.'

Heather thanked her, and leaving the phone to charge – 'Ten minutes?' – she held up all ten fingers, mimed a circuit round the concourse, and went back inside, but it had emptied out almost completely. There were a couple of car-hire places, neither of them manned, and an information desk where the two big men in overalls were monopolising the attractive girl behind it – but besides, what could she ask, without even a photograph on her phone? Whatever the men had brought in had disappeared.

Heather went back and got her phone. As she looked up from her messages – her request to connect with Sukie Alexander on LinkedIn hadn't been answered – she thought the girl behind the bar might have wanted to say something else but when Heather thanked her she just turned away.

The port materialised after less than ten minutes on the dusty road, rising up out of run-down houses and derelict garages, buildings that gradually looked less abandoned, washing hanging out limply in the thin sunlight.

There was a string of bars along the front and a handful of them were open in the sunlight. She showed the blurred photograph she had in every one and was rewarded only with a shake of the head, a shrug, curious looks. One barman, good-looking with bloodshot eyes, had leaned across his counter and touched her hand, lingeringly, on the pretext of getting a better look at the screen, and she'd jumped back.

There was a little booth selling tickets for the ferry and a teenage boy was in there, chewing gum, hoarse-voiced and with an impressive spray of spots along the line of his chin. He brightened though, when she spoke in English, and studied the phone seriously. He answered her carefully, practising his own English. 'I did not work yesterday, but my aunt did. I can ask her.' Heather began to say, no, don't worry, but he was already opening the booth's door. 'It is no problem,' he said, enunciating carefully. 'Where are you from? Are you from London? My aunt is here. She is here.' He shouted across the concrete jetty to where a little gaggle of older people sat on wooden chairs, apparently doing nothing. A short woman detached herself, and took her time coming over.

The woman looked from the photograph to the boy and then to Heather. Then she rattled off some Greek, thrust the phone back at her nephew and after another long curious glance at Heather, ambled back to her chair.

'She says,' the boy was eager, 'they bought the ticket to Kyros.'

'When is the next boat?'

'There is no more ferry to Kyros until Saturday.' His face falling as he realised that this wasn't what she wanted to hear.

Fuck fuck fuck, she thought, and then – so I can just stay here. Give it up.

'But . . .' He reached out a hand and then thought better of it when she flinched. 'There is a fast boat to the next island.'

She stared, began to turn away. His hand was on her arm now, and she turned back.

'My aunt said they went to buy something in this . . .' he hesitated, looking for the right word, 'boutique?' Pointing at a shop back along the harbour, with backpacks and jumpers festooning its frontage. 'The man and his girlfriend. Before they get the boat. Perhaps the lady who own, perhaps they talked to her?'

'Does she speak English?' asked Heather, still feeling the pull of surrender, just give up, mooch around here, go home. Forget it, Forget it. Forget him. 'The shop lady?'

She hadn't forgotten him in twelve years, was she going to forget him now? It was about time. But then there was her, too. There was the girl. Sukie Alexander. That look on her face in the airport coffee bar as she watched him walk away, the glance at Heather for reassurance that never came. Inside her something clenched tight.

The boy shrugged. 'I think,' he said.

'Okay,' said Heather. 'Thank you. Thank you.' He bobbed his head. She didn't know if she should give him money but he was already turning away, hurrying back.

The woman in the shop was wary. The girl bought a dress from her, she said, pointing up at a rail of them. The shopkeeper was edgy, uneasy. 'They are your friends?' she asked. Heather didn't know what to say. 'He was rude to me,' said the shopkeeper, folding her arms across her front. 'I didn't like him.'

Something kindled, warming Heather. 'No,' she said. 'He was rude – how?'

'I only asked if they were' – the woman mimed a ring on her finger – 'on the honeymoon. He told me to . . .' She said something in Greek. 'To shut up and do not ask stupid questions.'

Heather shifted, trying not to think of the girl's face, in the airport.

Then the woman said, abruptly, 'I think she lose her bag. Her clothes. On the flight. She only have a handbag.' She pointed at a row of sweaters. 'She was cold, and they were talking about a bag that must arrive.'

Heather turned, on instinct, back in the direction of the airport. That bag, slung between two men in overalls, lifted on to the airport information desk. She knew she'd seen it before.

Day Two, Thursday: Kit

At one of the long tables where they were supposed to share ideas in the sunshine – there were big windows, too, making the most of a bit of river view, but ideas from California didn't always translate, and the sky was low and grey – Kit sat with his phone in his hand. He had got in to work early and sat with his tea in front of him. It steamed in the reusable cup; Kit was scrupulous about that, and biking to work – he obeyed every rule, or always had done.

There must be a law against it, it probably counted as stealing someone's data. If she'd caught him, she'd have been furious. He'd never done it before, although he knew she didn't keep her phone locked. If she had secrets from him she'd have locked it, wouldn't she?

But the picture *was* a secret, that was for fairly sure. Still, the argument didn't hold water, she'd win that one. *We know what's private and what's not, and someone's phone is private.* There was a lot about Heather that was private, though. There was too much. After three years, sometimes the urge to know a bit more was overwhelming. And the way she had been holding her phone last night, between both hands, the expression at the table, just a bit glazed, elsewhere . . .

'What's so interesting?' It was Fred, baggy-eyed, smelling of beer.

'You're early,' said Kit.

Fred grinned, lecherous. 'Didn't get home, did I,' he said. Kit edged up, giving him space. It was the kind of thing Fred would do. Look through a girl's handbag, if he got the chance. *Because if she's got condoms in there, you know you're away.*

When she'd left the phone on the table to go to the loo she'd been so distracted she hadn't seen the screen still glowing, but he had. And he'd picked it up, knowing it was wrong. Fred wouldn't have hesitated. *You want to know if your date's got dick pics on there.* Although Fred didn't even take his dates out to dinner.

And in that mad moment – the waitress had seen him do it, a tiny question in her eyes before she decided it was none of her business, decided he was a Fred type and this was some Tinder date, she wasn't to know they'd been going out together three years and he still felt more like her brother than her lover – in the moment when the image appeared, he'd known on some instinct that it did mean something.

He had stared. A fuzzy picture of a long-haired bloke, fortyish – older? Dressed young – in an airport.

He'd had to be quick, snap, put his phone away and there he was with her phone in his hand at the restaurant table and the waitress moving between them with the food and

72

he had been handing the phone back to Heather. Had she noticed? He didn't know.

Plonking a latte down on the table before sitting down a bit too close, as he always did, Fred peered, shrugging. 'Who's the guy?'

'I don't know,' said Kit.

'Huh,' said Fred, looking closer. Taking the phone. 'Mystery man, hey?'

Kit hesitated. 'Heather took a picture of him,' he said. 'Not sure why.'

And now she's gone off on a mini-break.

'And you have the picture because . . .?' Fred frowned down at the image. 'Is he at an airport?'

He was at an airport and this morning she went back to the same airport, just like that, out of the blue. It might mean nothing. Or she might have left me.

'We ought to run him through the system,' said Kit, trying to sound nonchalant, or jokey, and failing. Fred was working on face-recognition software. But he didn't seem to be listening, he was squinting at the screen. Kit heard himself say. 'You know, as a control, or something. Random stranger.'

Fred eyed him, with amusement.

Over the three or four years he'd known Fred Kit had wondered if Fred's constant piss-taking where relationships were concerned meant he actually wished he had one. He could, couldn't he? If he wanted. He had an income, he had a place of his own. He was reasonable-looking, in a square-headed sort of way, not that Kit was a judge. Better-looking than Kit, anyway, who was ginger and freckled. What about the guy whose picture Heather had on her phone? Was *he* good-looking? The older man. Desperately Kit tried to close down that train of thought. This was irrational. Paranoid.

'Are you insane?' said Fred. Kit blinked.

Maybe Fred was just the smart one, and relationships were for losers. Kit decided he was going to delete the picture.

'What?' he said, defiant. Delete the picture, and then what? Pretend nothing had happened, like a mug? Or walk away? He held out his hand for the phone.

Then Fred looked up. 'You're kidding, right?' he said, just a trace of curiosity on his face. 'There's so much noise on that particular radar. Massive error margin, like sixty per cent. Never mind privacy issues.'

'Oh yeah,' said Kit, 'sure. Just – you know. It's fascinating. How it works.'

'Right,' said Fred, handing the phone back. 'Sure it is.' Not fooled. 'Later, yeah?'

'Later,' said Kit. There was an easier way, of course. He could just ask her.

Day Two, Thursday: Sukie

The path to the sea was rocky and steep between scratchy dark bushes: as they came down the wind dropped and in the sunshine it was almost warm. As they turned across a slope Sukie got a glimpse of the shape of the island. It was small, two pointed hills, one with the old village on top, a cemetery at the foot of the second, seagulls wheeling on the far hilltop. Around one bend she saw the scattered houses of the port town far below them, and the thread of a path down to it on the far slope, a villa with low walls and a collapsed roof, a neglected terrace of small trees.

'Are those olive trees?' she said, pointing at the terrace.

'Sure,' he said, dismissive, striding on.

'Your supplier?' She scurried, trying to keep up. He didn't seem to hear but she didn't ask again, not wanting to question him. He didn't seem to like questioning, out here. It had been all right before.

How long before a silence became uncomfortable? She resisted the urge to stop, dig her heels in.

'It must be lovely in spring,' she said, looking back across at where the port must be, although all that was visible of it from here was a handful of roofs on a cliff, where waves foamed white at the base.

Jake, ahead, turned to examine her. 'Oh, yes,' he said. 'Sure, it's . . . it's very pretty.'

'Maybe we could come back then,' she said, then blushed.

He laughed, an abrupt sound that he changed into a clearing of the throat. 'Of course we will,' he said, patting her on the shoulder, his rough fingers grazing her throat. She opened her mouth, then closed it again, uncertain. 'Just see if my little business works out first, hey?' he said, softly. She blinked, aware of things she knew nothing about, moving below the surface.

For a second Jake seemed to be examining her, then he

nodded past her shoulder and his smile was back. She turned to follow his gaze, which rested on the village above them, his village. From here she could see high up some rusty bougainvillea, an empty terrace, a faded sign swinging in the wind. 'And in the meantime,' he said, 'I've decided I'm taking you out to dinner tonight.' The eyes crinkled, rueful. 'The local taverna. No Michelin stars, I'm afraid – but they know me.'

'Oh,' she murmured. Things rearranged themselves: out to dinner. So normal. So comfortable. And in that moment she felt her spirits rise, suddenly she was ridiculously hungry. She leaned up and squeezed his arm. 'Thank you,' she whispered.

They walked on. Sukie looked back once, to try and get another look at the taverna, but it was in shadow against the sky, and Jake was striding on ahead again. Sukie hesitated, raised a hand to shade her eyes and, for one moment before she turned to follow Jake, she saw someone up there, a figure on the terrace jutting over the drop. A woman standing quite still, and watching them.

Chapter Nine

Day Two, Thursday: Heather

There was no Sam, never had been. How could she tell Mum — let alone Kit — that she'd invented him?

Walking back to the airport, Heather could smell the sea. She could hear the waves. She hadn't thought. She hadn't stopped to think, had she, that she was flying to an island, that the sea was going to be everywhere.

She'd avoided the seaside since leaving home for college. Mum often asked why she didn't go back and live there, so much cheaper. Mentioning those of her friends that were still around, people Heather hadn't spoken to in years.

The sound of the waves in her ears, the same rush and roar, Heather felt it closing in on her. She could see the mother-of-pearl light, the drift of travellers in and out, moving on before you could catch up. Brighton beach, under the pier while a DJ set played; a Greek island was his natural habitat, wasn't it? Here she was, and he was here too. Her worst nightmare.

She'd made Sam up on the spur of the moment on their first date or their third, back when she'd assumed she and Kit would be just friends. Made him up to make herself sound normal. If Kit had thought about it he might have wondered how her story echoed his own: *childhood sweetheart, we grew apart.* But the Sam she'd invented had stuck. In her head, he'd morphed, merged, with the man he was supposed to paint over. Her first: her rapist.

She'd taken one or two girlfriends to the police to report stuff, in the years since . . . it happened to her. She'd been firm with them. She'd gone along with them to emergency sexual health checks. She'd held their hands with a mixture of relief and guilt. She did the STD check after hers, not even sixteen years old and all alone, hoping no one in the dingy room would recognise her. They were mostly men, spotty youths with beanies pulled down almost over their eyes. A man in a suit. A couple holding hands. But she never went to the police.

She slept around a bit, afterwards, she didn't know why, to blunt the whole thing, submerge it, to show him it was nothing. It hadn't blunted anything, just left this sticky, dirty mess where her teenage years should have been. She managed to keep it from her parents and she managed not to get pregnant. Then she stayed off sex, until she met Kit.

Obviously she wasn't going to tell Kit about any of it. She was one of the lucky ones. Just sometimes – not often – she was taken by surprise. Sometimes she felt it again, undiluted: the fear, like she had on the airport concourse, turning from saying goodbye to her mother to see those two, in front of her.

And then she sat beside him, and she was back there.

That fear: the smell of his body, the smell of cigarettes on his hand over her mouth, that certainty that he was going to kill her. The thought that it would be easiest to die.

But she'd lived. And here she was.

Day Two, Thursday: Joey

Jake Littlejohn told her he might have had a difficult – an unsettled – childhood, but like lots of kids from that background, he wanted stability, normality. He wanted to go slowly, just like Sukie. Handholding, long walks.

I'm sort of alone in the world. And I sense you are too.

Yes, I suppose I am. I'm shy.

Joey almost couldn't bear to read it. Sukie seemed so transparent, so eager to please. To tell him what he wanted to hear. Joey didn't know what to make of *him*. He sounded like he was showing his vulnerabilities.

One long-term girlfriend. She was more adventurous than me, I suppose. In all sorts of ways.

79

Me too! I'm a homebody. No great gang of friends.
My parents died some time ago. An only child. I want
someone to be alone with, I suppose!

The sky was dark and rain spattered against the big plate-
glass window as Joey frowned at the screen, one last time.
There wasn't anything there. Or was there?

He seemed to be working round the subject, circling.
His loneliness, her loneliness. She scrutinised Sukie's eager
responses. She wanted to agree with everything he said,
come up with the answers he wanted, and Joey cringed at
the thought.

He mentioned his parents, she said nothing about hers.
A homebody, no friends – well, Joey thought, frowning, not
quite true. You've got me.

Joey sat back, staring at the screen. The emails said almost
nothing. But there was something in there, somewhere. She
just knew it. On impulse, she forwarded the correspondence
to herself.

And as she stood and stretched she felt it, heard it, it
whispered. *He doesn't know it, but you've got me.*

Day Two, Thursday: Sukie

As they picked their way carefully down the last steep stretch
to the sea Sukie could see that someone very old was
swimming out near some rocks, paddling slowly like an old
turtle, the gleam of a suntanned scalp, hunched shoulders.

A stony beach curved round a small bay and as they got
to it the turtle-shape was making his way back, paddling
and bobbing, face obscured behind goggles. Sukie paused,
somehow thinking there would be introductions – the way
Jake's gaze was briefly levelled at the figure in the water
made her think he knew him – but the swimmer found
his feet in the shallows and stood up.

The man was deeply tanned, and his wrinkled, sagging
body was – except for the goggles and a pair of flippers
that became visible as he flapped, one knee raised comically
then another, out of the sea – quite naked. And Jake didn't
stop, he didn't react at all. He just kept walking and after
a moment's shocked – no, just startled, she told herself,
startled – paralysis, Sukie followed him, stumbling a little
on the stones.

She didn't know, really, what had unnerved her more:
Jake's silence or the man's nakedness. Glancing back over
her shoulder she saw the man bending over some rocks,
retrieving a towel, and then he turned to watch them, at
the same time beginning to dry himself carefully.

'Up here,' said Jake, and coming round beside him she
saw another, steeper path between some big rocks.

Just an elderly nudist, thought Sukie, he wasn't to know
we'd come and surprise him, of course, making the explanations Jake wasn't making for her, because this was nothing
out of the ordinary to him, nakedness wasn't something
you were shocked by if you'd grown up in a place like this,
it wasn't something you sniggered about. Climbing behind
Jake, breathless, she felt the heat at her neck, burning her

cheeks. It wasn't until, after ten minutes of concentrated and difficult climbing that took them to a ridge from which the beach was no longer visible, that he turned, held out a hand to her and smiled. 'All right?' he said.

Out of breath, Sukie could barely manage a nod. It wasn't like she could say what she was thinking: that he needed a thin brown girl who could run up mountains and who'd grown up in some bohemian outfit; with parents who walked around naked and spoke several languages; not Sukie whose mother practically lived at the golf club; Sukie who was breathless after five minutes' climbing, pale and plump and frightened. That was why he hadn't said, *Darling, of course we'll come back in the spring.*

She needed to do something more, be something different, she thought, in a panic. *No you don't*, she told herself, but she could hear her mother, impatient, disappointed. *For God's sake, Sukie, grow up.*

'Fine,' she said, swallowing, looking past him uphill. They were in the lee of the little hilltop village, around the other side. She saw a lone tablecloth, flowered and faded, hanging out to dry, and a bleached-out sign painted on a stretch of peeling wall.

'Is that the shop?' she said, momentarily forgetting her unease. Jake shaded his eyes, frowning under his hand. 'Where you bought the bread?' she said. 'Can I . . . could we—'

'You don't need to buy anything,' he said, his mouth turning down at the edges, resting a hand on her sweaty shoulder. 'You're my *guest*, Sukie. Sweetheart.'

'No, but . . .' Again, she swallowed. 'I'd like to. I mean,

we'll need a few bits, won't we?' She longed for milk, fresh milk, suddenly. 'I'd just like to see what there is.' It sounded foolish, like she was some consumerist airhead, looking for sparkly mobile phone covers when she could be swimming naked in the Mediterranean.

Which reminded her: they'd charged his phone for him, hadn't they? In the shop. She opened her mouth to ask but he was looking at her with a frown of concentration and for an odd moment she wondered if he was going to say no. She closed her mouth, and he smiled. 'Let's go, then,' he said.

It was another ten minutes' steep climb, the only sound their hard breathing and the sound of seagulls, circling the far hill beyond the graveyard. There didn't seem to be any other birdsong. She briefly glimpsed the terrace higher up but there wasn't anyone there.

They came around the shop, and had to duck their heads to come indoors. The shop was dark and musty, with herbs hanging up, giant tins of feta and some unidentifiable fish in oil and an ancient cold cabinet. A middle-aged woman, reaching up to dust a row of cans, turned and grunted when they came in. In the recesses of the shop a man was dozing in a wheelchair and just inside the door a girl perched on a tall stool on her phone, her eyes following Jake around the room.

Sukie got out her phone, and looked from the woman to the girl, holding it out, miming a charger. The woman shrugged, pointed at a stand that had ancient converter plugs and dusty packs of batteries. The girl looked at her from under dark brows for a long second, then smouldered – or that was how it looked to Sukie – a foreign, angry, look, at Jake. Then the girl tossed her hair and reached for a big handbag and got out a plug and charger cable. Impatiently she gestured to Sukie and when Sukie took a step towards her plucked the phone out of her hand.

'I just need to tell—' Surrendering it with a quick blush of indignation, Sukie turned to Jake in explanation. 'It's not like I'm dependent on the internet or anything,' she tried joking, 'I just need to tell my parents I've arrived safely.'

The stocky woman had turned and was watching them, her arms folded across her front. In the dim shop's interior dust motes floated in a shaft of thin sunlight. Sukie smiled at her uncertainly.

Not a lie, exactly, although Sukie's parents of course had no idea she had even gone away – they probably would have thought she was making it up if she'd tried telling them it was with a *man*, or would have been bored. It was more she wanted to know that someone, somewhere, had missed her; she wanted to tell someone what it was like here, how strange it was.

And she wanted to ask what she should do, with the feelings of panic. She wanted to hear Joey say, comfortably, well, it's only another couple of days. Go for walks, or get a boat somewhere else, or find a hotel, or just come home. You can just come home.

But she wasn't ready. She hadn't given it a chance. Free accommodation, on a Greek island? What wasn't to like? She stepped outside to avoid the looks the woman and her disdainful daughter seemed to be giving her but as she did so she caught the girl's dark stare and a distinct, quick, shake of the head. *No.*

The message was obscure. Go away? You're the wrong one? Or – say no. The girl's back was turned now.

No to what? It came to Sukie that she just didn't know what Jake wanted. She knew he wanted something.

'You go on back,' she said to Jake, nodding earnestly. 'Why don't you? I'll wait till the phone charges up a bit, just check my messages and that.'

Talk to my friends. My friend. The thought of Joey's kind, worried, round face shook her, somehow.

There was a burst of chatter suddenly from inside the shop and she turned to go back in. Jake hadn't moved. The girl was bent over Sukie's phone screen, exclaiming over all the notifications marching up it, ping, ping, ping. She looked up when Sukie appeared in the door but wasn't looking at her now, but over her shoulder at Jake. Always Jake. Sukie supposed there weren't a whole lot of eligible men on the island; she supposed she must have known Jake since she was a small girl. A crush. Sukie shifted, awkwardly, because Jake was right there, and then moved inside.

'Popular girl,' he said, looking at Sukie's phone. He was smiling but there was an edge to it. Could he be jealous? Uneasily, Sukie edged out from between the two of them. Holding her phone still on its cable, she squeezed between a display of cleaning fluids and the giant can of fish.

'Just updates,' she said, eyes on the phone. 'You know,

85

that sort of thing.' Restraining an impulse to hold the screen up to prove it. She remembered his hand, helpless, palm up on a pub table as he said, *I'm not really the sociable type* and she, wanting to please, had said, *Nor me.*

Not all updates, though. Missed call, from her mother. Three missed calls. Answerphone message. Hardly anything to show off about. She held up a finger while she tried to contact her answerphone and Jake raised his eyebrows. The girl on the stool was examining her nails.

Sukie felt Jake's breath on her cheek. The answerphone was asking for a pin code, because she was abroad, and she had no clue what it was. Marsha never texted because she was too vain to wear her reading glasses, and therefore couldn't see the screen, but Sukie texted, anyway. *Sorry mum, I'm away for a few days in* – she hesitated, sod it – *Greece. Can't get the answerphone, hope everything's all right.*

A quick lurch at the thought that something might have happened to Dad, although that seemed unlikely, salad every day for lunch to keep his figure and Marsha never let him drive fast.

Then a text pinged up: sent last night, from Joey.

Hope you're OK. Had your mum on the phone because someone saw you at the airport. Don't worry, no one's ill, just nosy. Hope you're OK.

She turned quickly to see if Jake had read it over her shoulder, relief flooding her as she heard Joey's voice in her head, and happiness – Joey, Joey looking out for her, Joey being normal, Joey being funny – but he had his back to her, hands in pockets, nonchalant. She could imagine her mother's response to finding out from some acquaintance that her daughter had a boyfriend *at last*.

Joey had asked if she was OK twice. What was she worried about?

I'm fine she typed in quickly. *It's just my bag went missing—* Jake turned and she just pressed send. She smiled at him, placatory.

The phone was a quarter charged. She went to her mailbox, get messages. The little circle spun, hung.

'Seriously?' It was Jake, almost glowering, blocking the light. 'I mean,' more gently, 'we can't stay here all day.' The messages came in, spam, spam, work, spam, and a few things not quite one or the other. A connection request on LinkedIn. She hesitated.

'You can leave it here,' said the girl, startling Sukie with her English, and hurriedly she closed the email program. She seemed very composed now, hands folded, knees crossed, head on one side, examining them.

'Yeah?' said Jake, turning away from her already and steering Sukie, his hand on her upper arm, towards the door.

'Hold on.' She struggled briefly free and fished a crumpled five euro note from her purse and put it down on the wooden counter. 'Thank you,' she said, nodding earnestly. The girl still stared, not at her, over her shoulder at Jake. 'I'll come back for it.'

'Or I will,' said Jake cheerfully, hands on her shoulders,

jokily beginning to march her out of the shop. Sukie tried to turn to look at him but it was tricky.

'We're coming back up, aren't we?' she said. 'For dinner? I'll get it then.'

'Just concentrate on the path,' said Jake from behind her. 'It gets tricky when the light goes.'

Chapter Ten

Day Two, Thursday: Heather

The airport was almost completely empty by the time Heather got back there, except for a couple of policemen smoking at the exit. As she came through the glass doors her phone rang. She looked down at the screen a moment, then sighed.

'Kit,' she said.

'You landed safely, then?'

'I should have sent you a message,' she said. 'Sorry.'

'I saw a picture on your phone,' he said. 'A man at the airport. Who is he?'

'What?' she said. '*What?*' For a moment her mind was blank, wiped white. *He knows. He's seen.* 'When?'

Kit ignored the question. 'Who is he?'

Heather babbled. She never babbled. 'Just some . . . some DJ . . .' Shut up, she thought, but she couldn't. 'I recognised him. Thought I did. Stupid spur of the moment thing.' *Stop*. She stopped.

Kit made a sound of disgust. 'You don't believe me?' she said, and she heard the ominous quiet in her voice.

'Are you there with him?' Kit's voice was level, and angry. He was never angry.

She hung up.

Fuckfuckfuck. She stood, there on the dusty concourse. A pigeon flew in, at ear level, and skittered to a landing in front of her, immediately beginning to peck before it had even folded its wings away.

She'd thought it would be easy, when the time came to end it. She realised she'd always assumed it would come to an end. Not because she'd want someone else but because she'd want to be completely on her own, with no one else to think about.

That wasn't normal. She forced herself to contemplate that fact.

Sod it.

She approached a desk that read *Oversize and lost items*. There was a man in front of her being dealt with. She hesitated, because he was the right height, but then he turned and the face was wrong.

Her plan was sketchy, formulated as she listened to what the man ahead of her said: he was collecting for someone else. Eventually a surfboard emerged from behind a partition and as he set it against his shoulder, turning, she saw him retrieve his passport from the squat man behind the desk, and her heart sank.

She gave Sukie Alexander's name, the name she'd seen on the tag. The official looked back over his shoulder, considering.

'Yes,' he said. 'I know this bag, it is here. My colleague inform me of the owner. But . . .' His mouth twitched, but he let her go on.

'I don't know if Sukie – she's my friend, you see – I don't know if she called to say . . .' she began, grimacing apologetically when she got to the bit about needing the address because Sukie – her friend Sukie – had forgotten to give her the address.

The small man regarded her, sly. The answer, of course, was no. Sukie Alexander had not called to say her friend Heather would be collecting a bag. He glanced over her shoulder as if considering alerting the policemen at the glass doors, then he shook his head.

She had no idea how she would explain herself, if they came over. If they asked what she thought she was doing. But the man only leaned over the counter, and she could smell the cigarette smoke on his breath. 'You're friends? You and Miss – the Miss Sukie? Maybe they are on the honeymoon. You need your girlfriend on the honeymoon?' And he leaned back again, smirking. 'I don't think so.'

Heather stepped back automatically, repelled by the man, by what he was saying. The woman in the shop that had sold Sukie Alexander a jumper had said the same thing, and been slapped down for it.

A honeymoon, with him?

His name had been Jake, called himself BlueJ, those were

91

the only names she knew. She hadn't looked for him, googled him. He had never been a big name, or she would have seen him plastered on posters: he was a niche player. He was small. In her head, she made him so small she couldn't see him. She wanted him not to have existed, standing nodding behind his decks, smiling across at her over the heads, the fifteen-year-old her, thinking herself special. She hadn't said that name aloud, hadn't *thought* that name.

BlueJ didn't do honeymoon. There was something in the man's smile.

She stood there. What would he come out here with a girl like that for? Out of season, the wind was cold, the island little more than a reception centre for immigrants. A girl like that. Soft, unwary.

She could have got it all wrong. But she knew she hadn't. Whatever he'd put in the bag couldn't have been illegal, or they'd have taken her in – but that didn't mean Heather was wrong about him. She might have only seen him in the dark, she might have spent no more than an hour with him – it was probably less, she thought with the cool detached part of her brain, it was probably twenty minutes but it had grown, in her mind, it had mushroomed – she knew him.

'Of course,' said Heather, equably. 'I just thought I might save you and them the time. As I am going there myself.' He pursed his lips and she said casually, 'Is there an exchange desk, perhaps, in the airport?'

She knew very well there was an exchange desk, because she'd seen it coming in, but she took the little left luggage man's directions, his advice as to ringing the bell on the counter, with bright willingness. She needed him not to wonder why she didn't just leave the airport.

Creepy girl, stalker ex-girlfriend, spare wheel.

If the girl at the bar was surprised to see Heather back there, she didn't show it, instead she yawned sleepily. Heather, suddenly very hungry, asked for a cup of tea and a sticky little plate of baklava and positioned herself at a table on the edge of the terrace from which she had a direct view through the glass doors to the little man behind his outsize counter.

The baklava was good but the tea tasted of dust. The sun was dipping in the sky, a low golden gleam that glanced off the sliver of sea just visible from where Heather sat and she found herself yawning too – then something happened. Out of the corner of her eye she saw the man at the desk put on his jacket, disappear into the storage space behind his desk and emerge again – with a bag. Heather sat up hurriedly. *The* bag. He locked a shutter behind him and came around his counter.

It looked as if he was going to deliver it himself – Heather was wondering how she might follow him inconspicuously, because he'd recognise her – when something else happened. A battered car pulled up and a wizened elderly man in a hat got out, smoking. He raised his hand to the man with the bag, who was approaching across the concourse.

With hardly time to think, Heather made the decision. She slapped a five euro note on the counter, startling the girl awake, shouldered her bag and walked across to the taxi rank, deliberately unhurried, only glancing back to see the old man in the hat receive Sukie Alexander's bag. The lost property man didn't look her way: he was asking the driver to sign something.

Before she turned back, Heather saw that the bag – it was a roll bag, of nylon – was the one she'd seen with silver duct tape around it, as if it had disintegrated en route.

Once in the taxi Heather pretended to fuss over looking for something in her bag until the old man who had collected the bag climbed back into his car and then she pointed and said, 'Follow that car.' In films she always wondered why no taxi driver ever laughed, or asked why, but hers just started the car and moved into the traffic behind the old man, whose hat was visible in silhouette from behind.

They followed the hat as far as the harbour-front, where he parked his car, hoisted the bag out – bow-legged, wiry, stronger than he looked – and went straight to the ticket booth for the boats.

Heather – having paid off her cab, realising she hadn't taken enough money out, because her card wasn't going to be much use to her out here, fell into line behind him.

There was a little straggling band of passengers there now, stoical in the cold wind coming off the sea, their faces turned towards the last of the sun. The sun was almost down, dipping to the horizon, but that wasn't what they were looking at. There was a boat, low and long and fast, there was a hum in the air of engines.

There'd be somewhere to stay. She needed to keep going.

She heard the old man, the bag on the ground between

his feet, name an island, registered that it was the one next to Kyros that the boy had named to her earlier. The old man took his ticket and moved off, paying her no attention behind him. Heather asked for the same ticket. The woman behind the glass – it was the aunt, the boy's aunt, back on shift – said something she didn't understand, frowning with the roll of tickets in her hand. Then made a gesture with her seamed forefinger, to and fro. There and back. Return ticket.

Heather hadn't thought about it. If she had, she realised, she somehow thought this was it, this was all there was, the end of the line. But she had a flight home again, in two days. Home, that might have been another world.

And then the ferry was there, it was turning, thundering into reverse to draw alongside the pontoon, the curl of a leaping swordfish painted on its bow, the water slapping cold against it.

'Yes,' Heather said, 'return,' using the same gesture with her finger, there and back. And taking the tickets that spooled off the little machine, she turned and took her place among the other travellers.

Day Two, Thursday: Kit

'So,' said Kit. 'Will you give it a go?'

He was standing in the doorway of Fred's office. Fred had got his own office, of course. Ruthless and demanding was how you got ahead, or at least that was what Fred said.

'Sure, go on,' Fred said now, leaning back in his chair. 'Send me the picture. I'd like another look at him, anyway. What did you say her explanation was? She recognised him and took a picture, because he's some DJ?' He lowered his voice, as if he was offering condolences. 'I didn't think you'd have a girlfriend like that, mate.'

The smirk that followed made Kit so angry he felt dizzy. Or was it Heather's lie? Obvious lie. But he needed Fred's help.

'You'll do it?' said Kit stubbornly.

Fred shrugged, saying nothing, looking at him.

Kit stared down furiously at his phone, sending the picture. Fred's mobile pinged, and leisurely, he picked it up, nodding. 'You know I have no access to facial recognition databases, right?' he said, grinning.

'What?' Kit clenched his fists, feeling a surge of something he couldn't control. He felt like he was turning into someone else. 'So—'

'Calm down, mate,' said Fred, tapping the side of his nose. 'I can maybe help, anyway. The old-fashioned way, right? Show this around. You're not the type to go to DJ sets, I get that. But there's others do, it'd be easy enough to ask around, I've got enough mates involved in clubs. As long as she—' He stopped.

'As long as it was true, about him being a DJ,' Kit finished for him. There was a silence.

'So when's she back?' said Fred, clearing his throat. 'Your *lady*, I mean?'

'She comes back Saturday,' said Kit, tight-lipped.

'So,' said Fred, 'make the most of your freedom.' Kit stared at him. Freedom? Prison, more like. He wasn't used to jealousy, he felt like he was locked up with a lunatic. But he needed Fred's help.

Fred examined him. 'Pub tonight after work, right? No ifs, no buts.' He examined the picture again then raised his head and directed a look – glazed with satisfaction – at Kit.

'Right,' said Kit, but Fred was already leaning forward over his screen, one hand frozen in a wave of dismissal he couldn't even be bothered to complete.

Chapter Eleven

Day Two, Thursday: Sukie

Jake had kept his hands on Sukie's shoulders all the way back to the house. It had grown awkward, and at the foot of the wooden steps she'd dodged quickly out from under his touch, stepping aside to let him past.

Jake had given a little laugh, and Sukie had blushed.

She wasn't used to it, that was all. Physical contact. Her mother had never gone in for it; her dad had been very wary, as if she might scream, as if it was just safer not to. Sukie swallowed, smiled. Jake turned and went up the stairs and by the time she got to the top she could hear him in his room.

She stood at an angle to the half-open door, looking at the sliver of him she could see between its hinges. He was looking down into his unzipped backpack and suddenly she remembered and took an involuntary step back. Cup of tea, she thought, automatically.

It was just precautions. Condoms were just condoms. Like physical contact – normal people could handle that stuff. She had a sudden fierce longing for Joey, and then there was Jake, in the doorway.

'Sweetie,' he said, his eyes hooded. 'Are you all right? He stepped towards her and she made herself stay still. 'So pale,' he said, considering her a long moment until she blushed again and he smiled. 'I'd better have another go at that generator, hadn't I?' He lifted a hand and let it graze her cheek.

Left alone, unused to being without her phone for entertainment – although, like everyone sensible, she rationed herself, so this was good for her – Sukie took a book from the dusty shelf over the fireplace that was presided over by the horrible sculpture. There were a couple of dog-eared bestsellers from the eighties, seventies psychedelia – Carlos Castaneda, *The Dice Man*, *Zen and the Art of Motorcycle Maintenance*. Her eye skimmed over a battered Kama Sutra. She took down a Doris Lessing and sitting by the fireplace on the hard sofa stared at it, the words blurring.

There was the last of the thin sun through the windows but soon it would get cold again and Sukie had to suppress a sudden sensation of dread at the thought. The hard bed, the thin blankets. The night. She pulled the tasselled cotton rug up over her legs and got a waft of stale sweat.

Dinner. She needed to work out what to wear. Well – she didn't, it was either jeans or the tunic thing.

Two more days. Two and a half. It would be an adventure. They'd swim, they'd walk. They'd be friends. She would be able to tell Joey all about it. She squeezed her eyes shut a second, wishing it was now, the thought of the dark warmth of the YMCA bar they'd go to together, but she couldn't quite imagine herself saying, I found condoms. After all, most men would take one on a date. She felt tears at the corner of her eyes. Most women wouldn't be stupid enough to go away with someone they hardly knew. To think leaving their comfort zone would be fun: what was so wrong with comfort, after all?

But he'd done nothing. Nothing.

You don't have to do anything you don't want. Had Joey whispered that to her, when they'd said goodbye, or had that been her imagination?

Sukie could hear him moving about downstairs and suddenly on impulse she tiptoed back into the bedroom. A moment of panic, *where was it?* The yellowing plastic folder, which she was sure she'd brought in and left – yes. It was on the bed, in a fold of the covers, although she wasn't sure that was where she'd left it. She picked it up and looked around the room, which looked bare and comfortless in the fading light, the paint on the window frames peeling, the wood splitting. Had he really grown up here? It seemed so far away from normality. She tried to think of it as a home, and failed.

She padded back into the sitting room with the folder and sat, positioning herself so she could see the door down into the cellar, and carefully she extracted the folder's contents. The plastic was brittle and cracking with age. There was the map, with its names and crossings out. The ink must once have been green. Nat, Betsy, David, the shop was marked, a taxi number. Automatically she reached for her phone to make a note of it but that was when she remembered that she'd left it at the shop. She folded the map and put it in her pocket.

She could go up right now and get it, why not. She got up abruptly, losing her grip on the folder, and it all fluttered down, instructions, and the handful of old photos, lying at her feet.

She bent to pick them up.

It was Jake, some time ago, thirty, maybe more, bare-chested by a pebble beach. The sun was out but the sea was grey – it didn't look like Greece. It looked like England: she saw the corner of some ironwork jutting into the sea. Brighton? He had mirrored glasses on.

And then another. A family group, slightly wonky, on the sofa where she'd just been sitting. A man with a straggly beard and light eyes, a woman, square-shouldered and stocky with knees apart and staring at the camera with a weird expression, gleeful. She looked like Jake, a lot like Jake, if Jake had been a thickset woman, and the effect was strange.

Jake was in a corner of the sofa, she assumed it was Jake, at least, a skinny dark-browed kid of about fourteen, his face half covered with long hair pressed angrily into the corner of the sofa as if trying to get as far away from his parents as he could.

The man was holding something loosely between his knees and, peering, Sukie saw it was the wooden sculpture that still stood there on the mantelpiece. She stared, from the mantelpiece to the picture.

101

Downstairs, a sound. Sukie had become aware of sounds since she'd sat there but not the kind of thing she'd associate with the mending of a generator. No banging or noises of exasperation but slidings, shufflings, careful sounds.

The last picture was of a boy, just his body, naked. Young: maybe nine or ten, arms hanging by his sides. Whoever had taken the picture hadn't bothered to get his head in. Kneeling to gather the rest of the pictures hurriedly, Sukie pushed them back into the folder – and then she heard him on the stairs. Quickly she slid the folder underneath the cotton coverlet on the sofa.

He was back on the stairs and moving fast, quick and light, two steps at a time. He was whistling.

Her heart was beating so hard she thought he might see it through her tunic, he might hear it. Silly, she thought, silly, but she couldn't get the woman's face out of her mind. His mother. And then – the boy. She sat back down, on top of the folder, reached for the book, right way up, and when Jake appeared in the doorway she looked up, as if surprised.

She surprised herself. She'd never been a good liar. Marsha seizing her when she'd taken fifty pence from her purse to buy sweets for a girl she'd wanted so badly – SO badly – to be her friend. Marsha's fingers like iron pinching her upper arms. Sukie breaking down, *I'm sorry.*

'You look . . .' Jake hesitated, frowning. 'Much better.'

She felt her heart beat, knew her cheeks must have pinked, with the fear, the excitement. He frowned, head on one side, examining her. She put the book down and stood up, tugging at the tunic. It kept riding up.

'Oh,' said Jake, watching. 'They say your bag's arrived,' and he touched her lightly on the shoulder. 'It won't be here till tomorrow – but it's safe. Well – damaged a bit, they said. In transit.'

'Damaged?'

'The fabric. They've patched it up, they said. They put everything back inside.' He stroked her cheek. 'Don't look so anxious, little girl,' he said. 'You know how they throw things around. You didn't pack anything sharp, that might have pushed through? I hope there wasn't anything irreplaceable, anyway.'

She swallowed. 'No,' she said. Silk nightdress. Good knickers. She felt all wrong, uncomfortable. The wrong person with the wrong luggage in the wrong place. Her things scattered over some blowy runway. 'Nothing much,' she said. And abruptly he turned away. She went to the window.

Outside, the light was fading, even up here. Round the coast a single string of street-lighting identified the port, and the little bay below them was in darkness, no more than the odd glint off the water and the sound of the waves. It felt like she'd been pushed out to the edge of the world. Two more days. An adventure.

'I'd better change,' she said, turning back, and Jake just stood there a second before giving a little bow and going out of the room. She put her jeans back on: it had got cold. Brushed down the T-shirt she'd travelled in, and wrapped her big soft cardigan over it. It smelled of home. She buried her nose in it briefly then called, 'Ready?'

They went up in silence. When they got to the turning to the little shop Jake overtook Sukie on the path, to where the girl stood in the doorway. The boxes of fruit had been taken inside and half of the door had been closed: the shop was dark behind her. She took the phone out of her pocket, not holding it out, looking from him to her.

Sukie, hurrying, stumbled, and when she looked up he had it in his hand, and was smiling down at it.

Day Two, Thursday: Joey

It ticked away in Joey's brain, all the long bus ride home. There had to be something there she could work with, to find out more. She'd googled his name and found almost nothing. There were a number of Jake Littlejohns. One fuzzy picture of a guy that could have been him, more than a decade ago, standing behind some decks and a row of white Victorian buildings behind him that looked like a seaside town.

Joey wasn't one of nature's detectives. Even her best friends . . . even Sukie called her sleepy. Her brain ached all the way home.

Was it strange there was so very little about him? But then plenty of people didn't have much internet presence. People were savvier than they used to be about it, and she had a vague idea you could hide stuff if you knew what you were doing.

Or maybe she was just paranoid. Maybe Anastasia was right, maybe she was jealous.

Sukie had texted, after all, to say she was fine. If there was something wrong then she'd know by now, she'd have said. If Jake Littlejohn had turned out to be . . . not what he seemed. Surely by now he'd have . . . And then Joey swallowed.

What? He'd have what? Sukie had gone on holiday with a guy as vulnerable and lonely as she was. He had nobody. They were getting to know each other in an idyllic setting.

Bohemians, though. Was that what Marsha had said? The last thing Sukie was, was bohemian.

She flipped open her laptop and there was the correspondence. There was his email address.

She opened the browser and typed it in.

Bingo.

Day Two, Thursday: Heather

It was a long, bumpy journey, and Heather, tucked into a seat close to the gangway, was cold, and so tired she felt sick. The noise of the engines and the fast thud of the boat's hull gave her a headache. There was the smell of diesel and disinfectant and the cold sea, and food being eaten out of greasy paper bags inside the cabin behind her, and the sound of foreign voices.

In Heather's sleep-deprived state she could almost persuade herself she'd hallucinated the whole thing, from seeing him in the airport to standing there at the counter, impersonating a sane human being and demanding a ticket. Add to that fighting with Kit, and now following some old bloke on to a boat without any idea of what would happen when he got off.

She could see the bag, in the luggage rack on the other side of the gangway, which was why she was sitting where she was, but the old man had disappeared. Beyond the rack was a dark passageway.

Her own bag was clasped between her knees. She was stiff and awkward and uncomfortable, but still she was almost asleep when she felt someone sit beside her, and she jerked upright.

It was the old man, his hat between his hands. He said something in Greek and she shook her head, shrugged apologetically. She could feel his arm pressed against hers, all the length of it, but she couldn't edge away because she was between him and the bulkhead. A ticket collector appeared and took her ticket, gave her back half of it and made that same movement with his finger, there and back. He and the old man said something to each other, then he moved off.

Surreptitiously Heather tried to edge away but the old man was talking to her: it took her a second to understand it was English, or a kind of English. She half opened her eyes – mistake.

'Nice girl, English girl,' he was saying, pointing at the bag. Something leering in it. She pretended not to understand, just shrugging, but he kept talking, his hand went out, hovering over her knee, and she jumped up, unable to control herself, and turned into the cabin. Right inside the grubby glass doors there was a spare seat next to a fat woman snoring against the window and she took it. There was a handful of passengers, all dozing.

The old man came in after her, and sat down across the aisle. Heather sat stiffly, staring ahead; he was making a sound, a kind of small grunting. She knew what he was doing, she could even see his fumbling movements on the edge of her vision.

She wasn't afraid of a dirty old man.

She made herself close her eyes. She must have fallen asleep eventually, because when a change in the engine noise woke her, her cheek was pressed against the fat woman's warm shoulder and the woman was nudging her, not unkindly. The old man had gone from across the aisle.

The boat thundered, reversing. She could see lights through the glass door, and there were voices. They were docking and Heather jumped up, in a sudden panic, the fat woman murmuring behind her as she gathered bags together. Pushing in her hurry through the swing doors she almost fell over him, there was the hat, the old man in it reaching down into the luggage rack to retrieve the taped up bag. Heather stopped herself just in time and instead stepped back to allow the fat woman ahead of her, between them.

Over the woman's shoulder Heather saw a sign, giving the island's name: she was in the right place, the island she'd bought a ticket to. Slowly the fat woman shuffled and Heather hovered behind her. The old man was talking to a man in uniform who was leaning against a little booth on the water's edge plastered with bleached and ragged posters advertising boat trips.

As they came level with the pair the fat woman dropped one of her bags, and potatoes rolled out. Kneeling to help, Heather listened, peered up round the woman's flapping coat.

She thought the old man was trying to persuade the port official, if that was what he was, to take charge of the bag, pointing across the sea – she assumed to the next island – and he was saying no. The old man unzipped the bag and they both looked down into it: there was a laugh. She didn't like the sound of the laugh.

She could go. Climb on the boat and go back.

The potatoes were all stowed away and as she stood up Heather became aware that the fat woman was talking to her, stepping in front of her to make her understand but she didn't, couldn't. It was stupid. She had no clue where she was or what she was doing there. 'I don't understand,' she said. The boat revved behind them, and the old man called out.

The ferry's mate was uncoiling the mooring rope as the boat manoeuvred, there was a smell of diesel and the water churned. And she turned back and the fat woman was still talking: miming now. Miming sleep, two hands laid under her cheek, pointing towards an alley between houses.

And over the woman's shoulder she saw that the old man had disappeared, but then there was movement, no more than a blur, out of the corner of her eye, and there he was again, daring where she hadn't, stepping across the widening gap between the pier and back on to the boat with ease. He didn't have the bag with him. Turning, he stared at her, his face pale, and then the departing boat, and the face, were swallowed up in the darkness.

Chapter Twelve

Day Two, Thursday: Kit

'Fuck her,' said Fred, cheerfully. 'Or rather, fuck someone else, right?' Guffawing. The lift was empty apart from the two of them, because you weren't allowed to say things like that in public spaces, not even if it was all men. 'Big fucking Brother, right?' Fred said, reading his mind. 'Big sister, more like.' Stared up at his reflection in the mirrored ceiling and gave it the finger.

'Have you found anything out or not?' said Kit. He didn't want to play this game.

'Give us a chance,' said Fred, pretending dismay. Kit just glared. Fred tapped the side of his nose. 'I've put the word out,' he said.

'I'm going home,' said Kit. But he didn't move.

Fred put his hands in his pockets, rocking on the balls of his feet. 'They're all the same,' he said, good-humoured. 'Birds.

They'll fuck you over with another bloke or they'll eat you alive.'

The lift doors opened on the super-cool foyer, with fluorescent pod seating, and Kit walked out, and kept walking. *She wouldn't do that to me.* He kept the words in his head because he could hear Fred saying them, in a cry-baby voice. But when Fred caught up with him on the pavement, he let himself be led.

They walked along the river. Kit kept asking where they were going but Fred just tapped the side of his nose again, said, 'Leave it to Uncle Fred.'

Kit had never seen the pub before. It was on the water out on the eastern edge of the City. A little old place, two bay windows and small from the front, squeezed incongruously between tall modern apartment blocks but with the long low shape of an extension out the back. A small crowd of smokers in overcoats were gathered on the boardwalk in front of it and either side of the front door some chalkboards advertised forthcoming attractions. A stripper, an eighties night, quizzes. DJ sets.

Inside it was rammed, but they'd barely got in the door before Fred had spotted someone on the other side of the room and was shoving his way across, Kit floundering to get after him. By the time he got there Fred was bullying the barman for service.

There were three or four guys around him. Kit knew one of them vaguely, Ian, someone Fred used to work with who was now in the city somewhere. He had a big gold signet ring and his face was red and dripping with the heat inside the pub. Fred handed the beers round and they barged out on to the street. Kit leaned back against the frosted window and drank. They were talking tech so he zoned out and when he looked at his glass again it seemed to be empty, and he didn't feel quite as bad as he had.

Sod it.

'To what do we owe the honour?' said Ian, pushing his way out of the swing doors with drinks expertly held out in front of him, caged between his fingers. Another thing Kit had never been able to manage, along with drinking more than one pint without needing the toilet.

'Aren't you a married man?' Ian went on. Kit intercepted a warning look from Fred and worked out he must have been used as the butt of their jokes, at one time or another. 'Leave him alone,' said Fred. 'It's one of those "I need some space" things.'

'You married?' Kit said to Ian.

'No chance, son,' said Ian, puffing cheerfully on a vape.

'She's gone off somewhere,' said Kit, and the words seemed to take for ever to emerge. 'I'm not sure what's going on, tell y'the truth.' Very carefully he set his pint down on the window sill. 'Back in a minute.'

The pub's toilet was icy cold, and seeing himself in the little mirror over the washbasin Kit felt very lonely suddenly. *They're my mates*, he said to himself in the mirror.

Returning, he spotted Fred, in a huddle with the other two, showing them something on his phone. 'Hey,' he said stupidly. They looked up. And one of the ones he didn't know began to laugh.

Mates? Kit looked from one face to the next: they lived in another world, didn't they? They didn't know what relationships were like. They were all on Tinder all the time. Some of them thought it was great, others went along with it. He was in the wrong place.

Then Ian was beside him, a heavy arm laid over Kit's shoulders.

'Come on, son,' he said. 'What d'you want with a relationship anyway? More trouble than it's worth.'

'You pussy,' said the one who laughed. 'She's gone off with another bloke and she's asking you to vet him for you? Jus' go out and find another one.' He waved his pint wildly towards the pub window. 'They're gagging for it.'

Quiet, Fred stepped between them in time to stop Kit lurching into the bloke's face. 'Stop it, Gav,' he said.

Struggling, Kit turned wildly towards him. 'What've you been— Why'd you show them?' He could hear himself. *You pussy.*

'I showed them,' said Fred, patiently, 'because you asked me to find out who this bloke is.'

'Right,' said Kit, suddenly sober.

'Well,' said Ian, from the other side of him, 'I think you want to talk to the barmaid. Showed her your picture, and whaddya know. BlueJ, his name is, or the name he uses, anyway. She booked him here a while back—'

'Because he was cheap as chips,' butted in Gav, sloshing his beer.

Ian elbowed him out of the way, patiently. 'A bit past his best, apparently. But that didn't stop them getting friendly, if you know what I mean.'

Kit craned his neck, trying to see the barmaid, and only catching sight of hair in two plaits, like some German *bierkeller* dolly.

'By all accounts, he put it about a bit, anyway, so she—'

Kit had suddenly had enough. 'So he shagged a lot of women,' he said, making himself say it, trying to sound like them. 'Well, so fucking what? And she's fallen for it?' His head hummed and sang with pain. The men's faces blurred, and then there was Fred, in focus, filling the screen of Kit's vision.

'I think there's a bit more to it than that,' he said, softly. 'She's going to talk to us, when her shift's over.'

'I want to go home now,' said Kit, stubborn.

'In a bit,' said Fred.

Day Two, Thursday: Heather

If she'd panicked. If she'd got back on the boat.

'Yes?' said the big woman, bringing out the English word with satisfaction, more tumbling after it now. 'Yes? One night twenty euro.'

'Yes,' said Heather, giving in.

As they came past the booth, the port official was unlocking its door. He slung the bag inside and gave them both a glance. Heather hesitated and he stood there, keys dangling from a finger.

'May I help you?' he said. The big woman tugged at her elbow, hissing something.

'It's my friend's bag,' she said. He gave her an amused, sceptical look. 'Yes?' he said. Her heart dipped.

'I'm going to . . . meet her,' she said. His eyebrows lifted. 'I can take the bag, if you . . .' She faltered, changed direction. Of course he wasn't going to give her the address. But she could follow him.

'I understand.' She made herself smile, ingratiating, but she was weary suddenly with all this. 'I see that you have to deliver it yourself but maybe I can tell her when I see her, when it will arrive?' Desperately. But he only frowned at her, and the big woman was tugging at her sleeve.

The place was clean, a blue-painted door, a small white-washed room with a shuttered window. It stood across a tiny courtyard from the woman's front door. Stepping inside Heather looked around and saw a key in the door's lock and a socket where she could charge her phone, and nodded. The big woman hesitated in the doorway and thinking she was waiting for money Heather fumbled for her purse but the woman flapped her hand, into the future. 'After,' she said. And went, banging the door behind her.

Heather plugged in her phone and locked the door and with the sound she felt something lift, not all of it, but something, floating free from her. The man's small pointed face receding across the water, staring.

She lay down and slept.

At a certain point in the night she woke and heard the

waves, or perhaps they came to her in her sleep in the strange room.

With the sound of the water came the far-off coloured lights, the music. A certain guy, walking in and out of shot, always there, in the background, and Heather noticing him, as she drank cider under the breakwaters with her mates. One time she saw him on the decks, headphones, in silhouette. Assured, laid-back, cool. And it came to her, what he was, what his game was.

He liked to take his time. Grooming, it was called. He had watched her over two, three nights. He had chosen her carefully: known she would be a virgin, too naive to see what he really was, too young to fight, too ashamed to tell. He had wanted someone he could break.

You won't break me. You didn't break me. But her. Sukie Alexander. He'd break her.

She was under the pier, and darkness swallowed her, sleep swallowed her back up and Heather dreamed, turning, sweat cold on her, dreamed of the feel of stones hard under her back, the smell of dope, sweet and suffocating, of water lapping under the pier.

Chapter Thirteen

Day Three, Friday: Sukie

A bell woke her, ringing somewhere below, tolling on and on.

Sukie lay still with her eyes closed, everything reminding her she wasn't at home, the bell, the temperature in the room, some kind of odour in the air – what was that? What day was it? She calmed herself, counting. Friday. She opened her eyes.

Beside her in the bed was the back of Jake's head. His hair looked dirty on the pillow.

She struggled upright, her own scalp prickling, *what what what* and there was a sound from him, a grunting murmur, and she froze. The murmur petered out into a sigh and he was still.

Nothing happened. She blinked, trying to remember, she

let herself back down gently, deep breaths. They'd drunk wine. What had they eaten? She couldn't remember.

He had lit candles for them; when they stumbled back in she could see his face in the candlelight, deep hollows under his eyes, a glitter. Had there been another bottle of something? He must have stayed awake after Sukie because there they were on the table, they'd been blown out.

Then she remembered holding out a hand to him as she stumbled into bed. *Don't go.* She'd said that. Meaning, *look after me.* They'd talked about living without electricity, she remembered that. Close to nature, Jake had said, and she'd just looked at him, silently wishing for a plug, a lamp, a heater: something to put *between* her and nature.

Don't go. The alcohol must have made her needy. Now, warily, Sukie looked around the room. A thin morning light was leaking round the shutters; she couldn't seem to slow her heart down. She felt strange – her stomach roiled and churned, hotly – and suddenly she knew she had to get downstairs, to the toilet.

Coming back out of the loo, shakily, she paused at the foot of the stairs in the grey light in all the clutter. It must have been the food, whatever it was.

No Michelin star: he hadn't been joking. The taverna in season might, at a pinch, have been picturesque. A terrace looking down at the sea, the smell of woodsmoke. But on the terrace's cracked tiles leaves blew in circles under a single broken chair as they skirted it, and Jake, her phone still in his hand, had shown her to a lit doorway.

Inside, a table was laid for two – plates, paper napkins, a

large carafe of yellow wine – in what looked like someone's front room, with garish paintings, and when she saw the girl's mother from the shop standing there in one of those jokey aprons with underwear on it, cracked and yellowing, Sukie was glad she hadn't had her silk shirt to change into. The woman gave a stiff little bow, eyes fixed on Jake, and awkwardly they sat. For a moment the phone rested under Jake's hand and then he slid it across to her, screen up.

She'd looked: well, of course, she had. It was her phone. A message was displayed in its little box, *Sure everything's okay?* Joey. She'd heard a small sound, impatient, looked up and saw Jake frowning. Had he seen the message? She put the phone away in her pocket.

Looking for any kind of menu Sukie had realised quickly that you ate what you were given, which was a rich oily stew, pallid potatoes and stewed bitter greens. The overhead light had been too bright and she had drunk too much. Every time she looked her glass had been full, and quite quickly it had seemed easier – everything seemed easier – if she just drank it.

And now, standing down there outside the loo with her hand on the rickety banister, Sukie rehearsed it. *I don't think this is working out. I might take a room down in the village.* Her heart thumped.

She could hear her mother say it: What, *never?* Never spent a whole night in a bed with a man. What are you, a virgin? One of those LGBT demi-semi-sexual people? A *lesbian?*

That doesn't mean I'm a virgin, Mother.

119

Sukie had had sex with two people. She had lost her virginity at nineteen, a boy in college, shy, nice, or so she'd thought; weedy, and as hopeless as she was – or so she'd thought. Mostly she'd thought, it could have been worse. But then he'd spread rumours about her, after.

The other time had been someone drunk who'd cried in her bed after a party a flatmate had, before Sukie got her own place – the trigger, in fact, for her moving out. Sukie had patted him, a lot, and persuaded him to go before he fell asleep. She had wondered, then, what she was doing, and had decided that next time, it would only happen because she really, really wanted it to happen.

It occurred to her that Jake almost certainly thought she was a virgin. She'd told him she hadn't had a boyfriend, which was true, and had blushed, which might have been more revealing.

Her body felt strange, hot and awkward, now. She leaned against the banister and half registered the strange basement room in the dim light. Something was different: a suitcase sat on top of the chest freezer, its lid up. She tilted her head on one side, considering it, then she heard Jake turn over in the bed upstairs and carefully made her way back up.

Had he touched her? She suddenly couldn't remember. She couldn't even remember putting on her nightshirt, the one she'd rolled up and stuffed in her carry-on bag, just to be safe, it was a sensible one, with a cartoon character on it. She must have fallen asleep very suddenly.

He turned, and opened his eyes, and for a second she could tell he didn't know where he was, he was unfocused, quite vulnerable. 'Morning,' she said, timidly, and suddenly he smiled.

You sleep.

That was what he'd said. She'd said, *Don't go.* He'd said, *I won't* – and then, *You sleep.* And then it all made sense. She had fallen sound asleep because she felt so safe, she even, if she concentrated, thought she could remember lifting her arms, nightshirt over her head. She must have been dog tired.

And he sat up, he was rubbing his eyes but he was alert, immediately. He was bare-chested. 'Sweetheart,' he said. Sukie swallowed. 'You must have been still worn out from the journey, you were spark out.' And as he echoed the words in her own head, she sat down and let it all drain out of her, the panic.

'Maybe it was the wine,' she said, yawning, and he rolled over on his side and reached for his phone.

She picked up her own phone quickly from the side table: no signal. She held it against herself. Jake swung his legs over the side of the bed, and reached for his clothes. As the cover fell away she saw he was wearing underpants, at least, black but faded.

'I'll head down to the town again,' he said, pulling on his trousers. 'I've got a bit of business to sort out, maybe I can unearth the generator guy this time. But he was ancient, he's probably snuffed it.' And laughed, though Sukie didn't see what was funny. She thought of the little graveyard, lonely along the path, in the shadow of the far peak where the gulls wheeled.

'I can come too,' she said. A bit of business; she'd set a bit of store, she realised, by the idea of Jake as an olive oil importer. Her smiling at his side, charming farmers with him. Something she could tell her mother. 'Couldn't I?'

Jake regarded her. 'It's a long walk,' he said. 'Why don't you stay here and just chill?' He opened the shutters. 'Sun's out, at least. Explore. I'll pick up some more stuff while I'm down there.'

Sukie's stomach churned again and she sat, in a sudden sweat. 'And water,' she said. 'Maybe some mineral water?' She wanted her mother with a sudden sharp idiotic pang, her mother bringing her hot Ribena.

'Mineral water?' His eyebrows went up, mocking. 'How many bottles, for madam? Weighs a ton, that stuff.'

'Oh, no, I didn't think . . .' She was flustered, clutching the phone.

'I'll see what I can do,' said Jake, and he was gone.

Sukie made the bed. She found a broom and swept the floor, she washed up some cups, found teabags and made tea with UHT milk. It tasted sweetish and otherwise of nothing. Sipping, she looked around the room, the bright blue paint on the shutters and window frames peeling, the rough plaster greyish with dust. Whatever she did, trying to imagine him growing up here, meals and games, it refused to feel like a home. The image of the family on the sofa came back to her, frozen, the glaring woman. Maybe it was the wide arched fireplace, blackened inside with smoke, yawning dark and draughty at her. Maybe a fire would do the trick. Firewood.

She'd left the house and was halfway to the path down to the sea and felt the folded map in her pocket, before she wondered what had happened to the folder and the photographs. She'd left it there on the sofa but it hadn't been there this morning, she'd shaken out the throw. She stopped, turned; she could see the fig tree, the shuttered house opposite. She didn't know why she was panicking. Jake would just have found it and put it away.

The sun was weak and hazy, just barely took the edge off the cold, different pale colours glinting off the sea, and far off the long silhouette of a tanker moving lazily across the wide horizon. As she watched, though, its outline was already indistinct, the silvery surface of the sea turning dull and matte and for a moment she couldn't work out what was happening – and then she saw it was fog, drifting in, a soft grey blanket.

The walk, too, was good, the cool air and the pale sun and the smell of the sea. The going was slower without Jake, she didn't know the terrain and the path wasn't more than a goat-track. She heard the whump of a helicopter, loud in the silence, and turned to watch it disappear behind the far peak.

The trees she remembered were enclosed behind a tumbledown drystone wall, as the path disappeared around a curve in the hillside. Sukie thought they must be fruit trees of some sort, in rows, very old and gnarled, and there were plenty of fallen branches on the yellowing grass under them. She gathered up an armful and turned around – feeling warmed by the exercise, blood pumping – to see an elderly couple just a yard or two away, making their way around the hillside. They wore old-fashioned dark glasses, he wore beige trousers and she was in a faded floral housecoat, orange, and legs, her bare brown legs thin and dry as sticks underneath, feet in sandals. They were holding hands, the woman clinging, uncertain. Sukie waited politely for them to come alongside her. Not knowing what to say when they did, she bobbed an awkward little bow.

'Hello there.' The raspy voice was American, the man who spoke inspecting her from behind wraparound glasses.

'Hello,' said Sukie, hesitating, and the woman interrupted her.

'You have to be careful,' she said, anxiously. 'Iannis doesn't like people taking his wood, it's not like back home.' Looking up at her husband, if that was what he was. They both wore wedding rings, embedded in brown flesh.

The man patted her, shushing, and said in his deep voice, 'Back home,' he said, impatiently. 'The last time you collected wood back home on the prairie, my love, you were eight years old.' He nodded at the wood. 'And Iannis has been dead four years,' shaking his head. 'You'll have to forgive my wife,' he said, straightening, very upright. He still didn't take off his glasses. 'She doesn't always remember.' He loomed at Sukie, inspecting her. 'Are you Jacob's . . . Are you with Jacob? Jake? Have I seen you?'

'Yes,' said Sukie. Jacob's . . . what? She didn't know what he had told her. 'I came with Jake, we're . . . we're friends.' She held out a hand. *Sukie's always so polite*, Marsha would say, turning her back, stubbing her cigarette out in someone's cup.

'I'm Susan Alexander. Sukie. And you must be . . .' she hesitated, 'Nat and Betsy?'

The old woman in her housecoat straightened, dreamy blue eyes coming into focus, her face, her body language almost girlish suddenly.

Nat patted his wife's arm absently. 'Sukie,' he pronounced, trying her name out as if there was something funny about it, and she felt herself redden. 'Well that sounds about right. So Jacob told you about us, did he?' He sounded surprised.

'Well, I . . .' Of course, he hadn't told her. She'd been prying. 'Yes,' said Sukie.

'Of course you'll come down for a cup of coffee.' It was Betsy, she was confident now, the vague clinging elderly woman had receded.

'Honey . . .' Nat shifted, but his wife shushed him, riding the wave of confidence. 'This young lady hasn't had any breakfast yet,' she said, 'I can just tell.' Nat sighed. 'Well . . .'

'You have to be neighbourly,' said Betsy, beaming at Sukie. 'In this place, goodness, I remember when we were all in and out of each other's houses . . .' And she faltered. Nat took her elbow, resigned.

'I'm sure we can rustle up some coffee,' he said. 'I'm afraid we can't offer you much more than that, supplies are hard to come by up here, and Betsy does need her nap, but—'

'Oh, no, honestly, I really don't want to be any trouble,' said Sukie, uncertain, but Betsy, galvanised again, lurched towards her, the brown claw of her hand seizing her. 'But you must,' she said. 'She must, mustn't she, Nathaniel?'

And there was something then, a flicker of something Sukie wanted to understand, between these two, and the old neighbourly days, when Jake and his parents lived across the way. 'If you're sure,' she said, and she smiled, innocent, over the old lady's shoulder and into Nat's face. She could see herself reflected in the wraparound glasses. 'That's so kind.'

Day Three, Friday: Kit

The guy at reception looked up in surprise: sheepishly Kit lifted a hand in greeting and hurried past, fumbling for his security tag. He was never late to work, and he never came in looking like he'd slept in a wheelie bin. He left that to Fred and his lads, but today, he knew, Fred was already in, because Fred had texted him a string of suggestive emojis and a picture of his empty desk as he emerged from the Tube.

Kit had a hangover. That was what this was. That was all this was. Other guys got hangovers all the time. He waited for the lift. When the doors opened he had to make a conscious effort to move.

Obediently he positioned himself at the back of the lift. When it lurched, his stomach did too.

Waiting for the barmaid to go on her break, somehow more men Fred knew had turned up, and they all seemed have a version of his situation, via some kind of Chinese Whispers. People kept telling him to cheer up, plenty more fish in the sea. And then Fred himself materialised at his shoulder, curiously sharp among the beer-fuzzy faces.

'Come along with me, sonny,' he said, in a comedy accent. 'I didn't pick this pub at random. I got a lady here might be able to help you.' And then they were at the bar, not in the scrum but at the far end where there was a flap in the mahogany and the barmaid was lifting it.

'This is Jade,' said Fred. Jade was pale and pinched between her plaits, with suspicious little eyes. 'Five minutes,' she said, reaching back behind the bar for a big floppy cardigan, and Fred evaporated. They went outside where it had just stopped raining: the pavement was gleaming and empty.

She pulled the cardigan around her and got out a packet of cigarettes. She shook the pack towards Kit and he found himself taking one.

He fumbled for his phone to show Jade the picture, but she waved it away. 'Already seen it,' she said, inhaling deeply, offering him the lighter. He lit up, puffed tentatively, and immediately choked. 'So – you know him?' he said, when he got his breath back. She shrugged. 'Well I thought I did,' she said, blowing out smoke. She looked older than he'd first thought, and grim. 'He did a DJ set here a few times. BlueJ. Jake. He got the punters in.'

'Jake who?'

'Littlejohn,' she said, then, shrugging, 'At least, that's what he told me.'

'You had a . . . relationship with him?' Her chin jutted, angrily at his words, and he floundered. 'Well, Fred said . . .'

She dropped the cigarette and ground it out. 'He put on the charm, I fell for it, for a bit.'

'What ended it?'

He spoke casually but Kit could feel his heart pumping, chemicals in his system that he'd never experienced before, and for what? Because of a picture on his girlfriend's phone. Maybe he should have felt like this before, this need to know, this urgency.

'I saw him in another pub, on a date,' Jade said flatly. 'This was a few months back. He didn't see me. One of those city pubs, I knew the girl behind the bar and she told me, this was where he took his Tinder dates. Was in there a few nights a week, as a matter of fact. One of those old-fashioned places with the booths, you know, Victorian, fancy glass.' Her eyes narrowed.

'What did you do?' Kit said. He didn't know what he'd have done. He didn't know what he *was* doing, now it had happened to him.

'Oh, I told myself it was never serious, all that.' Jade eyed him. 'Then I found out he'd been dealing at my pub, using me as a cover, you know. And I went a bit mental, as you do.'

'Yes,' said Kit. *Dealing?* Heather would never go for someone like that.

'So you think your girlfriend has gone off with him, that it?' she said. Kit stared at his shoes. 'Got a picture of her?' He hesitated, then got out the phone, scrolled down. There was one of her at the seaside, wind blowing her hair, scowling at him. He loved that picture.

'Pretty,' said Jade, pursing her lips. Then she pushed the screen back at him. 'I dunno,' she said. 'She looks too savvy to fall for him.' Then she shrugged. 'He likes them impressionable, if you get me.' She saw what he was thinking. 'I'm not just saying that,' she said. 'Because I think it's what you want to hear. Maybe she—' She broke off. 'I dunno.'

Something occurred to him: how did she know what kind of girls he went after? 'When you said, you went a bit mental,' he said, warily. 'Did you . . .' He hesitated. 'Did you stalk him?' She glared, stonily.

He held her gaze, and eventually she sighed.

'Tell you what,' she said. 'Meet me there tomorrow night.'

'Where?'

'The place where he took his dates. It's called the Princess Alexandra,' she said. 'Holborn. I'll have something for you,' she said, pushing through the door and back into the heat and noise of the pub's interior.

'Something?' he said, hanging back. She turned.

'Someone,' she said.

Chapter Fourteen

Day Three, Friday: Heather

Too late. Shit. Shit.

Heather stood by the little glass ticket booth peering down into it. There was no one inside and the bag was gone. She turned, in thin sunlight.

The harbour-front was deserted, a couple of pretty little wooden boats bobbing inside a breakwater, one bar with tables outside and no one sitting at them. She sighed, and headed over there.

She'd meant to get up early; she felt like she'd hardly slept, for the rattle of water over stones in her ears. Perversely it had been the sounds of the port waking up – voices grumbling, cups clinking – that had sent her to sleep at last some time after six. And when she'd woken – her phone blipping notifications in her ear – the sun had been high enough to hurt her eyes, stabbing through the gaps in the shutters. Her mouth tasted sour and she could smell the night's sweat on her. She washed in the basin that sat in a corner of the room in a trickle of rusty water.

Outside she found her hostess sitting on a wooden chair in the sun, knees apart and peeling potatoes into a bucket. She stashed the money Heather gave her in a pocket in her apron. Hesitating, Heather had said, 'Kyros?' And mimed a boat going over the waves. Pointed vaguely in the direction of the port. The woman shrugged and said something in Greek that Heather understood as, *whatever*, and went back to her potatoes.

Now she pulled out a chair and sat. It was getting colder, not warmer, the sun more indistinct. A middle-aged man came out in a clean apron and she asked for coffee. 'Nescafé milk?' he said, grinning. She saw a gold tooth. 'Greek coffee,' she said.

When he came back with it, a tiny copper pan and cup and a little sticky square of cake with an almond on it, she went through the same boat-and-wave mime, the same pronunciation of the island's name. The café owner stared and then shook his head abruptly, waved his hand in the direction of the sea *no, no*, and went back inside. Heather sipped the sweet hot coffee; she felt almost light-headed, a hum of tiredness and tension like electricity setting up inside her. Her phone was on the table, face up.

Before she'd swung her legs out of the narrow bed she'd scrolled down the notifications, but none of them had been from Kit.

Kit hadn't texted, he hadn't phoned – but then it was

easier not to, wasn't it? That had always been the option Heather took, she couldn't understand women who moped over their phones. Silence was power.

Not always it wasn't, though, was it? Sometimes you wish you'd kicked and screamed, under the pier. Had she? She couldn't remember now; now it was all a great glaring white noise, the music, the sea, his face on hers, the sickly smell of dope and cigarettes.

She sat back, the phone was between her hands now, the little coffee cup drained, and felt a tug at the thought of Kit. Anger and misery mixed: how dare he? How dare he assume? She'd never given him cause to think she was interested in someone else. She never had been. She thought of his pale worried face, the freckles across his nose. His kindness.

Tough shit. She set the phone down.

From the other side of the harbour something moved against the faded colours of the houses and she wondered for a second if she was imagining things but then the movement took shape, two shapes materialised in the haze. A small wiry man and a fat one, growing more distinct as they approached. They nodded to her as they came past her and inside.

She picked the phone up again. Typed, before she could stop herself: *You don't know what he did.*

She got up abruptly, should she . . . and then with the movement all three men were outside, gesticulating around her. She looked down at her phone and blinked: she'd sent it.

The wiry man was talking to her in some confusion of Greek and English. 'What?' she said, her heart thumping at what she'd done, clutching the phone. The man took her upper arm and pointed out to sea, he said, Kyros. He mimed the boat, and said, Tomorrow.

'No,' said Heather, stubborn. 'Not tomorrow, now. Why not now?'

They all laughed then. Heather saw their teeth, the wiry man's edged with black from smoking, they were all pointing again. And then she saw the fog, rolling in.

And turning, Heather realised that she couldn't even see the coloured façades across the harbour any more. The port official must have looked at the forecast and taken the bag at first light.

She held her ground, folded her arms. No. Tapped the table with her fingernail. 'Now,' she said.

There was another scuffle and a pen and paper were produced and the wiry man wrote on it, a name. Kostas, and a mobile number. He gave it to her – or half did, holding on to one corner. 'Sixty euros,' he said. 'OK?' Heather's shoulders dropped, despite herself. 'Sixty?' she said in despair, fishing out the crumpled notes in her pocket. Two, three twenties and a handful of change. And she hadn't paid for her coffee yet.

'Fifty?' she suggested. And the little man's hand, hovering, descended to clap her on the shoulder. 'OK.' He grinned. 'OK. You wait here.'

And they evaporated, leaving her with the scrap of paper in her hand and the fog rolling in across the stones.

Day Three, Friday: Joey

Anastasia kept glancing over. She was subdued, and looking wan in an oversized sweatshirt. Perhaps the marathon shag-fest hadn't been all she wanted it to be. Joey knew she should ask, or commiserate, but she was finding it hard to focus on anything, most especially the historical novel she was trying to copy edit, whose timeline was all over the place and whose characters, who had been cheerful, raunchy robber barons when she started work on the book a week ago, were suddenly unbearable.

After last night's googling, Joey hadn't slept a whole lot.

She'd thought it was such a clever idea, to google using someone's email address. *His* email address. After all, you used it for all sorts. She knew vaguely how the browsers worked, how they filtered and arranged stuff.

Sukie wouldn't have googled him using his email address; she probably wouldn't have done much more than looking up his Greek island on Google Earth. She had thought she was scrupulous, but she had been trusting too much to her own instincts. Both of them, Joey and Sukie both.

So. Jake Littlejohn. jlky@gmail.com

jlky@gmail.com had posted a couple of reviews online using the same email address: one of a book about rave culture, another of an album by some band she'd vaguely heard of but she didn't know why, little alarm bells going off in her head. The reviews had been written in quite a different voice from the emails to Sukie.

*This c**t knows nothing.* That was the review of the book.

Posted on a slack forum, Joey thought, because generally this stuff would be deleted. Abusive stuff. Just over the line from a poorly regulated forum was the dark web, of course. Even Joey knew about the dark web, knew just enough not to want to think about it and what went on.

If Sukie had heard a man she was on a date with saying that, using those words. No way.

Sitting there last night, tense, at her desk, she had been able to feel herself testing something in her head. Testing the ground.

Then the review of the album. *You a god, man*, it had said. *You speak the language.* Joey had looked at it, frowning. There was a picture of the album cover above it, a man's white face thrust towards the camera, eyes in shadow, hanks of hair hanging black to either side. Goth, Emo, whatever. Not Joey's kind of music.

You speak the language. She had stared, turning that phrase over, at the words. What did that mean? Then the email address repeated. At the beginning, and then he'd added it in to his review.

`jlky@gmail.com` *You a god, man. You speak the language.* `jlkyr@gmail.com`

It was weird, unidentifiably, unquantifiably weird. She could feel its weirdness stirring the hairs on the back of her neck. She looked, and looked – and then she suddenly had the feeling that she wanted not to look.

All right, she'd said to herself. All right. And it had suddenly seemed very dark outside, a darkness that pressed against the windows of her little flat, and suddenly Joey hadn't wanted to look at this again until it was daylight. And slowly, slowly, she had lowered the lid of her laptop. And gone to bed.

'Hey.' It was Anastasia, sulky, standing at her shoulder, violet shadows under her eyes. 'Wassup?'

Joey sighed, pushed her chair back.

On the screen was not the historical novel but the same browser page, with Jake Littlejohn's email address on it. It had been sitting there a while.

'Hey,' she said. 'How was it?'

Anastasia yawned, wide as a cat. 'All right,' she said. 'Actually. Fun.' The shadow of mischief passed across her face. 'Not much sleep.' And grinned.

'Seeing him again?'

'Don't be soft,' Anastasia began to scoff, then shrugged. 'I mean, maybe. Yeah. He was quite . . . he wanted to. So – yeah.'

Joey pulled out a chair, glancing around. Heads hadn't begun to turn yet. 'Sit down,' she said, patting the seat. 'I need a bit of help here.'

'What's all this, then?' Anastasia leaned forward to get a better look. 'Eeow,' she said. 'That creep?'

'What creep?' said Joey.

'The band, that band,' said Anastasia.

'Oh,' said Joey, leaning back. 'Oh. Yes. Him.' Because she knew, suddenly, the reason she knew the band's name was because their lead singer had been in the news, a year or two back, maybe five.

'What did he get? Was it life?' said Anastasia, staring. Joey nodded. There'd been a lot of charges. 'Online child abuse, wasn't it?'

You speak the language.

'Grooming, I think,' said Joey, faltering. She didn't even know where the words came from, because it was the kind of screaming headline she always looked away from. 'Conspiracy to abuse a child, something like that.'

'Why's . . .' Anastasia was leaning forwards again, her finger at the screen. 'Do you think that's just a mistake?' She was pointing at the email address. Addresses.

jlky@gmail.com

jlkyr@gmail.com

One letter different. Anastasia rested her elbow on the desk, chin in one palm, frowning. She turned to Joey. 'Tell me what you were looking for,' she said. 'Who. Who is he?'

Chapter Fifteen

Day Three, Friday: Sukie

Nat and Betsy's house was dim and quiet and warm – at last, Sukie thought gratefully, feeling like she hadn't been warm in a week, settling back into a large ugly sofa in a ground-floor sitting room that was shaded gloomily by both by a veranda and the fig tree. Betsy went behind a breakfast bar to make the coffee but then just stood there and Nat sent her back to sit beside Sukie while he did it.

She learned – from Nat, talking from behind the breakfast bar without pause – that twenty-five years ago he had taken early retirement from the US Navy, Betsy was a *homemaker*, they had children – the kids, he called them, she assumed they were her age – back in the States. Betsy sat, quiet and obedient, nodding.

'Your . . . kids grew up here too?' she said and Nat laughed heartily.

'Oh, no, they were mostly grown by the time we came out, and besides, we wouldn't have . . .' He glanced at Betsy, who was turning her hands over and over each other anxiously. 'The schools here aren't up to much, between you and me.'

Sukie nodded automatically, looking to Nat behind the bar for confirmation, and in that moment he stepped into the light, sunglasses off, turning his head a certain way like an old bird, and she realised that he was the old man she and Jake had seen swimming. Had seen climbing out of the water naked. He was looking at her as if he knew what she was thinking, and Sukie babbled.

'The fog,' she said, grasping for something neutral, the weather. 'Really dramatic.' And it had been, mysterious and stealthy, unfurling like a carpet across the sea. 'Is it . . . does that happen often?' Speaking brightly.

Pathetic. Perfectly natural just to walk into the sea, he wasn't to know, was he, that there would be people?

'Is it foggy?' said Betsy, sounding alarmed, although they'd all three turned to watch it rolling in. Turning to Nat, pleading. 'Darling? Is it foggy? You must check the cellar door, Nathaniel, you must.' She leaned, confidentially. 'The boats come, when it's foggy. They're smugglers, you know.'

Sukie glanced back at the door, where a pale greenish light filtered in from the outside world. Smugglers? 'Oh,' she said. 'You mean the – migrants?'

'Betsy's been reading too many of her romances,' said Nat, coming round the breakfast bar with the tray, and obediently Betsy sat back and smiled, nodding. Taking his time he poured out three cups, offering cream. The coffee smelled delicious to Sukie, it smelled of home, and again she had that stab of longing, for her little flat, even for her desk, the framed picture of her aged seven holding her dog.

'Will you, though?' said Betsy, taking her cup. 'Just to be sure.'

'I'll do that, my sweet,' Nat said soothingly, looking from one of them to the other, standing over them. Sukie wished he *would* go.

'The mist comes in and gets into everything, you see,' said Betsy, confidentially, and Nat sighed. 'People come in too.' She smiled up at him. 'You know it does. It gets into the boiler.' She looked down at her coffee. 'Jacob likes the bad weather—'

'This is Jacob's girlfriend Sukie, Betsy,' Nat interrupted her. 'Did I say that?'

'Do go, Nathaniel, please,' said Betsy and with a sigh he set down his cup, turned and headed for a door at the back of the room.

'Jacob likes the bad weather?' Sukie said. Betsy leaned towards her, conspiratorial. 'It's when the boats come in,' she whispered, and winked. 'And they leave things in the cellar.' Sukie pulled back, disconcerted, thinking of the cellar across the way. She knew quite suddenly that Jake would disapprove of her talking to Betsy. As if on cue her phone blipped.

There was a message from Jake: *Bumped into some people. Back soon.* She saw that the phone was almost out of battery again.

She looked up from the phone. 'Betsy?' But Betsy's head was turned towards the door through which Nat had disappeared. Sukie could hear him taking the stairs carefully: he must, she thought, be at least in his late seventies. She hesitated. Some people? She thought of the island and the people on it and all the stuff she didn't know. *I might go for a little walk,* she typed, after a minute's hesitation. Send.

Betsy had got up, hovering, listening.

Then to Joey. *Fine sweetheart, stop worrying.* Then opened her mail program again, although she'd left an out-of-office reply, she felt sure there was something she'd meant to look at, something that needed answering.

Oh.

Only the LinkedIn. OK. She examined the profile of the sender: freelance film archivist, Heather Baxter. Well – OK. She clicked *accept.*

Now she turned it off again.

And then Betsy turned round. 'Oh, those things,' she said, seeing the phone in her hand. 'I'll do that for you, sweetheart.' Betsy held out her hand and abruptly was on her feet, the perfect hostess. She took the phone, unerring, to a socket where another was plugged in and, beaming, returned to her place.

'You're his girlfriend?' she said. 'But he's still so young.'

Sukie blinked, realising in the same moment that Jake really couldn't be called young, and that Betsy was living in an uncertain fog of present and long gone past. 'He's . . .' She hesitated, before going on, gently, 'He's over forty, Betsy.'

'Really? Perhaps . . .' Betsy drew her lower lip in between

her teeth, like a child. 'There was all that trouble, wasn't there? I remember he went back to Britain, I do remember that. Susannah – that's his mama – she used to tell us how successful he was, it was something to do with music.' She pressed her hands to her paper liver-spotted cheeks, like a girl. The movement raised her tunic and Sukie saw something, a belt with something attached to it, was it something medical, like a pacemaker? Or just innocuous, a step counter? Betsy noticed her looking and dropped her arms abruptly.

'So you're his girlfriend.' She repeated it with brittle politeness. Sukie smiled, uncomfortable. 'Have you been together a long time?'

'A . . .' Sukie hesitated, 'a few months.'

Betsy shifted in her seat, anxious, and glanced at the door through which Nat had disappeared. 'Thick as thieves, they are, every time he comes back,' she said, confiding again. 'Nathan and Jacob, thick as thieves, just a bit of business, he says, Nat says, nothing I need to worry my pretty head about, but I don't like it. It comes in with the mist, you see.' She shook her head and it was as if the movement cleared the thought because her face smoothed.

'Business?' said Sukie, disconcerted. 'Jake said olive oil.'

Betsy stared. 'Olive oil?' she said, faltering, glancing at the door. 'But they don't bring that on the boats, do they?' Head on one side, like an old beady-eyed bird.

Sukie gave up, searched for a neutral topic. 'It must be so lovely and quiet here,' she said. 'Now there's so few of you?' Betsy settled back, on safer ground.

'Oh, the children are such a nuisance, they run in and

out of here, all the little ones, Simon and David and the little twins; Jacob's the biggest, the ringleader, of course.' And she stopped, a hand to her mouth, half horrified, half delighted. 'David tells the most terrible tales.' Smiling, broadly. And then her eyes were shifty again, glancing from side to side.

'Terrible tales?'

'Oh, well, you know.' Betsy folded her hands in her lap and looked to the door and back to the window, satisfying herself that they were alone – it wasn't even clear that she remembered that Nat was in the cellar. 'Boys will be boys, although we do say it's neglect pure and simple.' She whispered, eyes bright. 'His mother – Susannah? Do you know Susannah? More interested in sleeping with other women's husbands. She drinks, of course, they both do, and who knows what goes on. We know better than to bring ours up here, they're at school back in the States, Nat insisted.'

'What was he like?' said Sukie, eager: she wanted to know, suddenly, now Betsy was back there, living in the past. Then there was the sound of Nat on the stairs, grumbling as he ascended, and something crystallised in her gaze, it was sharp.

'Jacob?' she said, head on one side. 'Well, there was that little girl from the shop told her tales about him, and David always was a milksop, Jacob was just one of those boys, I'm sure he never meant—' She stopped. 'Did Susannah die?' she said wonderingly. 'Did she *die*?'

Nat had stopped in the doorway. 'What was that, honey?' he said. 'Did who die?' Betsy's face was a mask of compliant sweetness. 'Sweetheart?' There was warning in his voice, and both their faces turned towards him.

Sukie spoke first. 'Oh, I was just asking about Jake's . . . family,' she said, some instinct guiding her. 'You must have all been so close. Their deaths – the car accident. It must have been a terrible shock. It was out here, is that right?'

'Was it a car wreck, honey?' said Betsy, searching his face, that was half in shadow still as he walked towards them, the bird-like silhouette thrown against the wall. 'Is that right?'

And he was between them, leaning down to pick up the tray. 'I think it's time for your nap, Bets,' he said, straightening, and, feeling something suddenly, something that had come up with him from below, the cold breath of the cellar, Sukie got hurriedly to her feet.

'You've been so kind,' she said. 'So kind.' And then she was backing, nodding, out of the door and into the fog. At the last minute she turned back and waved, faltering at their faces turned towards her in the gloom, the ghost of anxious appeal flickering on Betsy's and then gone, again, to blankness.

Day Three, Friday: Kit

You don't know what he did.

How many times had Kit looked at the message? *What he did.* He'd done something to her.

Tell *me.* That was all he had to write.

Better to talk to her. Kit needed to get information, not

a rebuff, not a two word answer, not, *When I'm back.* There was more to this than could be contained in a text message.

Taking a deep breath, Kit dialled. An odd long ringtone, two, then a pleasant recorded message informing him his contract didn't allow calls to roaming phones. He hung up. She wouldn't even know he'd tried, and he wasn't sure if that was a good thing or a bad thing. If only his head would stop hurting. There was a can of fizzy orange on the table in front of him: he'd gone up to the café on the top floor for it. He took a swig.

Methodical: that was the way to do it. Kit logged on to his service provider's webpage, with extreme difficulty remembered his password, selected the correct bundle of roaming extras, entered his card details. *Pay now.*

'Skiving again? How many times do I have to tell you, Mr Harrison?' It was Fred, his shirt hanging out, a large latte in one hand and an espresso in the other. He set down the drinks and pulled out a chair, with a loud careless scrape.

'You were getting on very nicely with our Jade last night,' he said. Kit looked at him. Hangdog was the word for what he felt. He couldn't think. He opened his mouth and closed it again.

'She liked you, I could tell. She even said something about seeing you again tonight.'

Was he taking the piss? 'Fred,' said Kit, as if through a fog. Fred held up a hand. 'You want the bucket of milk or the wake-up shot?'

Kit pulled the espresso towards him and knocked it back, feeling the dull jolt of caffeine.

Fred, who had been examining the latte with a grimace, lifted his head. 'Listen,' he said, 'I don't know why you give a shit. Join the real world. Join the lads. Play the field. Shag Jade, she's a sport.'

Kit stared. He got the words out, one after the other. 'My girlfriend,' he said, 'my girlfriend Heather, you've met her, Fred, I have a girlfriend. She is on the other side of the fucking world running after some guy who did something to her and I don't know what and I *need to find out.*'

Fred's face changed.

'I'm scared, Fred,' said Kit. 'I don't know what she's going to do.'

Chapter Sixteen

Day Three, Friday: Heather

Last seen at 3.30 p.m.

Heather made a noise under her breath. She'd never felt so urgently in need of a word from Kit, nor so frustrated by another person's failure to answer a message.

She could hear the boat, but not see it. The fog had thickened. Heather couldn't see much further than the black curled fronds of seaweed that bobbed and drifted like hair in the water below the stone pier where she was waiting. Kostas had answered her call in a raspy, smoker's voice. The good news was he spoke a kind of English, although he did use it to try and bargain her back up. He'd started at seventy euros. Because of the fog, he said.

'No, no, *no.*' She hadn't been able to restrain her despair, and, taken aback, he had agreed.

The sound of the boat's engine was high pitched, ghostly. There was no one on the pier, and Heather couldn't see back to where she'd sat in the bar. She clutched her phone so tight, her hand had seized up. Cautiously she released it and rubbed the cramped fingers.

She looked again. Nothing. What time would it be in England? She no longer knew. Two hours behind? Did the messaging app use their time or Greece's? Her brain was as foggy as the view.

It had been a mistake. She blinked her eyes shut to erase it. A mistake. She didn't even know what she'd said in the message any more, she'd deleted it straight away so she could pretend she hadn't opened her mouth. Maybe that was it. There had been no message.

What would be the point of telling, after all this time? Better just to walk away. And with that an idea came: she could block him, block Kit and then she'd have control again.

There was a buzz as it downloaded emails – she must have left the email page open. She looked down: blinked. *New connection*, it said. The girl – Sukie Alexander – had agreed to their connection. Heather stared.

'Miss! OK, miss!'

She looked down and saw the bow of a boat materialise in the fog, nudging towards her. Not a big boat: an inflatable of about fifteen feet, and a bearded man in a worn jacket standing at an outboard, scowling up at her. He was beckoning impatiently, then, when she moved towards the edge, pointing at a rusted ladder below her against the harbour wall. She slung the backpack on her back and began to climb down.

The bow of the boat bobbed precariously under her and she caught a gust of the smell, that under-the-pier smell, she swayed, Kostas shouted. She jumped, sprawled in the bottom of the dinghy, and immediately he was standing over her.

She looked up at him with the smell of the sea making her briefly dizzy, making her grab for the rubber sides of the boat, but there was nothing to grab, smooth and bouncy, her hand scrabbled uselessly. 'Hey, miss!' he said and his hand was on her shoulder, shaking her, his face was in hers and it wasn't him, it wasn't then, she wasn't under the pier. 'Fifty,' he said, and she scrabbled upright, undignified, sweating, cold all at once. She pulled the crumpled notes out of her pocket.

The boat swung round, bobbing, towards the harbour's mouth, negotiating buoys and moored boats. A gust of colder, fresher air blew in Heather's face and she looked back to see the ghost shapes of three men standing there between the bollards, hands in their pockets, watching them leave.

And then there was just the fog, and the sound of the outboard.

Day Three, Friday: Sukie

The mist hung just below the village. On the sea side Sukie couldn't make out the shoreline any more, or the path up from the port. She was walking towards the further peak

149

with the tiny walled graveyard at its base. The narrow road that led between the two hills was clear, but the mist hung just below the cemetery walls.

Just a little walk. There was nothing wrong with exploring, was there? Finding out about the place. She wondered how long Jake would be, with the fog – she calculated that it would be an hour, at least.

She brought out the map. Turning away from the view and retracing the narrow meandering path through the village Sukie thought she remembered something and consulted the map. She stopped. *David's house*: it was tiny, more a hovel than a house and shuttered up. A dusty old iron bath leaning against the wall. Whoever David was – perhaps he only came in the summer. Perhaps he'd died long ago. Betsy had talked about David, as if he was younger than Jake. As if— There was a tiny window without shutters or glass, only a grille, and as Sukie moved on she thought she caught a flicker of movement through it. 'Hello?' she said, but quietly, nervously – and there was no answer.

Jake hadn't talked about how he ended up in her bed. Maybe he thought this was a natural progression, just sleeping side by side. Maybe it *was* a natural progression. What would she know? She just wished she remembered a bit more about it.

But she had decided, she needed to be more adventurous. Taking a deep breath as she made her way down towards the road that led to the graveyard, Sukie reminded herself of that. That was why she was here: she couldn't expect it to feel familiar, and predictable, and *safe*.

And besides, he understood, didn't he? After all the cheesy jokes, all the bad movies, all the edgy guys who turned just a little bit cold, or excused themselves to go to the toilet halfway through dinner. All the uneasy struggles over the bill. There'd been none of that with Jake. He only listened, and smiled. He'd been shy, like her, lonely, like her.

Betsy must be confusing him with another child. Maybe this David had been the ringleader. She hurried on, leaving the little house behind.

All Jake had ever done was show his interest in *her*, to the point that she felt embarrassed of how little there was to tell, to the point that she'd just shaken her head sorrowfully when he'd asked about her parents. 'They aren't, they aren't . . .' Had she meant to say, they aren't interesting enough for you? He'd said, 'Mine too,' and by the time she realised he meant dead, it had felt too late to set him right. Also, convenient.

He hadn't talked about his mother's drinking. That might in fact be why he'd brought her here, to see if he could trust her with his past. Or perhaps Betsy had imagined that, too – but then Sukie thought of the photograph she'd seen: the woman in the picture sounded like the mother Betsy knew – hard-drinking, neglectful. Who had a picture of their son with the head cropped off? As she hurried, the fog swirled.

Coming out at the foot of the village beside a derelict barn, ivy growing out through its roof, Sukie found herself at the top of a path that became the hardcore road, that led across to the far peak. The mist still hung below, drifting in the scrub and stones, but she could see the other peak across the ridge, steep and treeless, with gulls wheeling over it.

There was a steady cold wind across the pass and when Sukie got to the graveyard she saw that it was more grim than picturesque. An iron gate squeaked as she let herself through, the cold wind whipped round her ankles and she tugged at the tunic. She thought longingly of the clothes in her bag, that perhaps Jake was at that moment bringing up the hill to her. *He's so good.* He must want stability. Someone to look after. To make up for . . . all that. She found herself smiling; me too, she thought.

There were a few graves but mostly it was long walls where ashes were kept. There were some plastic flowers on the graves, and stuck in tiny holders under the plaques. She came across two columns of these bearing the same date, November 1965, eighteen people. She was startled and then she remembered the earthquake Jake had told her about. She looked back at the village, perched precariously on the hill, and wondered what made them think it was safe even now.

She walked on, scanning the plaques, Greek writing she couldn't make out, and had almost given up when she saw, there they were, after all. In bold plain English lettering: Malcolm Littlejohn, died November 1996 aged fifty-two.

Where was his mother? The cold made her head ache. Sukie tried to remember Jake's mother's name, Betsy had said it. Susannah. She stumbled on along the wall, then back between the graves, checking each one, but there was no

Susannah Littlejohn. Sukie backed out of the graveyard. There would be an explanation.

Her head still hurt; the light was shifting and cold. Sukie had to make herself breathe. Fresh air, she told herself, hearing her own mother's voice, looking back at the teetering village and then the other way to where the seagulls wheeled. She walked towards them.

As she approached the gulls seemed to multiply, their cries accentuating her headache. Shading her eyes she looked up at the mountain and felt a sudden shiver of foreboding.

The road narrowed as the steep hillside loomed ahead of her; it was no more than a path now, a goat track turning across the slope, and Sukie slowed, one hand out, she moved stiffly now, feeling the unsteadiness under her feet. At least she had trainers. She spread her toes inside them, feeling for stability, feeling for traction. And suddenly out of nowhere had a vision of herself running, when she'd never run in her life.

No need for that. She swallowed. The locals came out here, that was obvious. They came around the side of this steep hill, and regularly, and she thought, of course, a church. A little blue dome, maybe a spotless bay beneath, and the thought reassured her, the hand out to steady her dropped.

And then a cloud of gulls rose, shrieking and calling and something rose with them, a gust of something. Sukie recoiled, she smelled it before she saw and then there it was, the view. Barely in time, she halted, steadying herself, leaning in to the hillside.

Just ahead of her a raw slope fell away, where land must

have slipped in the not too recent past: the end of the road. And tumbling down it all the way to a broken shore a sludge of rubbish, old fridges, rusting, horrible. And overhead the seagulls wheeling and calling.

Breathless suddenly, Sukie stumbled backwards, reversed a little way along the narrow path until it widened just enough, then turned and ran. When she reached the cemetery again, out of breath, passed it, she saw Jake, walking towards her.

Chapter Seventeen

Day Three, Friday: Joey

'Come *on*.'

Joey hesitated. 'Spill,' said Anastasia, arms folded tightly across her front. 'You think I'm going to be horrible? Look, I know more about this stuff than you and Miss Sukie do, face it.'

So she'd spilled. Well, most of it.

Anastasia was thoughtful. 'I think I've heard of that place, too, y'know. Kyros. They were all hippies and junkies and drunks.' She yawned suddenly, and Joey got a gust of stale breath. 'But this is something else.' She sat up, scratching her chin.

'You should go home and get some sleep,' said Joey.

'Maybe,' said Anastasia, looking round. The office was quiet but you never knew when the boss might emerge from her lair to look over shoulders. She pulled her sweater

155

up to her nose and sniffed, grimacing. 'I do need a bath, at least.' But then she frowned. 'She made him sound like a nerdy type, though. She didn't say anything about a wild background. Preferences for death metal and . . . worse.'

'People pretend to be things they're not, though, don't they,' said Joey quietly. 'I mean you . . . I mean anyone might get caught out.'

'I suppose just liking the band he fronted doesn't make you a . . . a paedo,' said Anastasia, uncertainly.

Was Anastasia thinking what she was thinking? Sukie's round, trusting face? A kid's face.

'You checked to see if his profile's still up?' said Anastasia, abruptly, turning the monitor towards her.

'Uh-huh,' said Joey. 'Practically the first thing I did do. He's taken it down. They both have.'

'Well that's a good sign,' said Anastasia, yawning again, standing up. Then something caught her eye through the glass partitions. 'Shit,' she hissed. 'Big cheese heading this way.' And her whole body language changing, stiff, upright, a nod as if they'd just concluded some official business, and she moved off.

Joey sat there, staring at her monitor, trying to make sense of it. *You a god, man.* And the email address. Two email addresses? She leaned forwards, abruptly.

She was distracted by a rap on the glass: Anastasia on the other side, drawing a finger across her throat. *Not safe for work*, she mouthed.

And Joey sat back quickly and angled the screen away from her just as Jeremy the editorial director stuck his well groomed chin round the door.

Joey leaned forwards and wrote the email address down on a piece of paper before she forgot it, hoping that when she looked up again he'd be gone.

He wasn't. 'Joanna.' When he sounded benevolent and fatherly you were in trouble.

'Yes, Jeremy,' she said meekly.

'I hope you haven't forgotten that I need *Blood Games* on my desk by the end of the day,' he said.

'No, Jeremy,' she said. 'I mean, yes, of course, Jeremy.'

'Well in that case I suggest you leave Miss Alexander's desk and return to your own, unless you would like her workload as well as yours.'

And reluctantly she stood up, hoping he would go, but instead he waited like a headmaster for her to go back to her seat. She caught Anastasia's face upturned through the glass as she moved, and nodded quickly.

When he was gone – fuck him – and Joey heard the door close behind him, she knew that before she did anything else, she needed just to hear Sukie's voice.

Hunched below the glass partition, Joey dialled the number.

The sound it made was different again from the last time. A long echoing note, then another. The foreignness of it, the distance, was overwhelming. Just come home, she begged silently. Just come home. It rang on and on. She should have texted – but should she? Again? How many texts were too many? She told herself she'd leave a message when the answerphone clicked in.

And then someone answered.

She heard shouting, there was shouting in the background and a woman's voice, quavering, frightened. Terrified.

'Sukie?' Joey whispered, terrified herself. 'Is that you?'

'I don't know,' said the voice, rising into a wail. 'I don't know.'

Day Three, Friday: Heather

Kostas was a man of few words, once he had his money.

'Kyros, yes?' she said. 'Kyros?' He grunted yes, gesturing towards the bow of the boat and she scrambled down there on hands and knees, pressing herself in against a wooden thwart with her backpack under her legs.

It felt very precarious, and quite surreal, the lifting and dipping of the boat, the slapping of the waves against the rubber sides and the muffling, blanketing effect of the fog. It wasn't dark, it was just that the light didn't seem to come from a single source, more that it was refracted through the fog into tiny particles, a dim sort of glow all around them as they pushed on into the mist.

He's a rapist.

Not the usual sort of message you got on LinkedIn. Heather stared at the words. She needed the girl to believe her. Sukie Alexander. She looked down the other contacts:

they had one or two in common. Assistant editor. Subject: HE'S A RAPIST.

If she'd been sent a warning.

He's a rapist. At fifteen, she'd had no notion of rape. It was all about love. Sex was supposed to be love. Like a great big suffocating cushion, pink and fluffy, as blinding and muffling and blanketing as the fog, it swallowed everything else up: your confusion, your pain, the bruises and the tears.

Were rapists entitled to start again? To find *love*. Was Heather entitled to break in on his new beginning, to smash up their world, just on an instinct?

Yes. Yes. Yes.

Contact me. I'm here. She typed in her number, and sent the message.

Shit. Even as she did it, she saw the signal blink down, 4G gone, 3G gone, one bar of signal, and that one a bit wobbly. Of course, they would be out of sight of land. She didn't know if the email had gone. Oh, yes, she did. It hadn't. *Your message could not be sent, we will try again later.*

She stared. The message was out there somewhere, she couldn't call it back. Wouldn't. Would it do any good? The girl, Sukie Alexander, had looked like she believed in love, in the big pink cushion that would soften every blow. But she wasn't fifteen. She might look like it. Was that why he'd chosen her? The LinkedIn picture confirmed it. The softness of her face, the wide, unmade-up eyes. Waiting to be twisted and hurt. And what else? Why bring her out here?

Kostas cleared his throat. Heather looked up and saw his head was turned, as if he was listening. She had no idea

159

about how many big ships there might be out here, moving between the islands, or what would happen if one loomed up out of the dusk. Yesterday as they set off she'd seen one, a long low shape at the horizon, very far off. She sat up and listened too, for any sign, a foghorn, or engines, but there was nothing. Or was there?

Something. The slap of waves, a rising murmur. Kostas called out something in Greek, then slowed the outboard. Someone called back, gruffly, then a small chorus of other voices, a shout and the calls subsided. Still nothing was visible.

Kostas cut the engine. She stared, and he put a finger to his lips, ferocious. He leaned over the engine, waiting.

Oh. It occurred to her, just as the change occurred – in the quality of the fog, the light – instead of blank white there was a patch of greater density and then a clump, of heads close together, materialised and one rising out of them, one standing arms out, the shapes all rocking as he did.

It was another boat, loaded – overloaded – with passengers, twenty, maybe, and the boat no bigger than Kostas's. It was drifting, like them. Heather glimpsed a woman in a shawl and something wrapped in the shawl, then as the boat rocked closer out of the gloom she saw enough to make out the long dark face of the standing man – his expression – and then Kostas whipped upright from the engine and in the same moment the outboard whined, roared, and they moved, veering sharply away.

Heather was tipped into the bottom of the boat, her

phone thrown from her hand into a swill of oily water. She scrabbled for it, it slipped and she grabbed again. There was a clamour of voices, strained and panicking, and then abruptly the boat was gone, swallowed up in the fog like it had never been there and the shouts drowned out by the whine of the motor.

Heather tried to ask him, pointing – holding up her dripping phone in a desperate attempt to suggest they should do something, call a coastguard – what had just happened but he just shook his head, sharply. And she knew, anyway: she'd seen enough news reports. Some of them had been wearing lifejackets at least. Maybe half.

They must have come under cover of the fog, like her, not thinking about the dangers.

They were gone, and around them the world was white and silent again.

Chapter Eighteen

Day Three, Friday: Sukie

'Darling.'

Jake was behind her as he murmured it, holding her by the upper arms – gently, but Sukie twisted a little, awkward. She held her breath. She could smell cigarettes again.

They were in the house's little kitchenette, the food he'd bought set out on the counter, candles. He'd only shrugged when she'd asked about the generator, and had gone on unpacking at the kitchen counter. Sukie was at the tap, half-way to filling the little furred up hob-kettle, and then there he'd been, at her back.

She hadn't told him about the rubbish cascading down the hill, she felt stupid, breathless with her own stupidity for trekking out there expecting some kind of paradise. And of course Jake must know about the rubbish. He grew up here.

The sight of it though, the sheer drop, the raw earth, the smell of rotting rubbish. It had felt like some kind of trick.

His mouth was in her hair. 'Darling,' he said again and she felt a sudden shiver. Then she remembered.

'Where is it?' she said, held fast, and then he released her, slowly.

'Where is what?'

'The bag?' she said. 'My bag?'

'Oh, that,' he said, nettled, turning away from her. 'They wouldn't give it to me. Because I had given your name at the airport, which was stupid of me.'

'Well, no – I mean it *is* my bag,' she said, puzzled.

'Well, *we* can go right back and get it, can't we?' he said and she heard a prickle of irritation in his voice. 'If that's what you'd like.'

'Yes,' said Sukie, hesitantly, 'I think I—' and then, 'Oh!'

She remembered her phone. She'd left it plugged in over the road.

'Oh?' said Jake, tilting his head sideways, smiling.

'Oh – nothing,' said Sukie. That LinkedIn request. Heather someone. There'd been a tiny picture of the Heather someone, dark shaggy hair. 'You said you'd bumped into some people?'

'Yes,' he said, vaguely, 'A bit of business. Something's come up.' A smile hovering at the corners of his mouth.

'Is this a business, trip, then?' she said, unable to stop herself sounding a little bit truculent. 'I thought—' and she broke off. What had she thought? Maybe a little bit of wandering through olive groves. Not all these . . . disappearances.

'Darling,' he said again, indulgent but something else in

there, and he put a finger to her cheek, pushed, gently, where she knew there was a dimple. 'Of course it's not. Where did you go on your walk, in the end?'

'I went along to . . . towards the cemetery,' Sukie answered.

'The cemetery?' He raised an eyebrow. 'Interesting.'

'Just to . . . Sort of get a perspective on the island? The shape of it.' She took a breath. 'Nat and Betsy asked me over for coffee.'

'Yes,' he said, looking at her as if he was sizing her up, somehow. 'I know.'

I left my phone.

'You do?' she said. 'You . . . did they . . .'

'I dropped in on them. They're our only neighbours, after all.' He smiled. 'I've known them since I was a kid. Betsy was tired, I didn't stay long. Just to ask, you know. Which direction you'd gone in.'

Now would be the moment. Maybe Jake's moment, to volunteer the information, to ask if she'd seen the graves. If Nat or Betsy had said anything at all, about the questions she'd asked. But he turned back and went on unpacking.

She could smell the food: he'd bought it from the baker's, he said, they cooked things in their ovens. Something with a thick rubbery layer of pale cheese on top, cold lamb, the fat hard and white, and all smelling of garlic in their little foil trays.

'The generator guy's sister says he won't come up here any more, so we'll have to just, I don't know, camp,' he said. He reached into a cupboard and got out a hurricane lamp

164

and a plastic jug of paraffin. 'Fun, right?' He set his hands flat on the table, regarding her.

'Maybe I should . . .' Her throat was tight. 'Maybe we should go down and find an Airbnb?' she said. 'Down in the port?'

Jake laughed. 'Airbnb? You millennials, honestly.' Cheerful. 'Of course, if you don't like it up here.'

'It's not that,' she said, stoutly.

'Sweetheart,' he said, still standing there quite motionless, a smile in his eyes. 'I don't have the money for an Airbnb even if Kyros had one, but do feel free.'

'Well, I . . .' she swallowed. 'Actually I left my phone over at Nat and Betsy's, charging. So—'

He raised his hands to either side, palms up. 'So we're free from the tyranny of technology.' He smiled; she hadn't noticed the droop to his eyelids before, the way the smile didn't quite get that far.

'Oh, it doesn't matter,' she said. 'I–I'm sure I can manage without it.' She squashed a sudden longing for the familiar little apps and all they represented. Information; friendship. Accommodation.

'I tell you what,' Jake said, watching her steadily. 'We'll go down together now and get your bag, and I'll ask around. I have to do a little bit of business. About an Airbnb. If you still want to by the time we get down there, that is. Would that do?'

Sukie felt a surge of the old panic, he thought she was a crybaby, a lightweight, a disappointment. 'All right,' she said, submissive. 'Yes.'

As they emerged on to the crossroads, she hesitated, looking across at Nat and Betsy's.

'She'll be having her nap,' said Jake, steering her past. She walked on but turned to look back. She saw two bags on the doorstep, plastic bags tied neatly, but Jake's hand was still on her elbow, moving her along.

There was a light mist between the houses. It was a ghost village. At the head of the path she turned. 'Are you sure we won't get lost?' His hand was on her shoulder.

'Look,' he said. 'It's clearing.' She was uncertain – where they stood, the mist did seem patchier out to sea. She could see a tiny boat, far away, and then it was swallowed up – and it was getting darker.

'But—'

'I could do it blindfold,' said Jake. 'Trust me.'

Day Three, Friday: Kit

Kit got to the Princess Alexandra just after five thirty, opening time. There was no sign of Jade. Jade whom Fred thought he should shag.

He shouldn't be here. Not because Heather might find out – Heather would be able to take one look at the situation and know the truth of it – but because it made him feel as if he was swimming in a sea of shit. Shit bobbing towards him from all directions. He took a sip of his lime and soda.

Also: Heather wanted to finish it with him anyway. He set the glass back down.

There was a boy behind the bar, with an elaborate quiff, who had raised an eyebrow at his order, unless that had been Kit's imagination. Kit got back up, leaving the lime and soda on his table, and ordered a double brandy, at random. As the boy raised the glass to the optic he realised that he'd ordered the drink not at random at all but because it had been what Jade had sipped from, behind her own bar. 'Make that two.'

He took the drinks back to the booth. From where he sat, he could see the boy behind the bar, and the boy could see the door, and there was a mirror behind the bar that would show a bit of everything to Kit.

Looking at the brandy, Kit took a sip. Pubs weren't too bad, after all, he thought as it went down. When they were empty, they weren't too bad at all. A whole future rose from the brandy glass like smoke: go to work, go to the pub, get drunk, go home alone and snore.

Like Fred.

He took another sip, then pushed the glass away. Was Fred nicer than he'd always looked to Kit? Kit had gone along to his office again, to find him scrolling through some social media search engine they were developing. A data scraper. When he registered Kit's presence he had straightened, eyes brighter than Kit had seen him. He was enjoying this.

'So what did you find out?' Kit knew he was sounding impatient.

Sitting in the quiet pub now, he knew he could phone Heather, right away. But he wanted to find out everything before he did that – or if not everything, then as much as there was to find out. So that all she would have to do was fill in the gaps. This guy.

He could be an ex who treated her badly. That would be the very simplest and most likely explanation. Heather could be a nut-job stalker who saw an ex at the airport and couldn't let it drop. And here he was waiting for another woman who'd admitted to doing the very same.

The lads would have you believe that the world was full of women like that. He'd heard them on the subject, at the long table with their lattes the morning after, joking about their hangovers and asking for a shot with that. They'd say, darkly, you had to be careful. Not careful about how you treated women: that precaution was way down on the list. But careful about what they knew about you.

Jade had stalked Jake Littlejohn, after all: she had hunted him down, and Kit was glad of it. It was why he was sitting here, why he had a chance to find something out, at last.

A lot of stalker bitches out there.

Fred hadn't said that, though. Kit had been waiting for the moment he did, because it would provide him with an excuse to walk away, but Fred hadn't given him so much as a sidelong glance, since he got on Jake Littlejohn's trail. BlueJ.

What he *had* said was, 'Sorry, mate, but the guy looks like a bit of a sleaze to me.'

Kit had stared at him from the doorway to his office. Sorry? *Sorry?* Because his girlfriend was cheating on him with a sleazebag? And then he realised that hadn't been what Fred meant. He meant, the guy's . . . not safe.

Fred had even patted him on the shoulder. 'You know what,' he said, and he looked thoughtful, for once, properly thoughtful. 'I might make a night of it.'

'A night of it.' Kit had been alarmed. 'I'm not up for—'

'I mean,' Fred said patiently, 'I might stay late with this. They're used to me doing that. There's something about your guy – your Littlejohn. I think he's got serious form. And you know me, I'm a night bird. My brain doesn't start working till after everyone else is in bed.'

Kit was staring at him again. There was plenty he didn't know about Fred, it turned out. 'So,' said Fred, focused on his screen again, fingers moving faster than Kit's ever could, 'I'll be in touch.'

And with a certain amount of relief Kit had left him to it.

Kit frowned down at his phone now, looking at the message again. Typed in a line. A handful of words, *send*. He looked away as it went.

Even as it sent, Kit had an idea. He stood up, sat down again. He had her number, after all. He could talk to her. BlueJ could have played Brighton, after all. He stood up again.

Just going for a fag, mate, he mimed a cigarette to the barman. The street was empty. He took a deep breath and dialled.

'Mrs Baxter?' he said, nervous. 'It's Kit.'

It took five minutes, maybe seven. He somehow knew what questions to ask. Heather's mum was breathless with anxiety and he managed to calm it down right away. *Just*

*one or two things . . . No, no, it's okay. Nothing to worry about.
I wanted to plan a surprise, that's all, I heard there was a particular
DJ she liked . . . No. She's fine, Mrs Baxter. I just wondered –
funny question – if you remembered . . .*

In the end, she told him what she wanted to know
without his asking. *Actually, that's when it started. We thought
it was just, you know, her age. Adolescence.*

When Kit hung up, the street was still empty, and the
pub too.

He sat back down, and reached for the brandy glass, and
it was then, some displacement of the dust floating, a gust
of air, and the boy at the bar – who'd paid no attention
when Kit came back in – smiled at someone Kit could
only see reflected in the mirror behind him.

'Ladies,' said the boy, bowing a little, and looked over at
Kit.

Ladies plural? Awkwardly he got to his feet, jiggling the
brandy glasses as he eased his way round the table. There
was Jade, the door swinging shut behind her. She wore a
cagoule gleaming with rain and as she came towards him
he saw she looked tired, slightly apprehensive.

'I got you a drink,' said Kit, awkwardly. She shifted slightly,
tugging off her rain mac, and he saw that there was someone
else behind her. A small, slight woman, a round face and a
lot of fluffy hair.

Kit who had been halfway to sitting down, bobbed upright
again. 'And what can I—'

'This is Emily,' said Jade briefly. She looked at him,
frowning. 'I said there was someone I wanted you to meet,

right?' Emily looked from one of them to the other, frightened.

'Yes,' said Kit. For a second he could only think that this was some really horrible, twisted thing, a set-up, a blind date, a trick. She looked nervous. 'What are you drinking, Emily?'

Emily asked for a diet Coke. She sat straight as if she was in school, narrow-shouldered, her hands on either side of the glass and just touching it with trembling fingertips.

Jade took a swig of her brandy. 'Emily?'

'Yes,' said Emily, 'Yes, I—' but it seemed to get stuck in her throat.

'Emily went out with him,' said Jade. They were both watching Emily. She had fair eyelashes that shivered against her cheek. 'Jake. BlueJ.'

'I didn't know he was called that,' said Emily. 'He said he was a graphic designer, on his profile.'

'You met him online?' Kit got out his phone, brought up the picture. 'This is him?'

Emily's eyes slid over the image and away, blinking fast. 'Can I try that?' she said, suddenly pointing at the brandy.

'How old are you, Emily?' said Kit.

'I'm twenty-five,' said Emily, flushing, scrabbling in her bag and thrusting a driver's licence at him. Bowed her head. 'He thought I was younger.'

Kit nudged the brandy towards her. She sipped, grimaced, a tear brimmed at her eye and she pushed the glass away from her violently.

'You came here on a date with him,' he said gently.

171

'I went *out* with him,' Emily said, the narrow shoulders stiffening. 'I went out with him for a five and a half *weeks*.' Her voice was high and shaky with disbelief and she took a gulp of Coke.

There was a sudden rush of sound from outside, the chug of traffic let in from the street quickly muffled as the doors must have closed again, invisible from where they sat, then men's voices. Out of the corner of his eye Kit saw the faces, overcoats, filling the etched mirror behind the bar.

'What . . .' Kit hesitated. It was like stepping out on ice. 'What went wrong?' he said, as gently as he could.

Emily looked at Jade, dumb, and Jade sat back, shaking her head.

'You don't have to say anything,' said Jade. 'But there might be someone else. Someone else he's done it to.'

Emily took a deep breath, and began to talk.

Chapter Nineteen

Day Three, Friday: Heather

.

It was getting dark now, and cold. Heather's feet were wet and she was chilled to the bone, in the bow of the boat. Kostas had not even looked at her since the dinghy full of migrants had disappeared into the mist.

She could do nothing but think, as she swayed and shivered with the movement of the boat. Think weird circular thoughts. This was all connected. This was all connected. The smell of the sea and the people clamouring, the sound of the waves on stones. Jake Littlejohn belonged in a place like this, after all, where people were desperate. She fumbled in her pocket and got the phone out with stiff cold fingers.

The sea was changing: the waves short and choppy, now. She was bumped and jolted; she felt sick and sweaty. The fog came in patches, drifting. She caught a glimpse of something – land? A hillside? – then they were swallowed up again.

'Hey,' she said. Kostas was looking the other way. 'Hey,' she said. 'Kostas.'

He said something in Greek over her head. 'What?' she said, desperate.

He gestured. 'We arrive soon,' and reluctantly lowered his eyes to meet hers. She tried to stand but a wave slopped, the bow rose and she sat down again abruptly. She edged towards him in the bottom of the dinghy, phone held out.

'Do you know him?' she said. He frowned down, waving a hand to dismiss her, shaking his head. She turned the screen to herself. She didn't know if it was her imagination, or if it was showing a different colour, everything pinkish. But the picture was visible. The tall figure, the shaggy hair. She felt abruptly sick, and swallowed. She turned the screen back towards Kostas. There was something in Kostas's face, of extreme reluctance, and pushing herself up from the thwart she stood, swaying, held it right in front of his face.

'Do,' she said, distinctly, 'you know this man?'

The boat lurched, and grabbing her shoulder with his free hand angrily he shoved her back down. It was quite dark now: the only light from the mobile in her hand.

'We *arrive*,' he said, his face, jaw set, thrust momentarily in hers. 'I do not know. I do not know this man.'

She looked back down at her phone; the pink glow was still there, yellowish round the edges, and the screen was cracked. It occurred to her that falling in the water could have done something to it. How many times had Kit told her to be more careful?

Heather remembered him holding her phone at the restaurant table. He'd only been trying to help, lifting it out of the way of the waitress, he must have seen the picture by accident, she could just imagine the succession of questions. *Who? Why?* And then she had just disappeared. Heather felt a wave of gratitude, and guilt – and something she hardly recognised. What was that feeling? She missed him. She wished he was here, to talk to, she could put her face into his shoulder and smell that smell of his, his ginger smell, washing powder and his skin.

Too bad. He didn't care: he hadn't answered. She blinked down at the screen again. It looked like a sunspot, now pink radiating to yellow.

Fuck it. Urgently she tried to dry it with her sweatshirt, rubbed it against her jeans. And just as she lifted it to look again, there it was. A message springing like magic in its little box on the screen, like a half-remembered magic from a different world. A message from Kit.

Jake Littlejohn. BlueJ. What did he do to you?

She stared: just the words made her hair stand on end. *BlueJ.* She could see the poster now, in her head, his silhouette with headphones, one arm raised, a crowd of bright faces raised to him.

The boat swerved and she grabbed quickly to stop

herself dropping the phone again. She stuffed it in her pocket.

The fog thinned, the smell changed from salt freshness to something else and there was a harbour wall. There were faces, the murmur of voices and a set of steps slimed and black with weed.

What did he do to you? Three words would describe it. *He. Raped. Me.* But it wasn't three words. It was thousands of words: it was no words. It was her running at him – *him* – as she had done so many times in her head, arms flailing, knives for fingernails, screaming, she would rip his skin off, she would scrape out his eyes.

That was what she was here for.

Heather stood like stone.

They came alongside, the boat rising and falling. Heather looked back at Kostas but he stayed where he was, made no effort to help her. She looked up. They were all men, standing between a set of huge iron bollards, and they looked back at her without moving. There was a groundswell of muttering and then one of them stepped reluctantly down and offered her a hand.

Stiff with cold, she stepped out. Kostas was securing the boat by a rope to a rusted iron ring in the seaweed-blackened wall. The fronds of weed rose and swayed under her feet, and then she was on solid ground, on the first step of the stairs, unsteady, but safe.

Behind them came the roar of engines as another boat came in, through the fog, a bigger one, and the slosh of its wake wet her feet.

They cleared a path for her, and she began to climb the stone steps.

Day Three, Friday: Sukie

It hadn't been an exaggeration of Jake's, to say he could do the path blindfolded. He stepped side to side, ahead of her, and Sukie was breathless trying to keep up.

At one point the path widened and ran alongside a fenced-off dust road and she tried to talk.

'Betsy and Nat were so hospitable,' she said. She could hear his footsteps, regular, focused, while her own skittered uncertainly. He had one hand in his pocket, turning something over and over in there like a charm, a lucky piece. 'Were they both there when you went over? Nat was busy with something downstairs, Betsy said—'

'Betsy's not altogether . . . reliable,' said Jake. He didn't look up, but went on, one step here, one step there. 'I expect you got that.'

'Is it dementia, do you think?' said Sukie timidly. 'She did have some funny ideas.'

'Such as?' He paused, in the dark, one arm resting on the wire-link fence.

'Oh, about the mist, and people getting into the cellar.' She could hear his quick breathing. 'Are there immigrants on the island, you know, just roaming around? That was the impression I had. Nat seemed to take it seriously, I mean, he went downstairs.'

She also said you and he were thick as thieves. Sukie didn't say that. Perhaps they were setting something up together, he and Nat, perhaps it was something to do with the packages in the cellar. It wasn't her business. None of her business, she didn't want it to be her business.

'Oh, Nat's very security-conscious,' said Jake. 'He has his supply of Jim Beam down in that cellar. I wouldn't worry about it. The immigrants—' He took a step and something glowed into life, his phone, in his hand and light was shed upwards. He glanced down – a message must have come in – then back up at her and when he smiled she recognised him again.

'The immigrants are just desperately poor people fleeing persecution,' Jake said, gently, resting his hand on her shoulder. 'Sometimes – sometimes the uneducated don't understand that. They're not a threat. I've thought of helping them myself, in fact.'

'That's lovely,' Sukie said, impulsive, feeling abruptly, stupidly emotional. 'Volunteering?' She had seen him talk to that man in the queue outside the immigration centre. She couldn't remember now, what he'd said they'd talked about.

'Anyway,' Jake went on, impatient suddenly, 'what else did Betsy tell you, while Nat was downstairs?'

Sukie was surprised that he remembered that bit. 'Well . . .' She hesitated. 'She talked a bit about your family, too.'

'Oh, she rambles,' said Jake. 'She gets all the families mixed up.' In the half-light for a moment Sukie thought he looked like someone she didn't know at all, his eyes were in deep pools of shadow.

'You went to the cemetery,' he said, his voice abruptly flat. 'You'll have seen my father's grave.'

'Yes, I . . .' She was about to come out with it now, to ask him, but something prevented her, something in his voice. She spoke brightly instead. 'Yes. And I-I found some pictures of your family, too, in the folder for visitors.'

'My mother's not there,' he said, making a gesture with his hand, brushing something aside, his voice quiet. 'You'll have seen that too, then.'

She was dumb.

'Did you ask them?' he said softly. 'Betsy and Nat? How my parents died?' She heard something in his voice, an alert, a warning, and felt herself stiffen.

'No – I . . .' Sukie stopped. It occurred to her that he would know if she lied, and there would be consequences. 'I might have mentioned it,' she faltered.

Did her father know when her mother lied? He never showed any signs of it. Marsha, brazening it out. Sukie had no idea what she would do, in this situation. She wouldn't let it happen.

Jake hesitated, then put his phone in his pocket and turned to face her. He took her hands in his. 'I might not have been completely truthful,' he said, still quiet. 'I told you they died in a car accident.'

'Yes,' said Sukie, subdued. 'Well, I—' She stopped herself. She didn't need to tell him yet.

'That was half true,' he said. 'My father crashed our car. But my mother had died the year before.' A silence, Sukie realised she was holding her breath. 'She took her own life.

That's why she couldn't be buried in . . . in a churchyard. She took barbiturates and alcohol.'

'But it could have been an accident,' Sukie blurted.

He stroked her cheek, thoughtful. 'She left a note,' he said, and let out a sigh. 'She was a troubled woman. She had . . . she'd had affairs. And if I'm quite honest . . .' He stopped.

'Yes?' said Sukie.

'I think my father's death wasn't accidental either.'

'You mean he was . . .' She didn't understand.

'I mean I think he couldn't live without my mother and he drove his car into a tree.' Jake let out another long, sad sigh. 'The priest turned a blind eye to it.'

'Oh.' Suddenly, impulsively, she put her arms around him and felt him standing quite stiff and still inside them. Jake was silent. She let her arms drop, and he stepped back.

'You can see why I didn't want to tell you straight away.'

'Yes,' she said.

The silence grew. 'Of course, bringing you here,' he said, 'I must have wanted you to find out, mustn't I?'

'Yes,' she said, uncertainly. She felt guilty: he might equally have not expected her to poke her nose in. In fact she felt sure he hadn't. She'd let him believe all sorts of things about her. That she was innocent and virginal and alone in the world.

She'd already lied. When had it been, date two, or three? *He'd said, you're an orphan, just like me, aren't you? I can tell.* And she'd nodded. There: it was out. She'd thought, if he met Marsha. If he saw her decking and her cocktail cabinet, if he heard her laugh,

Stupid that Sukie hadn't even admitted that to herself. She'd even said, quickly, do you mind if we don't talk about it?

Jake had turned and was walking on, quick and sure, almost jaunty. Perhaps he was relieved. Perhaps that was it. She didn't know. She didn't know what he was thinking. She hurried to catch up.

'Who was the message from?' she asked, at his shoulder, out of breath. They were closer now. She could ask.

A tiny fractional silence but he didn't pause or miss a beat. The air around them was still and white and muffled, not a sound, not a light.

'Message?' he said easily, but the next stride somehow took him abruptly away from her.

'On the phone?'

'Oh, that,' he said, but still he didn't stop or turn to look at her. 'A Greek friend, the guy I might be doing business with. He might be down there now. He's got a few ideas about helping the immigrants, as a matter of fact. He wants to meet up. '

'Oh,' said Sukie, rewarded, pleased: information. And the prospect of meeting one of Jake's friends somehow settled things around her, all her panicked ruffled thoughts. 'Maybe we could—'

But he didn't let her finish. He took her hand firmly in his cool hard one. 'We'd better stop talking and hurry,' he said. 'Or the agency where they're holding your bag will have closed.'

It was almost completely dark when they got to the

village, but the fog was lifting, and a handful of bars were open, there were lights on.

'There,' said Jake, pointing.

'Where?' said Sukie. 'What?'

'The travel agency is still open,' he said, taking her hand, almost tugging her. She couldn't see anything that looked like a travel agency. He pointed, and she saw a lighted window above a shop.

Along the harbour wall a small crowd seemed to have gathered: the mist beyond them at the edge of the darkness. A big boat had just come in and a row of men were looking down into the water.

Day Three, Friday: Joey

Joey and Anastasia were on the street in some unfamiliar part of the city.

On the phone, Joey hadn't been able to work out how many people had been in the room. A man shouting, another quieter man's voice, the woman – *not* Sukie, Joey had realised that almost immediately – babbling. Then one of the men had come on the phone. Soothing, apologetic. American accent, the voice of an older man, surely. Jake Littlejohn wasn't American, he was only forty something. He wasn't American.

'I'm so sorry,' Smooth. 'My wife has her confused moments. No, your friend left her phone here to be charged, she's out with Jacob.' A pause, the babbling receding, in the background. 'May I give her a message? Say who called?'

Joey had given her name, faltering. Shit, she thought, shit shit as she hung up. She hadn't even asked *their* names.

Anastasia caught up with her as she got to the lift. 'Trying to sneak off?' she said. Joey, still trying to process the phone conversation, just smiled weakly. She wanted to go home and think. 'We're friends too, aren't we?' said Anastasia, stubborn. 'It's not just Sukie, Sukie, Sukie. Sukie's on the other side of the world—'

'You don't need to remind me,' said Joey. She was tired and frightened. There was a limit to what she wanted to know about what you could see on the internet.

Anastasia grabbed her by the shoulders. 'Look,' she said. 'It's a matter of doing your research, this shit. Sukie isn't stupid, she'll work it out. One doesn't pan out, try another.' She grinned. 'Now let's go and get drunk. It's Friday night, isn't it?'

Was that even his name? He could be lying. That was the thing people didn't seem to understand: you could say what you liked on the internet. Most people just believed it.

'Joeeeeey,' Anastasia had pleaded. And suddenly Joey could see herself – it was too easy, just to slip away, back to her comfort zone. She was never going to understand this mess that way. She sighed and gave in.

'So,' said Anastasia now, turning at the big junction, a train rumbling overhead. 'Clubbing? Or what?'

'I don't think the answer to anything is to get pissed, Anastasia,' said Joey, warily. Anastasia looked at her.

'Spoilsport,' she said, but without much conviction,

tugging Joey towards a side street. Then brightened. 'What about a gay bar? Lesbian place.'

'Errr . . .' Joey was alarmed.

'You must know one?' Anastasia nudged her and she smelled something. Spirits.

'Why would I—' Joey was indignant.

'Joey, you can't fool me.'

'I'm not trying to fool anyone. I don't like picking people up for sex, Anastasia. I don't like it.' She tried not to sound prim, and managed to sound miserable.

'OK then.' Anastasia relented. 'There. There.' They stopped. A pub: an ordinary pub. No. Joey stopped in her tracks. Not an ordinary pub. This was the place. Maybe there were lots of pubs called the Princess Alexandra. It was where Sukie had gone for her first date.

'Just one drink, then home,' said Anastasia. Her eyes were bright suddenly, her face, pale all day, had pinked up, her tangled hair looked shiny.

A couple were coming out as they came up to the door. Anastasia pushed past, oblivious, into the noise of voices from inside, the smell of pub carpet, and beer, but Joey stepped back, against the wall.

The couple was a slight ginger-haired man and a young girl. 'Are you sure you'll be all right?' he was saying, earnestly. 'Shall I see you home?' She was small, tears streaking her cheeks, rubbing at her nose. 'No – I – no . . .'

And then an Uber pulled up, the driver leaning out of the window. She could see his illuminated screen inside. 'Emily?' he said.

The girl hurried forward and got in, the ginger bloke saying, *wait*, following her, leaning in at the car window. Joey couldn't hear what he was saying. You had no way of knowing, did you, what was going on, or when to get involved.

But then the bloke stepped back, turned, his face blank and strained and preoccupied – too preoccupied even to register Joey was standing there as he came past her, pushing his way back inside.

The car pulled off. Joey still didn't move. Uber – that was safe. There was a record of the transaction, your journey, of everything. The girl was safe.

The street was empty. She stood a moment without going into the pub, then another. She knew Anastasia, she'd have found someone to buy her a drink. Joey could just leave now, if she wanted to.

She stood there a long moment then turned and went inside.

Chapter Twenty

Day Three, Friday: Heather

Heather sat in the brightly lit bar, a glass of Greek brandy and a coffee in front of her. There were technicolour photographs of the islands around the rough white walls, white houses tumbling picturesquely to the blue sea, their colours faded, though, and some of them askew. Heather tried and failed to imagine summer. She had on pretty much all the clothes she had brought in the little backpack, and still she was shivering. What the fuck was she doing here? What was *he*?

At the harbour-front the boat that had come in after her was having trouble docking, or something. She heard raised voices: funny how you always thought you could hear English being spoken.

How old would he be now? BlueJ. BJ, which she knew now meant blowjob – which she had known, in fact, quite soon after, aged fifteen. He'd have been over thirty then, late forties now. He'd been very successful; he could have still been doing that, still running dance nights, festivals. But some of them didn't make it, did they? The ones that were still doing that were businessmen at heart, or so focused on the music that there's nothing else and he wasn't one of those.

He was in it for something different. The girls – and more than that, more than sex. The laid-back cool, the bouncing on his heels to the music, the nodding, the standing in the shadows, that was a cover-up, a veneer. He wasn't laid-back. There was something else he wanted.

That kind often veered off course, didn't they? Ended up in the gutter, panhandling or dealing, sponging off some woman. They didn't have anything to lose. Living for the next hit of someone else's humiliation. There was always someone.

That was what was happening here. The rest was detail.

Was that enough? Did she just mean to expose him? No. Whether Heather admitted it or not, she was after something else, too. He'd planted the seed in her. Rage.

After all these years of hiding from him, of thinking she saw him in the street only to discover it wasn't. Of feeling rage rise in her, seeing things, strangers in pubs, in wet dark streets – it might only be a man taking a sudden step towards a woman, a raised voice – and everything in her would be on the alert, ready for fight or flight. Just to have picked up a vibration that could mean something but might just mean, this is a couple who've had a row, or are about to split up, or have sex, or . . . or. It was like a sixth sense, for anger, and all she had learned had been to walk away from it. A vibration she had always made herself ignore, until now. And now it actually *was* him.

They walked past.

Past the café, they walked in the light it shed on to the cobbles of the harbour-front. Holding hands.

Heather sat up. Shit. Shit. The woman behind the bar who'd served her noticed the movement, and came around the bar wiping her hands on her apron, as if her sole customer might run off. Heather blurted something, feeling exposed in the bar's bright interior, and shoved the brandy glass at her.

'Yes, please, another, please.' She thrust notes at the woman who frowned down at her from under ferocious brows.

Outside they were walking on now, the café's glow falling on their backs as they passed into the shade, the girl, bare-legged – Heather shivered abruptly at the sight – was looking towards the harbour-front. Then they stopped.

Heather stood up. Her instinct was to get behind the barwoman, to hide, but once she was on her feet – the woman looking at her as if she was nuts – she saw there were some other tables the other side of the bar. Not quite out of sight but dimmer, in the recesses of the room. Picking up her bag she made for them, not caring if the woman stared at her, she just had to get out of sight.

Who was she kidding? It was fifteen years: he wouldn't recognise her. He'd probably forgotten her before he'd even got back to his decks on the beach, leaving her there under the pier, bleeding.

But *she* might. The girl. Sukie Alexander might know her face from the profile photograph attached to that LinkedIn message – if she'd read it. If she'd shown him.

Then *he* might remember her. He'd never known her name but he might have it all stored away. Like a trophy in his head. What she looked like underneath him, sprawled there, trying to hide herself, the expression on her face—

'Thank you,' Heather said, sitting down abruptly at a table in the furthest corner. 'Here, thank you.' She had everything awkwardly in her arms and as she put it down her phone dropped to the floor with a clatter. Leaning to retrieve it she saw that the screen was black, dead. Head down, from there under the table, she could also see their legs outside. The girl's were bare, downy – was she too young even to shave her legs? thought Heather – feet planted flat in trainers.

Is that his kind of girl? The legs shuffled, awkward, and the couple drew apart. Gingerly Heather straightened. She could smell the toilet, it made her gag. She felt strange and dizzy.

She told herself, don't. Don't move.

He was pointing somewhere, she was nodding. Then something got in the way: it was the woman with the second glass of Metaxa and she was blocking Heather's view. Heather stared up at her, but instead of going back behind her bar the woman stayed where she was. She was saying something Heather didn't understand. Then she did. 'Oh,' she said. The woman was pointing at the phone. 'Yes,' Heather said, shrugging. 'Dead.' The woman pointed at a plug in the wall at her end of the bar and belatedly Heather scrabbled

189

in the backpack, got out the charger and plug she'd bought at the airport and handed the whole thing over to her.

Still the woman didn't get out of the way, clutching Heather's phone and charger to her broad chest, looking at her with that angry frown. 'What?' said Heather, in desperation. 'What is it?'

And the woman touched her cheek with the back of her hand and for a second the touch, the cool hard dry touch of knuckles against her skin made Heather close her eyes with a little shiver. When she opened them again she realised the woman thought she was feverish. 'No, no,' she said, 'just some water, I'll be fine.' She had no idea if she was making herself understood but at last the woman got out of the way and Heather could see.

Whoever had arrived after her had emerged on to the waterfront: she was getting a warmer reception than Heather had. A middle-aged woman in a puffa coat and heels, gesticulating. A man in uniform had her by the elbow.

Sukie Alexander was nowhere to be seen but *he* was still there. Someone else was approaching, from out of the darkness, but she couldn't see who. Then he was talking to the someone else, light fell on him from above, something passed between them. Both men's hands went to their pockets, something had been exchanged. Money, for goods or services? Maybe it was how things were done here still. Envelopes of cash.

At the bar she heard the woman plug the phone in and rest it on the counter and one part of her brain was turning on that, on whether the thing would come back to life, whether she would ever hear from Kit again, on whether she would ever get home, on where she would stay tonight.

But that part of her brain had shrunk small, nothing more than a tiny cog whirring when all the rest of the machine had ground to a halt, frozen.

He was walking towards the bar. His hand was out to the door. He was coming inside, and the man he'd met, the man who'd come out of the darkness, was coming after him.

Jake Littlejohn. And the other man was Kostas, her boatman.

Day Three, Friday: Sukie

'Got to see a man about a dog,' said Jake and Sukie stared at him. 'What, you've never heard that one?' he said, nudging her gently under the chin with his knuckle. 'It means, there are some things a man needs to do on his own.' He put his hand down, into his pocket, feeling for something.

'Oh,' she said, none the wiser. Was he going for a pee? Or more business? 'Oh, all right.' She fumbled in her bag, that was battered now, if felt like she'd been here a lifetime, on a kind of adventure, that she'd dragged her bag through a jungle, getting lost. Retrieved her passport. 'I'll get down to the travel place, then?' He pointed along the façades. They were standing in front of a bar, its interior lit so brightly she turned away, blinking. 'It's on the end,' he said.

She had thought he might go with her some of the way

191

and looked back, hesitant, but he just stood there, watching her go. He smiled, she could see him turning something over and over in his hand. Black and shiny, a compact little thing: the shape of it was vaguely familiar.

When Sukie got to the grocery store that had the travel agency above it she turned back again but he wasn't looking any more. He was talking to another man, swarthy in a woollen peaked cap, their heads close together. Hastily she turned back and went inside.

Narrow stone stairs led up ahead of her, they smelled of a kind of fishy damp, they were dark and cold and with longing Sukie thought of her clothes, a pair of jeans, a sweatshirt. She couldn't remember what she'd packed. And then another leap, more feeble, more painful: home. Only another day and a bit and home and it would all be OK. But she couldn't make it real: it was as if there was a great rock, or something, between her and home. As if something waited for her, first. She paused. What *was* his business? She suddenly wanted to hurry back down the stairs and run out to watch him, to see where he was going and who he was talking to.

If it was just work, an olive grower or oil producer with his samples, why couldn't he introduce her? All this man-about-a-dog stuff. All he had to say was, *this is my . . .* My what? *This is Sukie.*

He hadn't even wanted to introduce her to Nat and Betsy, she'd had to do that herself. Because he was as unsure about her as she was about him, because it hadn't worked out? But he'd been sure enough of her to— She leaned a moment against the rough plaster of the wall, feeling her heart bump painfully. Sure enough to pack condoms – and more than one pack. She closed her eyes, felt them flutter under the lids, trapped.

If she'd imagined sex between them – it had been softly lit, something slow, something gentle, not some, some three-day marathon. And yet . . . And yet he hadn't even touched her. Could the condoms be for some other . . . some other purpose? There'd been something else in Jake's bag, among the dirty clothes, that flat cardboard box with something spilling. What had she seen written on its side? Something about surgical use. For some reason then the thought of Nat came into her head, the old wrinkled body emerging from the sea, his unblinking stare, the descent into the cellar. And then she thought of the lower room full of junk, and the suitcase sitting open there, and all the things she didn't know. The narrow space closed around her and she wasn't sure which way was up and which was down.

Gloves. The eruption of rubber fingers: a box of latex gloves. In Jake's suitcase.

She made herself keep climbing, her head buzzing. For work? And then there was the door, light behind it. She pushed it open.

It was warm inside and dazzlingly bright, and a plump, bored-looking girl with glasses sat behind a desk with a pink padded coat on as if she'd been waiting for Sukie before she could leave.

There were forms to fill out first. The girl wrote laboriously, pushing her glasses up her nose, so slowly that Sukie shifted in her chair, anxious, worrying about Jake, whether, where she'd find him again.

The thought sprang, surprising, into Sukie's head. She could just go. Now she had the bag. She could find someone to take her to the airport island on a boat, she could— She stopped. She was being ridiculous again. And besides, her phone had her plane ticket on it. At last the plump girl then pushed the forms across the desk for Sukie to sign.

'He is your boyfriend, Mr Jake?' she said, curiously, watching Sukie.

'You know him?' said Sukie, the forms in her hand.

'Beh.' The girl made a sound that went with her shrug. 'He is too old for you, isn't he?'

Sukie felt herself flush, thrusting the forms back at the girl. 'How old do you think *I* am?' she said, defensively. The girl got to her feet, padded in her coat that stood out around her, threatening to knock papers off the desk and shrugged again.

'I *know* how old,' she said. 'Is in your passport. Twenty-seven. But Mr Jake is nearly fifty, I know, because is five years younger than my mother, and you look like' – her upper lip curled – 'like fifteen!'

And then she turned abruptly, a swirl of bubble-gum pink, and went through a door at the back of the room.

Fifteen. Sukie stared after her. It was true: in her head, too. Fifteen, not twenty-seven. She shouldn't be here. She was too stupid to be out. And abruptly she felt disinclined to leave the little office, the warmth, the familiarity of contemptuous female companionship. She could be Anastasia, this pink-coated girl. But instead she was going to walk back outside and find Jake. Nearly fifty? Was he? These people knew him better than she ever would.

From behind the door came a shuffle and thump of stuff being moved around. Then the girl reappeared, hoisting the bag in front of her.

For a moment Sukie was going to say, that's not mine, because it had two broad silver bands around it – and then she remembered, Jake had said something about it being damaged and the silver was duct tape, crudely bandaging a tear in the top and side of the nylon. It was her bag. She reached for it and the girl handed it over, detaching a note from the handle as she did do.

The girl peered down at the paper then back at Sukie, pushing the glasses up her nose with the glasses. Shrugging. 'Was old, perhaps? Is not my responsibility, you know. Damage in transit, they say.'

Sukie looked back at the little pile of documents on the table. Unthinking, she'd signed to say she'd received the bag and accepted it.

Watching her beadily the girl shrugged again, a shade less patient, her English a shade less friendly. She looked at the note in her hand again. 'Something inside, have damaged the bag. Something hard . . .' The girl searched for a word. 'Or with corners. Inside. But the bag is here, so,' she shrugged, 'be grateful.' She tilted her head, curiously. 'How long is your holiday?'

'We go back tomorrow,' said Sukie and the girl raised her eyebrows.

'So soon,' she said, with a little laugh. 'Is just in time.'

But she looked suspicious, tugging the padded coat around her, and Sukie had a cold feeling; she'd thought this was an ally, but she wasn't. She wanted rid of Sukie so she could go home and gripe about foreigners. And what else? *Mr Jake.* That jeering tone. The girl was staring at the bag.

'I'm sorry.' Sophie retreated, the girl watching as she turned for the door but she should at least open the bag, make sure. Faltering, she reached for the zip. Behind the desk the girl let out an impatient sigh, but Sukie stood her ground.

It was all stuffed in any old how, and seemed somehow fuller than when she'd handed it over to Jake, perhaps the tape had bound it tighter. But there was a pair of jeans, legs twisted round each other, canvas shoes, a warm sock – Sukie had missed socks and began to root, suddenly needing to make sure the other was in there. 'Just . . . just one minute, I'm sorry,' she mumbled, and then the second sock was there, stuck around something, something with corners, that must be what had split the bag, only for the moment she couldn't remember what she had put in that was like that.

'Is all right?' The girl was standing, impatient.

'Yes, yes,' said Sukie, in the same moment hearing footsteps on the stairs.

The door opened.

'Jake,' she said, because there he was, frowning. She put a hand to her cheek, then hastily began to zip the bag back up before it all fell out on the floor, could it be a book? She didn't remember packing a book. 'Jake . . .'

'All right?' he said, only giving her a soft, enquiring look and then turning, her defender, Jake gave the girl a cold hard stare.

'Let's go,' she whispered.

They went out. On the stairs she mumbled, 'Do you know that girl?'

He shrugged. 'I don't think so,' he said. 'Not to speak to. Why?'

'Oh,' Sukie was still off balance, somehow, the bag bumped against her, 'she seemed to know who you were,' she said. 'That's all.'

'Really?' he said, but he didn't sound interested, pushing the door open. The mist swirled on the cobbles, in the soft haze of the light falling out of the window above them. 'Nothing better to do but poke their noses in, I suppose.'

Sukie followed him out in time to hear the bang of the shutters above being closed, and the light went. At the same time, from out in the dark of the sea came the sound of a boat with big engines coming in at speed, a light mounted on its turret that swung across the water, illuminating the froth of a bow wave, bobbing boats, the men on the quay in their hats.

Jake turned her, his hand on her elbow, towards the homeward path.

Ahead of them a man was taking pots and pans down from the frontage of a hardware store, stepping aside to let a woman out with her long package – then a figure flitted round the corner, a last-minute customer, or husband, boyfriend – and intercepted the departing customer.

Sukie stopped abruptly, the brief blurred image of the woman's white face bothered her, but now all she could see was the back of the man who'd stopped her. She felt Jake watching them too, then his hand was on her elbow, steering again.

'Let's go, he said, and clutching the bag against her, Sukie went.

Chapter Twenty-One

Day Three, Friday: Kit

'So.' Jade necked her brandy in one gulp. She'd taken off her cagoule. At the bar a girl that had come in as they were going out was being chatted up by a man in a suit; she looked half pissed already, or reckless, anyway. The kind of girl that Kit would have run a mile from but the men had all turned towards her.

'What d'you make of it, then?' said Jade and then, without waiting for him to answer, 'He's an arsehole.'

Kit suddenly needed another drink. He picked up her glass. She sighed. 'All right then.'

The doors opened again as he reached the bar and Kit, turning, registered the girl who'd come in – small but sturdy, with cropped hair and a tuft at her hairline – as having been outside when he went after Emily. She made for the reckless, loud-mouthed girl too and he heard *Anastasia*, as he headed back to the table.

He set down the glasses. 'I hope you're not going to ask me if she's telling the truth,' said Jade, reaching for hers.

'No.' At the beginning he'd thought only about Heather, her face superimposed on Emily's, *her* voice, halting, as she admitted things and he'd felt his fists clenching. And then, as she kept talking in that monotone, head down, it had been just Emily.

She'd needed some prompting.

'I met him,' Emily had started and stopped almost immediately, defeated already. 'I met him on a dating site.' Her shoulders dropped. 'He seemed . . .' she was miserable, 'so unlike the others.'

'In what way?'

'He didn't talk himself up. He was . . . quiet. He never talked about . . .' Her hands went up to her throat, crossed, as if she wanted to stop herself. 'About sex.' On the other side of her Jade shifted in her seat, laid a hand gently across her shoulders. 'He didn't ask for my private number or anything.'

'What kind of site was it?' he said.

'It was called "Respectful Dating",' said Jade. 'Yes, it really exists, I checked.'

'For people who want to be respected,' said Kit. 'Are there people that don't?' He felt stupid.

Pinched and white, Jade ignored the question. 'Or – obviously – for arseholes who want to prey on vulnerable girls—' she corrected herself. 'Women.'

'She looked so young,' he murmured. 'Emily did.'

Emily had sat there, turning her diet Coke round and round. Going quiet for long seconds.

'He took me to places like the park, on walks by the river, we went on a train once to a pub in the country. At first he wouldn't tell me about his family, he was a bit funny about that.'

'Funny?'

'He kept saying I wouldn't understand. Then I told him, I didn't see mine, hadn't seen them in years and years, told him my dad was dead. I just wanted to encourage him, really.' She flushed and sipped and went silent for a second.

'And?' said Kit.

'That seemed to do it, it was like, he needed to know I was alone in the world too? And then he couldn't stop talking about them, his childhood, living in Greece, how amazing it was, how beautiful it was, how creative and fun and . . . different his parents were. So much stuff. All the sunshine and the sea and the simple life, all that stuff.' She looked around the pub with fear in her eyes.

'It's all right,' Jade said quietly. 'It's OK.'

'I did ask him why he'd come to England if it was so great out there and he went a bit funny again.'

'What was it like when he went funny?' Kit was curious.

Emily bit her lip. 'He would look sad, like I'd upset him, and of course I'd shut up. But underneath – well. Something else was going on. Like . . . I felt it even then, and now it's obvious. Underneath he was angry because I'd asked him a question he hadn't got an answer for.'

She looked around again, fearful. 'Anyway, then he told me he'd come to Britain for his education and then he stayed because there were more jobs. I mean, obvious really, I don't know why you'd get funny about it.'

'Maybe there was another reason,' said Kit. 'That he didn't want to tell you about.'

She looked at him for a long moment, then reached for his brandy and took a sip. 'Yes,' she said quietly. There was a silence again.

'I feel so stupid,' she went on. Her cheeks were pinker, from the brandy. 'He told me straight away, he was . . . wasn't like that – he even said his previous girlfriend had left him because he didn't want sex enough. I was sort of . . .' She swallowed. 'I was sort of disappointed. I mean . . . I felt sorry for him. But I thought maybe I could . . .' She put her hands up to her face briefly. 'I thought I could help him.'

'That's an old technique,' said Jade drily and when Emily stared down into her lap, patted her. 'I'm sorry, love. All I mean is, plenty of girls fall for that one.'

'So what *did* he want?' He lowered his voice, a notch, but Emily didn't seem to notice and spoke clearly.

'He said he wanted me to come out to Greece with him. He said he had some business to do out there and it would be a nice little holiday, long weekend, we could stay in his parents' house. He sort of implied . . . maybe we could set up out there together. Him and me.' She frowned. 'I wasn't sure about that. But I didn't say so. I was getting a bit less sure, to be honest, now I think about it.' She faltered. 'There was something weird about the way he was with me. Like, touching me, looking at me, but always aware of what he was doing, how far he could go. Watching me.'

'That wasn't . . . just normal?' Kit was uneasy. 'Like . . .' he searched for the word, then said, lamely, 'respectful?' He'd always wanted to be respectful.

'I didn't really think about it, not consciously,' said Emily. 'Until there was one night, we went out and I asked him up to my place for coffee. I live with another girl and I thought, assumed, she'd be there but she was out somewhere with her boyfriend. And he started walking around the place as if he was checking it out, looking at the things on the walls, where the rooms were, all that. I made him the coffee and all the time I was worried he thought there was more to it, that I was ready to . . . you know.'

'To have sex with him,' said Jade. She was watching Kit.

'But you weren't,' said Kit. He couldn't get the picture out of his head, of the anxious Emily, the man checking out her flat.

'He was very careful never to freak me out but I just thought there was something underneath,' said Emily, her head so low they couldn't see her face. Then she looked up. She was very pale now. 'He got out some dope.' Eyed Kit, elaborated. 'Marijuana. He said it helped him relax. I didn't really know what to do or say, so I let him. He offered it to me and I-I did try it. It made me feel sick and a bit . . . out of it, sleepy. I . . . and then I did fall asleep, for a bit.' She looked down at her hands, Kit could only see her cheek but it was flushed.

'And then she came back,' she mumbled, head down still. 'My flatmate came back, that's when I realised I'd been asleep, the sound of her key in the door, and he was standing by the window and it was open. She was a bit annoyed, I think maybe she could smell it. But he was very calm.'

'And then he left,' said Kit.

She lifted her head and nodded.

'And afterwards I could see, you know, like he had been getting pleasure out of that part. The waiting, the pushing me out of my comfort zone, seeing how far I would go. Because after . . . because when . . .' She stopped. No one spoke.

'And how . . .' Kit spoke very, very quietly, 'how did it end?'

Emily sat up, composing herself with an effort, hands in her lap.

'He wanted to buy the plane tickets,' she said. 'We were out walking, in the wetlands, out near the Olympic park. It's always so empty. I hadn't invited him back to my place since . . . since. And I said, I said, I didn't even think, when he mentioned it, I said something about my dad going to Greece a lot, I used the present tense.'

'Because you'd told him you didn't really have family.'

'Yes,' said Emily, grabbing the drink, gulping it. 'And he went very quiet. He said, I thought your dad was dead. I said . . . Well, then I just thought, I'll tell him the truth. I told him my dad was alive and while we weren't on bad terms he had remarried and lived in the Isle of Wight so as good as – I tried to make a joke out of it – as good as dead. And he was smiling, and smiling.' She put the Coke down so hard it splashed up the glass, she put her hands down to either side of herself, jammed down on the banquette. 'I told him, my dad's a policeman, retired. And then he . . . he . . .'

Kit saw that Jade was holding her hand, fingers entwined, so tight their knuckles were white. Emily's head came up again.

'I was still talking,' she said. 'And he punched me in the face, right then. Right then. I just fell over backwards and then he was on top of me and he punched me again. And then . . .' She stopped. 'Then he . . .'

'He raped her,' said Jade.

'He went over it all while he was doing it, like he'd memorised everything we'd done since I started going out with him, every expression on my face, everything I'd said. He imitated my voice.'

For a second Emily's face had contorted, like she was back there, then it was still and pale again. 'He remembered every single thing I'd said,' she said.

Kit had stared at her. *If Heather . . . if Heather. If he'd done that to Heather.*

She'd got to her feet abruptly right then. 'I've got to go,' she said, fumbling with her phone, and suddenly she had looked terrified. 'I've got to go.'

And now, as he sat dumbly next to Jade in the hot, noisy saloon bar of the Princess Alexandra, Emily in her Uber on her way back to the shared flat, Kit stared into the distance, blank.

The two girls were making their way through tables

towards the booth next to theirs: it must have been free because they disappeared behind the screen. With their retreat, the room seemed to turn quiet, a lull descending as the guys at the bar turned away, pretended they hadn't been trying to pick anyone up.

'Respectful Dating,' said Kit, in disbelief. Behind the glass, behind Jade, he could see the movement of the girls' heads, the small cropped one, the tangled one.

'Yeah,' said Jade, thoughtful. 'He'll have disappeared from that site. Emily told me she tried to file a complaint but they just fobbed her off, and no doubt she didn't tell them everything.'

'And you just came across her,' said Kit, warily. 'Just got talking about abusive boyfriends.'

Jade looked at him expressionless for a long moment, then said, 'He did a job on me,' she said. 'Jake Littlejohn did. He groomed me, so he could deal in my bar, and the sex was . . . well, the last time wasn't nice, let's put it that way. He'd stored up every bit of hatred.'

Jade stared down into her brandy. Her white-blonde hair, kinked from its plaits, was dry as straw. 'I don't like that. I don't like being conned, I don't like being used. So I asked around. Other barmaids, other club workers. DJs can't afford to change their names. I thought, if he could do that to me, to *me*, and get away with it, what happens when he meets some kid? Someone like Emily?'

'Right,' said Kit, his voice hoarse. He felt as if he'd been shouting, as if he'd had this guy, Jake Littlejohn, in front of him and had been screaming at him.

Jade let out a long sigh. 'Anyway. A friend of mine is Emily's flatmate is the short answer. The flatmate – she's called Carmen – who turned up unexpectedly when Emily was there with him, and saw the state she was in, wondered if she'd been taking drugs. After the attack, the rape, Emily confided in her, eventually, and Carmen tried to get her to go to the police. When Emily told her his full name – he'd only been Jacob up till then, Emily's new boyfriend – she remembered I'd been looking for a Jake Littlejohn, and came to me. I've been trying to talk Emily into going to the police ever since, but she won't.'

'Maybe she will now,' said Kit.

'Don't push her,' said Jade, with a warning note in her voice.

'All right,' he said, holding up a hand, 'all right. But what I don't understand is, why she didn't go to her dad. Ex-policeman?'

Jade gave him a long, level look. 'You don't?' she said. 'There's not a whole lot you know about women, is there, Kit? The dad's divorced, a tough bloke, miles away. But even if he'd been none of those things – talk to your dad about being raped? He's the last person she'd have told.'

Kit thought of Heather, and how much she had loved her father, and stared down at his hands. 'I suppose not,' he said, hearing his voice crack. Not for the first time, he was glad Fred wasn't there. Briefly he wondered if Fred was really back at the office, trying to work this one out, or if he'd got lucky on Tinder.

'And besides,' said Jade, 'the guy knew what he was doing.

I don't know, maybe he'd got in trouble in the past or maybe he just enjoyed it, the game. He was obviously after a girl with no one looking out for her, no parents or estranged. Her dad being an ex copper must have made him very angry. But you see how scared she looked, when she left?'

'Yes,' said Kit, but he didn't understand.

Jade stood up, pulling on her rain jacket. 'He knew what he was doing,' she said. 'She told me. Mr Jake Littlejohn had an insurance policy, didn't he.'

Chapter Twenty-Two

Day Three, Friday: Heather

For a long five minutes after they left the café, Heather just sat there, feeling weirdly light-headed. Her hands and feet felt very cold but her cheeks burned.

They'd come straight up to the bar without noticing her in the back room. Heather hadn't been able to see their faces and she told herself, keep your head down. Just stay still. She heard Kostas order coffee, curt and rude, and heard the woman clattering cups by way of reply.

In her corner, back pressed into the wall, Heather had her Greek brandy, that burned the back of her throat, she had the dregs of her coffee. If she moved fast, she could be out of the door.

Her phone. Her phone was on the bar, plugged in. Around the far side, by the wall, probably face up, she didn't know how close the men were to it. If it came back to life, if the water hadn't got into it. If a message came in.

If it rang.

If it came on and there was his picture, right there, was it the last thing she'd looked at? Heather felt hot, then cold; again she shivered.

Stop panicking. No one was interested in her phone. *Now is not the time to panic.* And besides, what was she here for? She was here to get him, and here he was.

That cooled Heather down. Planning was required, for what she wanted to do. Planning – and maybe some cash. Just out of the wide rectangle of light shed from the bar someone stood, a dreadlocked beggar, cap in hand, shifting from bare foot to bare foot, a figure in loose dirty trousers made indistinct by the constant nervous movement.

At the bar she heard Kostas saying something, urgent. She leaned cautiously to peer and when she looked back the barefoot figure was gone. Man or woman, she hadn't really seen enough to tell.

They were talking Greek, and Heather didn't understand the words but there was something in the tone, the muttered tone of a question, that made her lean round the bar again, to look. If she went on like this they'd see her. Littlejohn had asked the question, and that voice, very soft. They stepped away from the bar, their backs to her, and Kostas pointed, with both hands outlined a female shape, patted at a height, Littlejohn nodded. Kostas was telling him he'd brought a woman over on the boat who'd shown him Littlejohn's picture.

Something moved in the corner of her eye and she saw that the woman was looking at her from behind the bar. Heather brought a finger to her lips and the woman turned away.

Money. A cash machine? Think.

This is what you get, BlueJ. If you go through life doing that to enough women, one day one will come after you. One of them will be brave enough.

Was it brave, though? Or was it − was *she* − crazy?

The two men walked together, to the front of the bar, the wide glass window − Littlejohn lanky, Kostas burly and squat − and Heather eased herself back, as far into the corner as she could. They would still be able to see her, if they turned. If.

Of course, even if Kostas turned and pointed, *that's her*, Jake Littlejohn still wouldn't know who Heather was, which one she was. There could be an army of us, she thought. He stood there with his back to her, shoulders thrown back, hands in his pockets. He didn't look afraid. He should. He should look afraid.

Then he seemed to come to a conclusion, one hand came down to clap Kosta on the shoulder, while the other reached for the door handle to leave.

But in that same moment, on the bar, level with her eyes, her phone came to life. It glowed.

Day Three, Friday: Joey

The bus swayed, out along the Holloway road, the shop-fronts sulphur-yellow in the street lamps, a crowd still on the pavement outside the big pub on the corner. From the back row of the top deck Joey looked down on their heads, men stumbling and shouting, their aggressive moon faces turned to look at the lit-up bus, and pressed herself further into her corner.

Anastasia was mumbling on her shoulder, half asleep, the corner of her mouth damp.

'Take me home with you, Joe,' she'd said, looking round the pub blearily. 'Absolutely not,' said Joey, but the first Uber they'd called for her took one look – one whiff, and drove away. Trouble was, she felt responsible – she should have collared Anastasia and hauled her out of the pub.

But instead she'd stood and looked around the pub full of men, and seen the ginger bloke who'd put the girl – tear-stained Emily – into her Uber, sitting back down in a booth with another woman, and something about them – something. And just in that moment the booth next to theirs coming empty, and she'd just taken Anastasia by the elbow and said, 'Let's sit down a minute.'

No harm in it. Anastasia stumbling, spilling her drink but doing what she was told.

And then sitting there in the booth with Anastasia moaning at her for dragging her away from the bar, Joey had heard his name.

She hadn't been sure if it was the man or the woman

who'd spoken it, in the next booth, and if there hadn't been that lull right then in the noise from Anastasia's abandoned admirers she probably wouldn't have heard anything. But she did. *Mr Jake Littlejohn.* Muttered, with contempt, but audible.

'Mr Jake Littlejohn had an insurance policy, didn't he?'

She'd had to hiss at Anastasia to shut up, a minute. Finger to her lips, Anastasia pouting and sulking, her chin in her hands and making eyes at the guys at the bar. Joey had leaned closer to the glass between them.

The girl called Emily had been one of Jake Littlejohn's exes, and recent. And he'd fucked her over.

Joey wasn't sure what this stuff about an insurance policy was: the woman had lowered her voice so she had to strain to catch any of it. Something about smoking dope, something about pictures. Anastasia had been getting restless at that point, had got up to get herself another drink, and Joey had let her go, so she could listen. The woman's low angry voice muttered on.

'So sweet kind Jake's a serial rapist, revenge-porn artist, and he likes them young and innocent. And if you ask me, there's more; if you ask me he had a plan for little Emily and finding out she's got a dad and he's a policeman—'

Clear and angry, and the guy shushing her. And then in that moment two tables between her and the bar stood up en masse and began to move towards the door and when they'd cleared and Anastasia was wobbling back towards her, pouting because the guy behind the bar had refused to serve her, the next door booth had been empty.

The bus swayed and the brakes wheezed as it slowed down. Joey nudged Anastasia off her shoulder.

'Hey,' she hissed. 'Wake up, sunshine. This is our stop.'

Chapter Twenty-Three

Day Three, Friday: Heather

Heather had the feeling someone had been following her when she turned from the cashpoint – not Jake Littlejohn, because she knew where he'd gone, she had her eye on him. Not him.

She'd seen Littlejohn go into the door beside the grocery store at the end of the row. Was that where he was living, with the girl, a room above a grocery store, was that what he'd brought her here for? And for a second Heather saw him in her head, turning in some dingy room to lock the door. At least under the pier he'd got off and kicked her aside. At least she hadn't been shut in with him. She'd got away.

She stepped off the pavement to look up and saw a lighted window, a faded sign painted on the wall for a travel agency. Hesitated, then turned back again. She needed money, and quick. The woman in the bar had told her where to find the ATM.

Back in the bar, there'd been a split second in it. If the phone had made a sound *before* it glowed back into life, rather than after. If they'd moved to seize it – she and the purple-haired woman behind the bar – just a little bit faster, rashly enough for their movements to have been detectable in the window, or even audible, before his hand had met the door handle and its rattle and creak had not drowned out the sound and movement behind them, at the bar. If Kostas had stayed behind – or if either of them had been polite enough to turn and thank their hostess as they left.

But they had walked out without looking back. The woman had got to the phone first, holding it against her broad bust, watching after them, then, only when the door had closed behind them and they were gone in the darkness, did she look at Heather. She thrust the phone at her.

'No,' she said before Heather could even ask the question. Shaking her head so violently her earrings jangled. Holding both hands up against her, palms out, the international gesture for *keep me out of it*. Heather tried sign language – *Where does he live, don't tell him* – but the woman's face was like a closed door. She relented only when Heather gave up and, opening her purse to show how empty it was, mimed putting a card in an ATM. Then she marched Heather to the door and pointed.

Two missed calls and a message from Kit, late afternoon. *Don't do anything stupid. Don't. Come home, I love you.* For a second it was like a shaft of light in a dark room, and then she turned away.

The cashpoint was down a narrow alley off the row of façades that ended in the grocery store. From where she stood, impatiently waiting for the ancient machine to process her information, Heather could see a sliver of the harbour-front at the end of the alley. On the corner a shop was still open, pans dangling in silhouette. If Littlejohn and Sukie Alexander walked back the way they'd come, they'd walk past, across the opening to the alleyway. They didn't.

As she looked a man came out with a long pole and began unhooking the pans. Hardware shop, she thought, her brain churning on a dim interior, rows of tools.

The alley was dark further in, and in the glow of the cash machine Heather could see the mildewing on the white-washed house fronts, she felt the cold. Was it that that made her shiver, or was it a fever that made her imagine things? There was a snap and a jolt and her card was disgorged then the notes emerged and she grabbed them and ran.

Still nothing. And no one. Had there been a rustle, a movement in the darkness at the end of the alley? Kostas, sent to find her?

No. Because there was Kostas, smoking on the quay and talking to a woman with a basket. He shifted, and she ducked quickly inside the hardware store.

The place was a haven, it smelled comfortably of oil and paraffin and varnish, of her dad's workshop, the garage at home; behind the counter were even the little niches for castors and screws and washers and tacks.

The man wrapped her purchase carefully in brown paper without a word or a question, took her money, counting it out on the scarred wooden counter. Then he reached for his pole and came around her, heading back outside.

As she got to the door she saw them. Jake and Sukie, lovely couple. The girl looked pale, clutching the bag to her front as if it might break open and spill. Heather stopped dead, the girl's eye passed over her and – Heather could tell – was about to look again, look back, break step, say, that's her. *That's her.*

Because even if she hadn't seen the email Heather had sent on LinkedIn, she would have checked out the profile picture, must have, in order to say yes. *Make connection.* Everyone – well, every woman – would do that.

Was about to double-take, and then something happened, the shop owner with his pole had stepped out of her path and round the side of the shop but someone else was there, in between her and the approaching couple. She clutched her package against her, long and flat, wrapped in paper. A tall skinny frame shrouded in dusty brownish clothes and a smell of sweat and patchouli and dust that made her nose tickle, with the memory of old days, of student days. Dreadlocks.

'It's you,' he said, because it was a man, after all, the figure shifting nervously from foot to foot outside the bar, the cap on his head now, and framed by the dreadlocks that hung dusty to either side, brown skin stretched over hollow cheekbones, scabbed lips, pale, pale eyes. A ghost, a ghost from long ago, from another world, from another life.

'What?' she said, desperately, trying to peer round him after them as they vanished into the night. 'What? I'm sorry, I think you've got the wrong—'

'Heather,' he said, and she saw he was trembling like a dog. 'Heather?' And he brushed the dreadlocks back and she saw the eyes and looking into them she remembered someone, from out of the past, the overweight fresher who'd wanted that gang to go off for the summer on the magic bus, pleading, the boy who needed friends. Who'd grown up somewhere abroad. Grown up here: it was how she knew the name. Could it be him? All the puppy fat long gone, he looked like an old man, but the eyes were the same. She searched her memory.

'David?' she said. 'Is it David?' And it was as if she felt the tug of an invisible thread, connecting them.

He stumbled awkwardly against her, a quick bony hug and then he stepped back. 'What's wrong?' he said. 'Are you sick?' She couldn't see them, she didn't know where they'd gone.

'Heather?' he said, and her teeth chattered as his face loomed into hers, blocking everything out.

Day Three, Friday: Sukie

They walked back past the tiny bar and Sukie turned towards the light, as if she was in a dream, her heart fluttering, thinking only, one more night and all this will be done, I can tell people, I can tell Marsha and what will it look like when I get home? *Lovely holiday, weather a bit mixed. Getting to know each other.*

She saw a man reaching up for a bottle of bourbon and a skinny man banged a tiny glass on the bar, impatient, a man in a fedora hat.

'Was that,' she said, half to herself, but Jake had strode on, 'Nat? Was that Nat?'

'What?' Jake turned round, and she saw something flicker in his face. In the same moment the man in the hat inside the long narrow inside space of the bar turned too and it *was* Nat. He came towards them stumbling, pushing the door open.

'You seen her?' he said.

'Seen who?' said Jake quickly, stepping sideways so he was between Sukie and Nat. Nat barked a laugh. '*Betsy*, of course. She came down here.' Sukie leaned to try and see his face but as she did Jake moved again and she couldn't see. She heard a string of muttered things but Jake had moved closer to him, muffling the sound. Something like, tracked her? She stepped back because she had the sudden sense of intruding. *Tracked* her? Like a dog?

Jake was murmuring, soothing, something about something being erratic, unreliable, *maybe the batteries*, she heard. Then, *not to worry.* Then he stepped back.

'We'll keep an eye out,' he said, hearty. 'Won't we, Sukie?'

Nat stood there, under the light shed from a lamp outside the bar, his face greenish, unshaven, and he swayed. 'You didn't see her down there? On the front? There was people down there, right? I know she wouldn't,' he began, then veered, '*You* wouldn't. She's just senile, poor goddamned, poor goddamned—'

'It's all right,' said Jake, soothingly, and he shot Sukie a quick complicit glance, weary, shrugging. 'We didn't see her, but we'll keep an eye out, on the way back.'

'I shouldn't have gone down to swim without her,' said Nat. ''S my fault. You'll look out for us, right, Jakie? You scratch my back I'll scratch yours, right, Jakie?'

Jake laughed. 'Right, Nat. Don't worry. She'll probably be home before you are.' And firmly he turned Sukie, propelling her ahead of him, lifting a hand to wave Nat off. She turned to see him just standing there under the light, still swaying.

'She's always wandering off,' he said, keeping his hand on her elbow, and sighed, theatrical. 'Put me out of my misery if I get that way, right?'

'Right,' said Sukie, doubtfully. His hand dropped.

As they turned by the lantern that marked where the footpath met the edge of town, Jake stopped and turned to her, reaching for the bag. 'Let me take that,' he said.

Sukie pulled back away from his hand, she could feel a corner digging into her. 'I can manage,' she said, and he stopped, under the light, hands in pockets.

'Is something the matter?' he said, frowning.

'No,' she said, 'no, I just . . . I was worried about Betsy. She does seem . . . vulnerable.'

'Well, yes,' said Jake, eyeing her, reasonable. 'She is. Nat going out and getting drunk doesn't help.'

'What did he mean,' she said, uncertain, 'about tracking her? Did he say that?'

'Oh, he has some . . . I don't know, some tracking thing going on. Tracking device, not sure what it is. On her mobile, or something.'

'She has a mobile?'

He shrugged. 'I guess. Doesn't everyone?'

She hadn't seen one. 'Let's not let it spoil our last night,' said Jake, breaking in on her train of thought.

'No,' said Sukie, with an effort. 'No, you're right. Let's just get going.'

'That's the girl,' he said. His hand was still held out for the bag, and she gave it to him. He slung it over his shoulder and they began to walk. After five hundred metres or so, in the soft dark, his free hand came out to hold hers. He talked to her as they climbed. There was a moon, but it was behind clouds, silvering their edges, and his voice was pensive in the dark.

'Not long now,' he said. 'I mean . . . not long to go. Only one more night.' He spoke sadly, with resignation. 'I'd hoped we'd get to know each other a bit more, and it's all been a bit chaotic, hasn't it?'

And Sukie suddenly saw into the future: the flight back, in silence, Jake looking out of the window. He might shake her hand when they said goodbye – would it be at the airport? Would he make up some excuse for not travelling with her on the Tube, with her bandaged-up roll bag? Their last night.

'I feel like I've got to know *you*,' said Sukie, hesitating. 'Well – just a bit.' Jake stopped abruptly; not realising, she took one more step and found herself bumping against him, felt her ungainly softness meet his lean length. He was warm to the touch as her hand grazed his arm, and she had the sense of his body running hot, like an engine. His face turned, very close.

'Have you?' he said.

She couldn't answer.

'Do you think it's possibly to really know someone?' he said. 'I've been lonely for so long.'

Sukie felt something inside herself lean towards him, she felt tears come to her eyes, because she knew what that was, even on this dark hillside – anxious, confused, disturbed – she could understand loneliness. He just wanted a hand to hold, like her. An orphan. Except she wasn't.

'I think maybe I need to be . . . braver,' he said, touching her cheek. 'About . . . about opening up. About . . .' He hesitated, sounding agonised. 'About intimacy. Don't you feel that?'

She held her breath, then let it out carefully, on a whisper. 'Yes.'

And then suddenly the moon came out from behind the silver lace edge of the cloud, and they were walking on, in step, his hand in hers.

At the crossroads she paused. 'My phone,' she said, uncertain. 'I could go and see if Betsy's in there, and get it. Can I?' He held both her hands a moment, loosely, in hers.

'You need it?' he said softly.

She looked across at the neat square house, the veranda with its untidy vine. The windows were shuttered, and it looked dark. She hesitated. Something was different, from how it had looked earlier. A piece of the picture was missing.

'She's probably gone to bed, if she's back,' he said.

'Nat was worried,' she said, uncertainly. 'I thought . . .'

'What did you think, darling?' he said, smiling, indulgent. 'Look, Nat had had a bit to drink, hadn't he?' *Darling,* she heard, *I'm his darling,* and remembered what was different. Maybe he had taken it down, taken the bags of rubbish down, that had been left outside the house. *But. But.*

'Do you really need that little screen,' he said, interrupting her train of thought, 'on our last night together?' And he smiled so she saw that deep line one side of his mouth and he cupped her cheeks in his hands, so gently. And just as she was getting used to his touch, the warmth in his palms, he took his hands away and turned to cross to the fig tree, the little rickety balcony.

'Our last night,' he said, softly. 'Let's leave the phone out of it. There's so much to talk about.' Fitted his key in the lock, opened the door on the dark interior of the little house, swinging her bag in ahead of him.

'Let's make it special,' he said, turning to her in the dark.

She followed him in and he closed the door behind them, she heard the click.

Day Three, Friday: Kit

Weary, Kit let himself in. Someone was snoring on the sofa: Friday night. Just another Friday night. He was bone-tired, but he felt it hum and buzz inside his system.

He'd felt himself go hot and cold as Jade told him, in an

undertone, what Emily hadn't been able to. What Jake Littlejohn's insurance policy had been. And then Kit had stood up in the booth, not knowing what he was doing, not wanting to hear any more and not knowing how to climb out of the dumpster full of shit people did to each other, except just to walk away.

Some instinct had told him that the shuffling at the two tables between him and the door were getting ready to leave and it had jolted him to his feet, the thought of being in the place a minute longer, hemmed in between gangs of lads and the knowing looks of Neil behind the bar. Serial rapist. Revenge porn. His brain scattered. *You don't know what he did to me.*

And in his head, in the dark room with somebody's mate turning over on the sofa in a room stuffy with beer and farts, Heather's face appeared in his head, white with determination. And he realised that he knew her, after all, inside and out. Over these three years he knew what she looked like before she woke up in the morning, restless with dreams; he'd seen her spring out of bed. He knew that she didn't stop before a job was done, she knew for absolutely sure the difference between right and wrong.

Warily he skirted the sofa, went into the bathroom to pee, in the dark. Swaying.

Heather might have gone there not knowing what she was going to do. But she knew now. She was going to kill Littlejohn.

He hesitated, weighed up cleanliness over waking up the stranger on the sofa, and flushed the toilet. Made his way

225

to his room as if sleepwalking, and in his head it all went round. She's gone all that way and she doesn't want me involved. She hasn't even told me where the island is: she doesn't want me scrambling for flights. She doesn't even want me calling the Greek police.

He sat on the bed and struggled with his socks. His phone fell out of his pocket on to the floor and shone its blue light up at him. He squinted down at it.

A message from Fred.

BlueJ aka Jacob Littlejohn accused of rape in 2009 and 2010, rape and false imprisonment in 2016, none of the cases went to court for lack of evidence. Keeps his head down for a bit after that. Companies house: Jacob Littlejohn registered as the owner of nail bar in Streatham since 2018, profits surprisingly high, considering a manicure is seven quid in those parts. Probably moves money through there, or something, I'd guess drugs, from what Jade said. If you had any more search terms, I might be able to get further.

He hesitated. Fuck it. He forwarded it to Heather, entire, complete. His finger hovered over the screen. What did he want from her? The truth. He typed.

Chapter Twenty-Four

Day Three, Friday (night): Heather

Her phone buzzed. It was from Kit: a forwarded message that began *BlueJ aka Jacob Littlejohn . . .*

Then Kit's message to her.

Was it drugs? Did he rape you?

Heather looked up, feeling hot then cold, looking around the foreign landscape, the shopfronts, and seeing Streatham, of all places. A different row of shops, people waiting at bus stops. London.

'Heather?' He was shaking her shoulder, but gently. David from way back when. David who'd grown up here.

A rape accusation that didn't stick: he'd done it again then. Another woman had been braver than her. False imprisonment. She looked down at the paper-wrapped package in her arms.

'Have you got any money?' His face was too close, so close she could see he didn't clean his teeth. His breath was not good, she could smell it now as she sat beside him in the car on the bumpy track.

'David,' said Heather, wonderingly. 'David.' It was him. The needy boy whose memory had nagged at her all the way here. At college he'd been fatter, a plump bullied kid, always trailing round after people. She couldn't remember if she'd been nice to him or not. In her memory, she'd just avoided him. She wished she hadn't avoided him, she wished she knew what he was like. Whether she could trust him; she wanted to be able to trust him.

It turned out he wanted money for a taxi. The winking lights of the harbour spun around them as she searched in her bag for her purse, panicking that it had gone and then she realised she still had it in her hand, clutched against the awkward package from the hardware store. 'Here,' said David, eagerly, his hair stiff as twigs round his face, reaching for the purse, and she surrendered it to him. But when gently he tried to take the package from her as well, stubbornly she hung on.

'I'm not trying to rob you,' he said, lip trembling, wounded, and she patted him weakly.

'I need somewhere to stay,' Heather said, and he brightened, sly.

'That's right,' he said. 'You said that already. You can stay at mine, I told you.'

'Did you?' She had missed something. She remembered babbling, babbling at his face when he knew her name.

'The taxi guy's coming,' said David. 'He's just finishing his dinner. There's only one.'

'His name's not Kostas, is it?' she said, and he frowned, shaking his head. And for some reason she thought of the boat loaded with refugees, out there floating in the dark. There were the helpless, and the people who made money out of them, and that was all. She didn't know which one David was. She clutched at the package until it dug into her hand.

'Let's get you a coffee, first,' he said. 'A . . .' he looked around, nervously, 'a drink.'

'Cup of tea,' Heather said, and thought of Kit, thought of tea in bed, thought of safety, blinked. 'I've already had a drink.' Was that her problem? The two brandies.

'All right,' he said, encouragingly, steering her towards the lit front of the bar. He felt nervous against her, a shivering dog still, or was that her? She did feel strange.

Looking down she saw the ragged hems of his trousers, his filthy bare feet. 'Have you got a bath at your place?' said Heather, hearing her own voice as if from far off and anyway he didn't seem to be listening.

He took the notes out of her purse in front of her. 'That all right?' he said, displaying them, and she just nodded. She got out her phone and looked at it: the screen still had that odd pink tinge, with fading round the edges. Her screensaver was a picture of the river – other people had pictures of themselves, or their loved ones, didn't they? She found she couldn't quite control the direction of her thoughts, they surged, dangerously. She went to her messages and blinked again. *Kit. Kit.* The longing for him was quite odd, it was unprecedented. He was missing from her. She needed that bit of her back. He didn't even know where she was, how was he supposed to come and get her? Help her?

There was a sharp exchange behind her at the bar, the woman interrogating David – it was very late, maybe she wanted to close up. Rubbing fiercely at her eyes she looked up to see him returning, sheepish, empty-handed.

'She's bringing the drinks,' he said, and sat. He was humming a little and grinning, nervous. She saw at least two of his teeth were missing. 'Doesn't trust me.'

The barwoman set the tray down in front of them. A tiny teapot, yellow Lipton tag hanging from it, cup, no milk. Never mind. Also a large glass of brandy. The woman didn't go away. She said something in Greek, gesturing at David and giving Heather an interrogatory look. She put the change down in front of Heather.

'She wants to know if you're all right,' said David. 'If I'm bothering you.' He looked anxious and under the table, his knees jiggled, and perhaps it was the brandies or feeling so strange but Heather felt a surge of pity for him that unbalanced her. She nodded and smiled at the woman, and patted David on the shoulder to show her it was all right. As she turned away Heather registered how terribly thin he was.

'Was that all she said to you?' she asked, pouring the tea, watching it come out, pale gold. David wasn't looking at her, he was looking at the brandy, amber-coloured in the glass, she could smell it. 'Take it,' she said, suddenly dead tired. 'It's for you, isn't it?' And his hand darted out so quickly she knew what his problem was.

'She's worried about you,' he said, avoiding her look, and drank half the brandy down in one gulp then set the glass back down, his gaze on it as if fascinated. 'She thinks you're ill.' He giggled nervously.

'Ill?' Heather didn't know what that even meant, for a moment, and reflexively she sipped her tea – it wasn't very hot, but it was all right. She poured another cup and drank it straight down. She must have just been thirsty.

She couldn't remember if David had been a drinker, back then. An eater, maybe. One compulsion or another: she'd always avoided them, herself, or thought she had. The order she put in her days, in her life, maybe that had been her compulsion. Counting frames per second, calculating, living in one archive or another. She looked back at David and saw the brandy glass was empty. He had the drinker's body, skinny arms and legs, a sad pot belly under the thin loose tunic. He sat back and she saw the jitters had gone out of him. She shouldn't have bought him booze. But she was so tired. Dead tired. She shivered with it.

Someone was tapping on the window. A man held up a bunch of car keys.

'That's us.' David jumped up and the cup rattled in the saucer.

'What else did she say?'

'She said I should look after you.' Heather looked from him to the woman and she thought the woman nodded.

When she looked back David was collecting the change from the table.

'Tip?' he said and Heather nodded her assent. He walked as far as the bar and she could hear him thanking the woman. She doubted he'd give her all the change but she didn't care. Sometimes you had to just decide; some people needed stuff that you could give. She got out her phone again.

Outside there was some argy-bargy going on, a middle-aged woman trying to get their taxi. The woman who'd come off the boat behind them? David seemed to register the fuss and moved off from the bar, shambling outside, passing Heather in a fug of brandy. He'd used the change to get another.

But Heather just looked down the messages, the exchange between her and Kit. She scrolled back, even to a time before all this, when it was just, *Cinema?* Or *Drink?* Or *See you at six*.

So few. *Kyros*, she typed, feeling tears come into her eyes. Send.

And when she looked back up there was no sign of the competition for the taxi and David was beckoning to her from the door.

Day Three, Friday: Joey

A missed call, from Sukie's mother Marsha.

Joey lay in the dark, with her hands round the phone clasped on her chest. She tried to rehearse the conversation she would have to have with Sukie. *You see, I found this stuff on the internet. You see, I overheard this woman in the pub.* She forced herself to think: am I doing the right thing? Am I inventing all these dangers because I'm jealous?

On the sofa Anastasia grumbled in her sleep, but Joey couldn't even close her eyes. When she closed her eyes the room was full, humming with dangers, so she left them open, watching the headlights of passing cars move across the ceiling. The room was stuffy and hot. Her bedsit wasn't meant for two, unless they were in the same bed, and Anastasia, even when sober and sorry, was not reading from the same hymn book as Joey. Nor was Sukie.

This wasn't jealousy. This wasn't romance. This was friendship, this was a powerful feeling something was wrong, and only a small amount of evidence. She needed more before she worried Sukie with what might still be nothing.

Good job tomorrow was Saturday. Or was it today, already? She lifted the phone off her chest: it was only ten o'clock. She saw the little red circle on her phone app again, telling her she'd missed that call. Marsha had phoned at five thirty, although for some reason the alert had only come through later. Joey would have taken the call if she'd heard it ring, she was too polite not to, but she wasn't going to phone Marsha back.

It wasn't Marsha's fault, she had to tell herself that. It was as much hers as Marsha's. Call herself a friend? She shouldn't have been so passive. Just sitting there and smiling and saying I'm sure it'll be all right and how lovely and enjoy yourself.

She should have said, *Are you sure?* Should have said, *How much do you know about this man, really?*

Were these dating sites meant for people like Sukie? They were for people who played the system. That prompted another thought, meandering, her and Anastasia staring at the screen in the office, springing apart when that face loomed behind the plexiglass. *What's that?*

She'd written it down, hadn't she? Joey had. Written it down, the email address, the one with the typo in it, written it down and . . . She leaned down for her jeans and fished in the pocket. No.

On the sofa Anastasia let out a string of unintelligible nonsense, then a laugh, and slumped back into sleep. Joey looked back at the phone: 10.05. Silently, another little red circle bloomed on the message app and her heart jumped, then dropped again. This number called at 17.30, and left a message. Marsha had left a message. *To listen to the message, dial . . .* Inwardly, Joey sighed.

Perhaps she could remember the email address. Jklyr? Something like that. Gmail. The phone nagged at her. Jlkyr? She gave in and clicked on her answerphone.

Hello? Hello, Joanna? the voice barked, and on the sofa Anastasia stirred again, whimpering. Why did Marsha have to be so loud, so imperious, why did she have to SHOUT? There was a lot of background noise Joey couldn't understand or interpret, it sounded like she was in a bus depot or something, an engine roared. Then what sounded like, *I'm here,* and that was it. Joey stared at the phone and set it face down. She needed a pee.

When she got out of the bathroom there it was, on the floor by her jeans. By her bed. The piece of paper.

Evidence.

OK, she thought. I'll just try this. One last try, then I'll call Sukie.

Chapter Twenty-Five

Day Three, Friday: Sukie

As they came into the room it wasn't pitch black, there was a trace of bluish moonlight coming in from somewhere. In front of Sukie Jake stopped and was still a moment, a dark shape ahead of her. Then a soft movement as he set the bag down, a muffled clunk as it met the ground.

Hearing the sound, Sukie wanted to bend and retrieve it, *her* bag, but he was in the way, between her and it. Then he turned.

He closed the door, fumbling, and a light came on, over the stove. She blinked.

'Surprise!' he said. 'I fixed the electricity, internet and everything.'

She stared. 'When?' she said, bewildered. His face was dark with stubble in the low light, his eyes glittered.

'Oh . . .' but he just waved his hand vaguely. 'You know,'

he said, sidestepping the question. 'There's another bag you could use, we keep a spare here. A suitcase.'

'All right,' she said uncertainly.

Then he turned and the light went off again. 'But let's have candles anyway, shall we?' Smiling in the dark. 'More romantic.'

She stood there. When had he fixed it? For a second she wondered if there had never been a problem at all. But why would he do that? It had made them feel so . . . cut off. She smiled uncertainly.

'Shall we eat first?' he said, and she turned to the sound of his voice. *First?* He was almost whispering and she saw the sharp planes of his face in the light, the deep-set eyes, she felt something momentous coming closer to her, something she had to do, something he'd set in motion. Every word turned her towards this moment: first. And then he looked away and down, the match flared and the blue light warmed, softened.

'Perhaps you could lay the table,' he said, smiling, ducking his head apologetically. Mechanically she went over to get the cutlery out.

She had to live. She had to embrace life. She could hear Marsha say it. Once, hunting through the drawer where her mother kept her belts and scarves, Sukie had found a packet of condoms. Always poking her nose in and finding things that were supposed to be kept secret. She blinked her eyes closed. These were practical things, safe sex. Normal people had sex and you couldn't have a relationship without it and why was she being so bloody precious, anyway? But the gloves? Latex *gloves*? Her thoughts veered. She couldn't go on being like this.

'What is it, sweetheart?' he said, and she looked up. He was closer than she'd expected and she gasped just a bit. He was examining her face as if she was worrying him, troubling him. 'Don't worry,' he said, stroking her cheek. 'And look,' he said. 'Here's the bag.'

There at his side was an old suitcase. It was the one she'd seen downstairs in the dim cellar.

'Thank you,' she said, obediently, and he moved on past her then stopped. She got the cutlery and went to the table.

He was doing something with the food, getting the foil trays out with his back to her, when they heard the unfamiliar sound of a car, coming closer, on the hillside below, and his head turned, quickly. Sukie, sitting, obedient, caught the quick movement because until that point everything had seemed to be in slow motion, a slow-motion game where she was finding her way in the dark, and kept finding dead ends.

In the quiet of the night there was the sound of a car approaching.

Jake turned, moved to the window with the foil trays in his hands, again, with that stillness like an animal listening – then he moved. He came over to the table, set the food down, served them both, a generous helping for Sukie, but his head was still cocked to listen the whole time. Sukie found herself listening too, as she ate. The sound of the car's engine came and went, she thought of the bends and dips on the dark road. Jake poured them wine, more of that very yellow wine that was like licking fence posts. She took a big slug, remembering that it tasted better after a bit.

The food was rich and oily, vegetables and meat baked together and a herb Sukie couldn't identify, bitter, gone cold. She could tell it was good but her appetite seemed like something from a distant past, those evenings eating takeaway with Joey round her table. Jake was doing no more than moving his around the plate but Sukie ate dutifully. She was glad she'd found napkins, because the oil lingered at the corners of her mouth, she could taste garlic, but when she dabbed at her mouth they smelled musty, and were damp. She took another mouthful of wine and everything smoothed out, just fractionally.

'It'll stop at the bottom of the village,' said Jake, breaking the silence. 'Maybe it's Nat coming back, too drunk to find his way up the hill.' There was the trace of something in his voice and she remembered his mother, the drinker, she remembered the folder of photographs but when she looked up he was smiling and she found herself smiling back.

'Dear old Nat,' Jake said. Somewhere from the other side of the village, at the far end of that narrow winding alley where the weeds grew between the stones, a car door slammed. She liked the sound; it was the sound of company, people, life. This little village full of life, children running between houses. A kind of newsreel played in her head, but distant, a montage of old photographs and landscapes, a steep peak, a walled cemetery, it flickered against a far-off screen. Jake pushed his plate away and put his hands across the table to her, palms up.

'I hope he found Betsy,' said Sukie, but she was suddenly so ridiculously relaxed – because it was their last night? Because tomorrow she'd be home? – that she felt sure he must have found her.

'Let's forget them, shall we?' he said. 'Make the world go away.'

Sukie didn't know what she was supposed to do; she felt a giggle and suppressed it. Her hands crept across the table, and he took them loosely in his. 'I've got something for us,' he said. 'A treat for our last night. Just to help us . . . relax.'

'Something?' she said. Smiling. 'I'm relaxed,' she said, and the weirdest thing was, as she said it, it seemed true. She'd felt like something tangled and knotted, a lumpy mattress full of springs – she almost giggled again – and now she was all smoothed out. He lifted her hand as if he was leading her to a dance floor and brought her into the middle of the room, where the fireplace was. And there it was on the mantelpiece, that sculpture, that silly sculpture that looked like a— He turned her, one arm was on her waist.

'I need you to do something for me,' he said. 'Will you do something for me?'

'If you light the fire,' she said, finding stubbornness because there was something about the cold ash and the smell of a dead fire that was sad, distracting her. He leaned back to examine her a moment, holding her in a dancing position, his forearm and hers raised together and very still again with the listening, watching look of an animal deciding which way to jump.

'Sit down,' said Jake, soft and cool, and he lowered her arm with his and gave her a little push. Sukie sat on the sofa, sleepy, and watched him, like it was slow motion, or a film. First he stood and moved something to the centre of the low brick shelf around the conical chimney breast, his head lowered. Then he knelt to light the fire and his movements were hurried. She frowned at his haste, trying to work him out – there was no hurry, was there, after all. She could only see his back, the nape of his thin neck that reminded her of something far away, long ago, or so it seemed. She could see the shape of his shoulders, the rough skin on the backs of his heels as he knelt.

But she couldn't work him out. He looked unfamiliar. Unless this was the real Jake, the one you saw when his back was turned. Funny.

Funny haha, or funny peculiar, that was Dad's phrase. Jake wasn't funny haha.

Jake stood and turned and she saw the fire flicker behind him. 'That better?' he said. A little watchful bow. 'Is that to Madam's satisfaction?'

His hands were nervous. Sukie felt a smile spread across her face. 'Don't worry,' she said, looking up at him. She did feel so strange: *don't worry* was what he had been saying to her.

Jake laughed, then, shifting, and she saw that the thing he'd moved to the centre of the fireplace was the strange ugly sculpture, the wooden penis.

Sukie put her hand up to her mouth. Of course, that was what it was, *I mean, I have seen one before.* And he saw her looking, and he rested his hand on top of the sculpture, just gently. She looked from the hand to his face. Gentle, she told herself. That's what he is: careful.

There were other things he was, Sukie knew that; she'd made a tidy list of them because this had been about getting to know each other, parts of him, sides to him that she had glimpsed and then they were gone – but they were too scattered, now, something had loosened their connections. She felt it warm her, whatever it was he'd given her, she felt it spread, relaxing everything that had wound tight. And why not? Maybe it was what she'd needed, all along. She just sat there, her hands in her lap, smiling.

And then Jake's hand lifted and he was moving again, he was behind the kitchen counter and he came out with her bag and dropped it beside her on the sofa. 'Just in time,' he said, giving it a little push so it pressed against her. 'I bet you packed a few nice little bits and pieces, didn't you?'

She nodded. 'I did,' she said, still smiling, bringing it into her lap. The silk and lace nightie, she closed her eyes a second remembering how it had looked when she'd held it against her long ago and far away. She'd been too superstitious to try it on, or something, she preferred just to hold it up and shimmy it a little bit. She did think now, the way she was feeling, she might put it on. He seemed to know that.

There was a tiny sound – that somewhere in the recesses of her mind she knew was an alert – on someone's phone. Was it his?

'You wait there,' he said. His mouth was open, just a little as he watched her, looked from the bag to her. She could see his chest moving, up and down. 'Just sit there,' he said. 'I just need to . . . sort something out on my laptop.'

He went into the next room, and closed the door. She watched the small fire struggle in the grate, and leaned to balance another dry stick on it.

'Jake?' she called. The flame licked and crackled. It was easier to ask when he wasn't in the room with her, she realised, smiling at how silly, *how silly*. Getting to know each other was what all this was about. And in her strange dreamy state this one question seemed to hold all the other questions, all the odd embarrassing questions about condoms and pale latex gloves like octopuses and what his business really was, inside it. 'Jake?'

Easier to ask when he might not hear.

She reached for the bag. She could put the silk thing on in front of the fire.

'Jake,' she said, and pulled the bag on to her lap, hugging it as if it was a cushion, but it was hard, it had that hard thing inside it.

'Your mother, Jake,' she murmured, half to herself. *Mothers, mothers, mothers.* Her own mother had sent her here, after all, as good as. 'Why did she do it?' Looked up, into the flickering candlelight. 'Why did she kill herself?'

Day Three, Friday: Kit

Sitting on the edge of the bed, hearing the city outside his bedroom window without having to listen, any more – there was music throbbing far off, shouts somewhere down the street, police sirens coming and going – Kit googled *Littlejohn, Kyros,* on his iPad.

He got a new tablet, whatever the newest thing was, every six months or so. And whatever his flatmates didn't give a shit about – washing up, privacy, noise – they loved their high-speed unlimited internet. But somebody was probably in their room downloading a mega-update on the latest version or the latest game, because it hung.

Bare feet on the manky carpet that had seen dozens of tenants, the blind too thin and the yellow streetlight. Soon he would be able to put down a deposit on a place, he'd always thought somewhere on the edge, where there was a bit of countryside, woods and fields, somewhere for kids to play. Not seaside, she didn't go for the sea. Kit tipped his head from side to side, and it was as if all that he knew about her, all that painstakingly accumulated knowledge, rolled inside his see-sawing skull, from one corner to the other. He hadn't asked her if she wanted kids but he knew she did, with someone. She'd never asked *him*, so it maybe wasn't him, that someone. She hates the seaside but she's gone a thousand miles, more, to be surrounded by it.

The page was taking too long to load. Kit raised his head. What was he doing this for? When he next saw Fred, on Monday morning, would Kit even still *have* a girlfriend, the girlfriend he was going to ask about where she'd like to live? With him.

She's a nutter, mate. He could almost see all the heads turning in the pub, all laughing their identical laughs.

Damaged, mate. That'd make them laugh like hyenas. Damaged goods, never mind having kids with her, put her out with the bins. The page opened, line by line.

Fred though. Fred hadn't said, *She's a nutter.* Not once he started looking.

Ancient microfiched headlines appeared on the screen. Someone's job to put this stuff online: thirty years ago. A front page: a fuzzy photograph of a steep hillside and some men in uniform standing in a circle on the slope, silhouetted against the horizon. The backdrop of the wide sea, even down the distance of years, the pixellated image further degraded by transfer, the sea had that soft fuzz of luminescence that suggested blue even in black and white, the deep clear blue of the Mediterranean. For a moment he just gazed at that, the sea, his first sight of the island she'd left him for. Kyros.

There was a smaller photograph, from further off, that showed the strange pointed cone-shape of the mountain where the men stood, and in the foreground a tiny cemetery, the kind they had abroad, walled, spiked with plaques and monuments. So far away.

A headline.

The men were looking down at something at their feet. One man was pointing, another was frozen in the act of pushing his uniformed cap back on his head. The curled shape at their feet was covered with some kind of sheet. One of the men had his head bowed. His vision blurring, Kit rubbed his eyes and swiped.

A gallery of photographs. A woman with a thick mop

of frowsty blonde hair in dark glasses, with her arm held across her face to block the camera. And a sullen family at a restaurant table: a blonde woman, glaring, a dark man with his arm resting across the shoulders of a boy. A pale lanky boy, hunched over a glass, drinking from a straw, staring at the camera. Staring.

Kit swiped back to the photograph of the policemen on the hillside. There was a scattering of debris below where the men stood and blowing up the image Kit saw rubbish, an old fridge with the door hanging open, bulging plastic bags. His finger on the screen he went back, up: he zoomed. There was a shoe on the ground, a high-heeled sandal, on the ground beside the sheeted shape.

The headline said:

WIFE OF ABUSE SUSPECT COMMITS SUICIDE

Kit stood, so abruptly the iPad slipped out of his hand and clattered to the floor, but the words were in his head, they skittered and chased each other.

Body identified as that of Susannah Littlejohn, wife of Malcolm Littlejohn recently interviewed in connection with the rape of a minor. Mr Littlejohn was released pending further investigation. The couple have a son, aged fourteen, who may not be named as he is a minor.

Chapter Twenty-Six

Day Three, Friday: Heather

David was leaning forward, talking to the taxi driver excitedly, between the seats. They were talking in Greek.

David, she thought. There'd been something about him that had warned her, all that time ago. Almost a smell about him of shame, of fear, and she'd avoided him. Guilt shoved her into a corner of the taxi. She thought about the message Kit had forwarded. Turned out he knew stuff, he could find stuff out, he could be unprincipled.

A nail bar. *So weird*, she thought as the taxi bumped slowly up the hill, so weird. Thought of the nail bars she'd been in, skinny girls and boys with masks over their faces, cash only. Who needed money laundering? Gangsters, criminals, Mafiosi, drug dealers.

And she could smell it, dope-smoke under the pier, his brown fingers holding it out to her, dirt under the nails, the joint's glowing tip upwards as the water lapped on the stones. The figures that moved to and fro behind his DJ decks, the hand slapped into another hand. Was that it? Was that what he needed her for, this girl, with her wide pale face and her startled eyes? Was that why he needed Sukie Alexander? She sat up.

'Do you know someone called Jake Littlejohn?'

Her voice sounded clear and loud and from the front seat David's head turned quickly. And she could see the whites of his eyes, not white but yellowish, she could see him pale under the tan, a sickly grey, and his finger went to his lips in a panicked gesture, *shh*. The taxi swung, its wheels spun on the bend and she was thrown back, clutching at the seat, her heart bumping.

'He's from here, too, isn't he?' The words came unbidden. Kostas had known him, the barwoman had known him. Jake Littlejohn had grown up here.

Funny how she cared, suddenly, about not going over the edge, the car rolling, rolling and all of them flung down and Kit or Mum having to take her home in a box and wondering who David was, sprawled between the seats, both their necks broken. The headlights swung across the hillside and the taxi righted itself and the driver was looking round now, grinning, changing gear with a flourish. David staring stiffly ahead, she could only see the back of his neck, thin and vulnerable and scared.

And then Heather remembered, hazily, some night round someone's student house, and David. He must have been not long into the drink then, still cheerfully tipsy, affectionate, she could see it now, all of them trooping back with kebabs and six-packs to a house in a terrace just like a hundred others, a student house with flimsy partition walls, only this one had had a cellar that the landlord had neglected to dig out and turn into a sixth bedroom.

They'd been playing a stupid game, what was it, hide and seek? Still kids, in some ways, most ways, that was the weird thing about college. You could put things behind you, because no one knew you, you could start again. The game had been sardines.

Through the seats now, through the dusty windscreen, Heather could see a hilltop, feebly lit, a single lamp illuminating the side of a small house and the one next to it, the dark shapes of further houses above it and the shadow of a tree blown wildly by invisible wind against a bare wall.

She looked back at the phone: Kit hadn't replied. After all, it hadn't been much of a message, had it? It hadn't been, *I love you*. Was the phone dying? It looked like it. She felt a rising wave of despair, something she'd never felt in all these years of fighting, fighting, to stay on the surface. She moved her finger over the screen and there it was, the little string of messages. She blinked away the feeling. There *was* something she could do, after all. She could tell the truth. And she began to type.

It was slow, at first, halting, and then the new feeling came, a kind of hum inside her of energy, like the singing of a railway line when there's a train coming. And when she was done, she pressed send, and laid her head back on the split leatherette of the taxi's back seat, she could smell it, hair oil and warm plastic. When she looked back at the phone it was dead. Perhaps the message hadn't sent. Perhaps it would come back to life, perhaps it wouldn't. Perhaps it didn't matter, any more.

It felt so strange, for her brain to be meandering like this, back to a London terrace and a lot of students blundering about in the dark, but she knew there was a string that led back there, from here, there was a trail of crumbs. In that house someone had begun screaming, and that someone had been David, in the cellar, behind the door, shaking at the doorknob in the damp dark. Screaming, screaming, screaming, and then all the lights had gone on and someone, some girl kinder than Heather, had spoken gently to him. *It's not locked, David. No one locked you in.*

That was memory, wasn't it? You blotted out the memory of things you didn't want to think about, behaviour you weren't proud of, people whose faces you didn't want to see because they spoke to you of your own weakness.

Shit, though. Shit. She felt the same shrinking as she'd felt then. Nutter. David's a nutter and you're going back to his place, in the middle of nowhere?

And on cue, the taxi drew up beside a peeling wall, under the sulphur-yellow lamp and the leafless tree. The driver kept the engine running and Heather peered out through the smeared glass: they were under a village of tumbling dwellings; in the flickering dark it seemed half ruined. Feeling the sudden need to be out of the smells, the old cigarette smoke and hair oil and plastic,

250

Heather reached for the door handle, setting her shoulder against the door, but it didn't move, it was locked, and both the faces turned to her. She sat there feeling panic surge and thinking, *Who's the nutter, here, am I the nutter? Was I the nutter, all along?* And then the driver gabbled, grinning, and belatedly Heather understood, she had to pay him first.

It wasn't till she'd given him the notes and the driver had released the lock and they'd climbed out and Heather was standing there watching the taxi's tail-lights recede, not until she was turning to see that between the houses there was a dank alley leading uphill – that she remembered David had taken money for the ride already. And there he stood, fumbling with something between his fingers, bare dirty toes clenching and unclenching and she could tell, even if it had been a scam, he'd changed his mind, the money wasn't worth it.

Jacob. Jake. BlueJ.

Back then, ten years ago, if she'd mentioned that name, in the student bar or waiting to go into a lecture, might it all have got ironed out? Might they have gone to the police together, she and him, or a shrink, or something?

Too late to wonder.

Heather turned with her back to the village and looked outwards. Below them wound the road and the taxi bumping down it. To the left, across a kind of valley, a cone-shaped mountain against the last of the sky, and at its foot a cluster of tiny winking lights in the blue dusk.

'You *do* know him,' she said.

'You grew up here together? He's how much older than you, ten years?' She looked around and saw the dark hillside falling away, the feeble string of lights below them at the harbour, the wide sea, just glints of light on a great expanse of emptiness. So lonely, so cut-off, so far from anywhere.

'What did he do to you?' she said.

And there was a sound of footsteps behind her, of skittering stones, and turning there was movement, breathless and hurried in the shadows between the houses. Someone was running in an uncontrolled, unsteady rush, down towards them.

Day Three, Friday: Joey

It's just the internet, Joey told herself, prising the laptop open on her desk. It's just following a trail, it's detective work.

Her familiar screen gazed back at her. Her screensaver was a collage. Pictures of her and her mum, her and her dog, Stanley, a couple of her and Sukie. Sukie always looked happy when she saw Joey, too. There was nothing complicated about them, her and Sukie.

Joey didn't do dating sites, and if she did she wouldn't do the kind Jake Littlejohn went to. She didn't even want to start.

She had the piece of paper in her hand, picked off the floor. First of all she typed the wrong email address in by mistake, the original one, and got the same results, mostly vanilla, just that one rogue comment posted on Reddit, the praise for a singer who'd abused children. Or wanted people to abuse them for him.

Joey swallowed. She should be doing this by daylight. She held the piece of paper up to the screen and cross-checked it, yes. Two email addresses differing only by a single extra character. With trembling fingers she opened a new page and tried the other email address. The search engine didn't find many results: five, it said at the top. But five was enough. One of them was a link to a page she knew her computer would not allow her to access unless she disabled most of her security systems.

Joey stared at the few words surrounding the link. The email address was attached to his profile on a different kind of site. Not Respectful Dating, this one; a different kind of niche, a dirty little niche, a moving row of pictures of sex, but not as she wanted to know it. She didn't know if it was legal or not: she knew it shouldn't be, not legal to hurt people, to lie to them, to shock them and frighten them and abuse them. She didn't know if she'd get into trouble if she clicked, if a police car would arrive at her door.

What if it did? That decided her. She didn't care: she welcomed it, the car at the door, the uniformed officers: she wanted the authorities involved. Joey disabled her security, one system after another — she had four, she wasn't stupid. She clicked on the link.

There was a profile picture, not the same as the one he'd used on respectful dating, in this one he had cartoon devil horns; in this one his tongue was just visible between his lips.

What next? What next? What was he doing, still registered on a site like this when he'd ditched Respectful Dating, when he was on a break with Sukie, her best friend, careful, sensible, trusting Sukie? *What was he doing?*

Joey didn't want to know what he was doing, what he might be doing with her, with Sukie, for viewers, what *insurance policy* he might be constructing to get Sukie to do what he wanted, now and later, maybe on and on for ever. Revenge porn? Joey felt like her brain space had been blown, her shields all down. She didn't want to know this stuff.

Evidence. Something to hold up in front of Sukie. Not hearsay, not chatroom messages: evidence.

There was a little box. *Connect.*

But you had to know. You had to find out. If she turned off her computer, what then? If she just slowly closed the lid and walked away, what then? No. *Connect.*

She clicked. Waited, a beat, two. It would send him a message. But he was with Sukie, he wouldn't answer . . . Wait. Something inside her told her to wait. Two minutes. Three.

She wanted more than anything to close the laptop: her hand went to the top of the screen to pull it down—

He was live. He was online.

His face filled the screen, examining her, she could see nose hairs and then the face – long, stubbled, bloodshot eyes – drew back. She could see what was behind him, in low lighting: a whitewashed wall, blue shutters, one hanging loose, some kind of hippy hanging with tassels and embroidery, a Kama Sutra scene of a naked man with eyeliner, his groin against a kneeling woman's backside.

Joey was looking at what was behind him because she didn't want the foreground, she didn't want to see what he was doing, fumbling in loose pants, bringing it out. His mouth was moving, slack, and then he said words. 'Now you show me,' he said. His eyes were fixed on her, he must be able to see her, white and pinched with fear in the tiny screen, as she could see herself in the icon in the corner. She hadn't thought. She hadn't given herself time, to protect herself.

Are you scared, little girl?

A silence, only his breath, she could hear his breath. And then a voice. From behind him, calling, Sukie's high, innocent, untroubled voice—

So she's all right she's all right she's still all right

She was calling his name, and his eyes glittered.

Jake Littlejohn, one hand still moving up and down in his lap, turned towards Sukie's voice and Joey heard it in her head but in the same moment it came out of her mouth, she couldn't stop it.

Sukie. 'Sukie?'

She fumbled for her phone. Surely, for God's sake. She held it in her lap, out of sight of the camera. What had she thought would happen? He mustn't see her phone, he mustn't.

She had to keep him talking.

'Coming,' he said, breathless. And his head turned back to Joey.

'What did you say?' he said, and his head tilted, like a predator's.

Day Three, Friday: Kit

999.

Kit had never called the police in his life. And what did he think he was going to do when they answered? Fire, ambulance, police would be the choices. How long would it take – for him to hang on, then to explain, stuttering, stupid? His heart sank.

This wasn't a game, it wasn't a spy thriller, he didn't even know if there was a way 999 could get you to someone so far away, Interpol was for the movies, wasn't it? James Bond shit. A sleepy policeman on a Greek island, getting him out of bed, and for what?

He knew he had to get everything he had together, first. He had Emily's name and number. But they'd never forgive him. Not Emily – and not Heather. Heather would never go to the police. She'd never make the accusation, be interrogated in a police station, she'd rather die first. What if he called and then tripped over himself, fucked it up, hung up out of embarrassment?

He stared at his phone, at the dial pad. And the message came in, and it wasn't for him, it was for them. For the police. It was her statement.

And as he gazed at it he felt something crack, something break; it was so sad, it was all sadness.

Yes, he raped me. My name is Heather Baxter of 113 Leytonstone High Street, flat 3a and the man I now know to be Jake Littlejohn then calling himself BlueJ, gave me marijuana and alcohol and possibly another drug then raped me in 2002 in Brighton, under the pier, when I was fifteen and I did not report it because I was ashamed. Me and probably other girls before and since, and the younger the better. Definitely other girls, perhaps boys.

Not just sadness.
He deserves to die.

Chapter Twenty-Seven

Day Three, Friday: Heather

David didn't have time to answer but she saw his face, she saw *him*, a kid, locked in a dark place.

'He raped me,' she said, the first time she'd spoken the words out loud. 'Did he hurt you too?'

And then the figure emerged from the alley into the yellow light and they both turned to him.

It was an old man. Older than Jacob Littlejohn, much older. This man was over seventy, lean and leathery, and his face sagged when he saw them.

'David,' he said flatly. 'It's you.' He wiped his mouth distractedly, then passed his hand over his forehead. He was unsteady on his feet, and when he leaned to support himself against the wall Heather smelled alcohol. She stepped back instinctively from the two of them.

'Nat?' said David, sounding bewildered.

'It's Betsy,' said the elderly man, swaying. 'She's gone missing. I thought it might be her, I heard the taxi—' He broke off. 'The tracker said she went down to the harbour, I went down for a swim and when I got back she'd gone.' He staggered back against the wall in despair.

Heather saw David stiffen, as if the man's distress had sobered him, and she stepped closer. 'Who's Betsy?' she asked, wondering if he was talking about an animal, a dog.

'His—'

'My *wife*,' said the man, Nat, his eyes wild as he turned to her, but she heard anguish, released maybe by the alcohol. 'It says she went down to the harbour not long after I did, so I followed her down but I didn't see her. I asked Jacob and his . . . that girl he's brought here but they hadn't seen her.' He peered at Heather again. 'Do I *know* you?' he said, confused.

David stepped between them, and his hand fell on Heather's a moment, squeezed it, dropped it. 'No, this is an old college friend of mine,' he said. She just stood there, his name between them and that squeeze of the hand, Jacob, and then something the old man had said just didn't make sense.

'*What* says?' she asked, stubborn. 'What says she went down to the harbour?'

'Her *tracker*.' Nat glared.

'She wears a tracking device,' said David, pale, shivering a little. 'Betsy has trouble remembering things, and sometimes she wanders off, so Nat has this thing – he put a thing on her belt.' He tapped at his waist, then made a shape with thumb and forefinger, walnut-sized.

'I've always found her before,' said Nat, pleading now. 'It's always worked. I shouldn't have gone swimming so late but Jacob said, he came over for the girl's phone, I told him . . . he said . . .' and Nat looked back up the alleyway, and she thought he looked afraid. 'Stupid woman,' he muttered. 'Stupid woman, always talking too much.'

David intervened. 'She's not well, Nat,' he said. 'It's not her fault.' He looked sickly suddenly. 'What did Jacob say?' but he muttered it, and Nat didn't seem to hear.

'We've always found her before,' he said, and everything about him collapsed a little. 'She doesn't like the dark.' His head flipped up, an old tortoise. 'Did you see her? Did she get into . . . a boat or anything?'

With it all tumbling in her head, the woman lost in the empty dark, Jacob, a girl, his girl, her phone – her *phone* – Heather turned to David. 'There was that woman down at the port, who wanted our taxi.'

'No, no, that wasn't . . . Betsy's not . . .' David was distracted, she could hear his distress. 'That was someone else, that woman was English, I didn't know her.' He turned to Nat. 'I'll go back to mine and get a torch, you must have a spare, Nat, we can go and look, you'll help, won't you, Heather?'

Heather shrank back, holding her things against her, feeling it dig again, the package. The knife, the knife she'd bought, feeling its edge through the paper.

In Deep Water

But David reached for her wrist, she could see the tendons in his stringy neck. 'Nat needs our help, though,' he said, and she knew he could see what it was, in the package.

And he pulled her towards him as he spoke, he leaned in and she could smell his breath sour with brandy; with their conspiracy.

'I'm sure it won't take long.'

Day Three, Friday: Sukie

Sukie could hear something, from outside.

And she paused, the bag still on her lap, the fire flickering in front of her, giving out hardly any heat. She crossed to the window, feeling the unnatural dreaminess about her like a blanket, muffling everything. She couldn't get it open for some reason so she pressed her ear against the glass, feeling the cold of the night outside. There were voices, one of them a woman's. Footsteps.

She went to the door but that seemed to be locked too. She called again, back into the room. She was alone in here. Why was she alone? She felt the real world tugging at her, trying to get her attention; she felt a tiny prickle at the back of her neck. Why had he got up and walked out of the room? The question wouldn't go away. A weird thing for him to do. The words marched across her consciousness. Weird. Not me, him.

'Jake?'

When he answered his voice *was* odd, or was it her

261

hearing? Sort of high, as if he was laughing, or out of breath, before righting itself. 'Coming,' he said.

She turned to look at the bedroom door, that he'd closed behind him. She wasn't sure what it was she could hear, from behind it, whatever it was, was soft, muffled. Was maybe none of her business. She went back to the window and again the glass was cold against her cheek.

The voices stopped, further down the narrow alley that she thought of as the village's high street; she could visualise the hand-drawn map. David's? David had company. He seemed to be the only other person in the village apart from Nat and Betsy and the family who ran the shop. She rested her head against the window. What had happened to that map, and to the photographs? Someone had found them and put them away.

The fire was feeble now and she left the window to put another stick on, hardly logs, just damp branches, the last one, and it hissed and sighed, then Sukie, turning, saw the bag. Crossing, she sat and opened it. And it must have worked its way to the top because it was the first thing she saw — well, a corner of it. Bigger than a book and not so flat, it was something in a box, a boxed up something and she pulled it further out.

I didn't . . . I didn't . . .

Her hand was at her mouth and she wasn't sure what she was seeing. Her eye went from the box to the wooden sculpture on the mantelpiece. There was a sudden brightness of revelation in her head and then it went dark, as if she was looking into a kind of tunnel, a dark place where men loaded things on and off conveyor belts, bags were thrown into cages and a bag split open.

Sukie fumbled down below it, below the boxed thing. Where was it? Her nightie, her silk and lace chemise they called it on the website – she hadn't gone into a shop for it because of what they might say, the looks they might give her. And a shop that sold underwear, they sometimes sold these.

It was a . . . a . . . she knew the words, she knew what it was. A sex toy. A dildo. If someone had made her say these words out loud she would have run out of the room. Sukie breathed, in and out.

Had someone put it in her bag, for a joke? Her brain scrambled for a scenario in which luggage handlers, or the women in their uniforms at luggage check-in, or all of them, identified a bag – by the address label? Sukie's address, Sukie's name, did it scream, silly frightened little virgin? *I'm not.* And did they keep a cupboard with these things and stuff them in for a joke, if a bag was left unlocked, or split open?

At school once, someone – she didn't know if it had been a boy or a girl – had put a condom on the classroom door handle and Sukie had been the one to touch it, she'd been the one who hadn't looked, hadn't been wary, she hadn't even known what it *was* at first, until she heard the burst of laughter in the room behind her, and someone said, *It had to be her, didn't it?*

She'd seen condoms, hadn't she? She hadn't run away screaming. She'd seen them and told herself, just sensible, just in case, just taking *care.* And she was as bad, poking her nose into other people's luggage.

The nightdress was in there. She pulled it out, sad and crumpled, the lace smudged with dirt. Had they seen that, and decided, those men with dirty hands in the dark tunnel?

Her brain ticked though, she couldn't stop it. Sukie wanted to go back to the dream state, where a wooden sculpture was just funny. Breathe, she thought. Breathe.

Next door she heard Jake's voice, talking velvety and low. Had he taken a call from someone? He said he had something for her, he said he had a treat. She walked back over to the side and found her half-full wine glass and took a gulp. Maybe that would help. She could hide the thing, or throw it away, or – she swallowed some more – take it out of the box and set it beside the wooden sculpture and they could laugh together.

But her scalp tingled, her brain ticked. The wine slipped down but there was something in her blocking its action, some chemical in her bloodstream that held her on alert.

The box had been what *split* the bag, so it had been in there before. *They* didn't put it in, those men hauling things from conveyor belt to luggage cage.

Don't show it, don't. Don't make yourself laugh about it. Don't

And then from far off, from where she'd sat on the stool in the airport coffee shop in her head, Sukie saw his back as he walked away from her down the concourse. That glimpse of the back of his neck, Jake's neck, that had told her he was old, too old for her, had told her – like his smell had told her, his breath, his hands, everything – that he was the *wrong* one. That he had done things. He had

264

learned things she didn't need to know. And back then she'd looked away. Looked back into her latte.

And when they'd arrived in Greece, Jake pacing by the conveyor belt. Jake grilling the woman, insisting.

Jake looking at her around the curtain in the shop, Jake wanting her to feel his eyes on her, wanting to see her tug at the hem of the tunic. And then, now, this evening, Jake seeing the split in her bag and something adjusting in his mind, rearranging everything, his plans, and when they got back that gleam in his eye of something new, going straight away to find another suitcase for her, here, you can use this one. And there it was, standing against the end of the sofa. She leaned down and picked it up.

His voice was still there, low as a hum, next door. She opened the suitcase and looked down into it. It was empty, but it had a sort of padded base and she put her fingers to it, walked them across it.

Here's a suitcase for you, here's a tunic for you, here's a dildo for you. Here's a little house on a hill and the doors are locked.

Something made a sound in the room. A familiar sound, a sound Sukie knew, because it was the sound of her own phone's ring.

Day Three, Friday: Joey

Would he see? Could he see? Stonily Joey stared at him, at what he was doing with his dick, but whatever her expression was, it must be enough, because he kept on jerking at himself. His face was like an uplit mask in the dim room. Behind him the candle flickered in a draught.

In her lap the number glowed, as the phone rang, on and on. Could he hear it, wherever it was? Could he see it? Don't look round, Joey told him in her head, don't wonder if you can hear anything. Finish. Finish.

Because if he did, if he came in front of her, it would buy Sukie some time. Wouldn't it?

And with that second's doubt Joey faltered, she blinked and the thread between them, the horrible sticky thread was broken. Jake Littlejohn's glazed look turned to something else: he was suddenly, silently, absolutely focused. He took in everything, her minute glance downwards into her lap, her fumbling, her desperation at having been caught out, exposed: he was intent, and full of rage.

She lifted the phone from her lap, still ringing, swiped to load her camera, snapped the screen, fuzzy, cross-hatched with computer light.

'You little bitch, you . . .' He seemed to rear up in front of her screen – and then it went black.

Chapter Twenty-Eight

Day Three, Friday: Heather

David's place was worse than she'd thought: Heather could smell it before she got to the door. Damp and stale and piss-smelling. She had to squeeze past a grimy ancient bathtub upended beside the door. Behind her Nat stood unwilling in the narrow lane. Light came from somewhere further along the alley, a thin light, showing the hollows under his eyes.

'I told you, Nat.' David's voice was shaking as he fumbled with the latch. 'I told you not to do anything with him. Don't get involved. He's dangerous.'

'Oh, *non*-sense.' But Nat's attempt at schoolteacherly calm didn't ring true, it was shrill.

'I know what you were doing for him,' said David. 'Those little packages delivered to your cellar, when the right boats came in? I know because he wanted me to do it and I said

I wouldn't, not for any money, not whatever he did to me.' He was stiff.

'Alcohol's a drug too, Davy boy,' said Nat, drawing himself up a little, then backtracking, his voice pleading. 'And besides, all I did was receive packages for him, I didn't know what was in them. Goddamn, if you had my responsibilities—'

'And look where that's got you,' said David, suddenly, startlingly cruel. 'He uses people. Haven't you understood that? That's what this fucking place teaches: you use people or you get used.' Heather felt him holding himself rigidly upright beside her and she had the sudden sensation that he was burning through his reserves, that he might just suddenly dissolve, collapse. She put a hand out to his shoulder – he didn't seem to notice.

Nat was on the defensive, sullen, panicky. 'Besides,' he muttered, 'I didn't ask the goddamned woman to have the girl over for tea, I didn't ask her to start babbling about the Littlejohns. The old days, the bad old days.'

David froze, the door creaked inwards, but he was looking at Nat. 'She talked to Jacob's girlfriend about the old days?' White under his tan. 'So now this girlfriend knows.'

'Knows what?' said Heather, warningly, but neither of them seemed to hear. Nathan turned away, mumbling. David was reaching inside the rancid cluttered interior in a sudden urgent hurry, thrusting his hand around by the door, and when he turned back he was holding an ancient torch in his hand.

It shone feebly, playing round the weedy alley, into the

house. She glimpsed a sink piled with pots and dishes, a bucket on the floor. Empty bottles. Many.

'What are you talking about?' said Heather, letting her backpack drop to her feet. She kept hold of the package though. 'What happened?'

Wordless, David turned her, pushing her ahead of him, and she stumbled towards Nat in the street. *Kit*, she thought, *Kit, how did I get here?* The torch cast barely a spot of yellow, and Nat's face was ghastly.

'Do you want to tell her?' said David.

'No, I . . . no, I . . .'

David turned towards her in the narrow space. 'Nat had the brains to send his kids back to the States, you see,' he said. 'Get a nice clean education. They don't see each other much, of course. But none of them has committed suicide, none of them is on their third marriage, none of them abuses drugs – or human beings. None of them rapes little boys and girls. That right, Nat?'

Nat mumbled, looking pleadingly up the alley.

'His mother killed herself because the police were investigating the family. His father was an abuser and I know because he started on me. Did they do it to Jake, their own kid? He would kill you just for asking: he turned it into something else. Something he did: following in Daddy's footsteps. He was in the UK by the time it all blew up. DJing in seaside towns, dealing. I stayed well away from those. He could get people to do and say whatever he wanted by the time he was fourteen so now he's nearly fifty . . .'

Seaside towns. Heather's eyes felt like two stones, her scalp prickled.

And David was out of breath, as if that had used it all up, as if it had all come out like a bout of vomiting, leaving him weak and helpless. He staggered against the wall and Heather stumbled back out of his way, wanting to get out from between them and out of this narrow space. She felt as if she was suffocating. She couldn't see. She got out her phone, for the light, for the sense that it connected her to Kit, but it was still dead.

'Did your wife tell J-Jake's girlfriend all this?' she said, incredulous, trying to breathe.

'Not all this.' Nat's head swung from her to David and back to Heather as he spoke, gabbling, panicking. 'Just hinting, you know. And I told her, Betsy gets confused.'

'Betsy lives in the past,' said David, leaning his cheek against the rough wall. 'It's not the same thing. There are things she remembers clear as day. There was no proof because we were all scared to say it, to take the lid off. But he was an abuser before he left. He took me down around the mountain to do it, past the cemetery. Where his mother killed herself, in the end, where he said he'd kill me, if I told.'

Nat's old mouth moved, but he couldn't say anything.

'I didn't say a word.'

'I thought he'd kill me, too,' said Heather and they turned to look at her. 'I told him I'd never tell and I never did.' She held Nat's gaze. 'Did he know what your wife said?' Nat's lip trembled. 'Because if he found out she'd been saying things . . .'

'He wouldn't, he wouldn't . . .' he mumbled. Then something shifted, his voice was a monotone. 'The tracker,' he said. 'It showed her going down to the port. And . . . and then it looked like . . .' His head turned, wildly, in the ghostly light.

'What?' said Heather. Thinking of what she'd seen, on the waterfront, the people ambling leisurely in the fading light, the glow from the shops, from the bar where she'd sat, like a stage set. The way he'd stood there, BlueJ, still among the moving figures, waiting. And Kostas, the boatman coming up to him, obedient.

'He wouldn't,' said Nat again, looking from one of them to the other, pleading.

'It was him told you,' said David, his voice flat and tired. 'When will you get it? It was him told you to go down and swim, told you to leave Betsy behind? And you did. You left her behind with *him*.'

And then, into the sudden silence, from the far end of the village, perhaps further, came a horrible noise that echoed in the dark hills. It was the sound of something lost, the sound of terror and shame and loneliness and it drew a circle round them. It pointed. There.

Heather was the first to run.

Day Three, Friday: Kit

Kit just kept saying, over and over, But can you do anything now. It needs to be now. *She's there NOW.*

He wasn't going to confuse it by saying, She's going to kill him. The first operator – a male – just took everything down, wouldn't engage with him except over factual details. Kit told him everything he knew: the names, the dates, the places. Kyros: offered to send him the picture she'd taken.

The responses were always level, cautious, scrupulous. 'So your girlfriend has made this statement to you by text message.'

Kit felt as if he was being buried under a mountain. He wasn't used to being aggressive, pushy, angry, he wasn't used to demanding anything, ever. He was a born back-room boy.

He was polite. Did the operator sound weary, impatient? He felt rage simmering near the surface. If Fred was here . . . For a moment he imagined Fred had decided to come round, he was at the door and would just walk up, take the phone off him and give the bloke both barrels. Kit was polite: he remained polite.

And then there *was* something in the operator's voice. 'Would you mind holding a moment?' A quickening of interest, of urgency. '*Please?*'

Kit held. The music was something stupidly jaunty, then a message reminding him it was being recorded, thanking him for his patience.

And then there was a woman on the line. CID. She told him her name, said she was a detective inspector, said something about international liaison but he wasn't listening hard enough, he wanted her to stop introducing herself and ask him the right question or give him the right answer so he'd know, she got it, she knew.

'He's on our radar,' she said. 'Jacob Littlejohn, flagged up for narcotics most recently, though witnesses are hard to pin down. They disappear. We've looked into him over rape allegations, and then some intelligence more recently on drug trafficking. He's on our radar. And has been for some time.'

And Kit sat back, drained, suddenly, as if all the energy had been sucked out of him just by hearing someone confirm, it wasn't her imagination, or his.

'And your girlfriend's gone after him? Having recognised him in an airport? On her *own*?'

That just made Kit want to hit his head against the wall. He didn't care what she thought, he didn't need patting on the back – except of course he did. 'She needs help,' he said, desperately. 'This place, this island . . . It's in the middle of fucking nowhere.' He stopped. 'Sorry. But . . .' and he hesitated. 'I think she wants to do something . . . stupid.'

'To herself?' The detective was quick.

'I . . . I don't know. I don't know.' Him first then herself. 'All I know is she won't stop till she finds him.'

'He's there with a young woman,' said the detective.

'How do you know that?' The hair rose on Kit's head and he thought of Emily, whose fingers wouldn't keep still, who wouldn't raise her face to him in the pub. 'He's raped since,' he said. 'I met a girl . . . Look, can you get in touch with the local police force, or can't you?'

273

'It's a one-man band out there,' said the officer. 'But it sounds like he knows his territory.'

'What?' said Kit. 'You're already in touch with the police on . . . on . . .'

'Kyros,' she said patiently. 'We are.'

Kit sat up. 'Has something happened?' he said, and desperate he stood up, paced, one hand tugging at his hair. He caught sight of himself in the mirror, his freckles looked black against the whiteness of his face. 'What's *happened*?' he said.

'We're not sure,' said the police officer. 'Maybe nothing, yet.'

'So how—'

'You aren't the only one with someone to protect, Mr Burton,' she said, stiff, warning. 'You're not the only one who wants to stop him doing it again.'

Chapter Twenty-Nine

Day Three, Friday

On the waterfront the shops had closed up, one by one. The hardware store was dark, its row of knives, in order of size against the wall, gleamed in the light from the row of lamps along the water.

Offshore in the darkness, where the island's lights couldn't reach, an overloaded dinghy waited, more than one, bobbing in the silence and hoping the forecast storms wouldn't arrive till dawn, waiting till the coastguard had dropped off to sleep. Somewhere between three and four was the time they chose, depending on the season, which coincidentally is the most common time for a person to die.

Only the police station was still lit up inside, and with an illuminated sign over the door, a flag that hung limp above it. Inside, a middle-aged woman was shouting, in

English, about her child. Behind the desk the policeman offered her his hands, palm up, and shrugged.

Day Three, Friday: Sukie

The phone was ringing. Looking around the dim room – lit only by one candle, the flicker of the fire – in that moment Sukie could only see that it was all closed, all closed in on her: the blue shutters, the door he'd turned to lock as they came in.

She turned, and turned in the room, seeking the sound.

And then she saw it: a rectangle of light in the pocket of a jacket that hung over the back of a chair, and it pulsed with the sound, of her phone. Her phone. Was in Jake's pocket.

She hurried, clumsy, between chairs. *Quick. Stop it, shut it up before—*

Before what? Stupid with panic, she didn't know if she was more frightened of him seeing her hand in the pocket of his jacket, or of the explanations he would give.

She couldn't remember what he'd said. No, she could. Nat didn't mention the phone, he said. Leave it over there, he'd said. He'd gone over to Nat and Betsy's. Betsy's pale blue eyes looking up at the mention of his name. Inside Sukie something turned over, monstrous. *She'll have got back and gone to bed.* And then, *Do you really need that little screen?* When he had it all the time, and Betsy wasn't there, not back, not asleep.

And the rubbish bags gone from her doorstep and Jake turning something over and over in his pocket, not her phone, something smaller. Jake handing it to a man on the harbour-front, a small black something, the size of a walnut: the thing she'd seen on Betsy's belt. The tracker.

Fumbling, Sukie reached for the jacket, the sound went on, the jacket swung, the pocket was on the inside, she couldn't . . . and then there it was, her hand slipped in and grabbed it. The ringing stopped.

What is my phone doing in your pocket, Jake?

In the same moment she heard the sudden scrape of a chair and Jake's voice from behind the door, saying something. Hissing it. But the roaring in her ears – of things she had seen but not seen, had been told but had not heard – meant the words were lost.

The scrape of the chair, the muttered violent words – then silence.

Looking down at the phone Sukie's eyes were blurred, her hands were trembling, clumsy. She blinked. Missed call, it told her, and a list of other things, calls, messages. And then maddeningly – this always happened – it began to announce all her emails, marching down the screen one after another, *Stop it, stop it . . . wait.*

Still silence, from behind the door. Where was he? Surely she must be mistaken. Surely . . . and she saw that raw slope, littered with rusting fridges and burst open bags of rotting rubbish, she saw the sea below, cold and blue and empty. Betsy trying to warn her of something, Betsy's frightened eyes. Noises in her cellar.

And what was Jake doing now? Who had he been talking to, behind that door?

Sukie looked back at the phone, at the emails, still marching down the screen, but there'd been one – it was the subject that had caught her. Flagrant. A LinkedIn message with a subject title like that.

HE'S A RAPIST.

From the woman who'd asked to connect, she couldn't remember when it had been. Only yesterday? A woman whose name she didn't know, whose face had not been familiar, and yet. And yet.

Had he seen the email? Had he read it?

A sound and her eyes moved from the tiny screen, her glance skated over the object still in its box she'd left on the sofa underneath the crumpled mess of silk and lace that made sickness rise suddenly in her throat. A sex toy for her, placed in the bag.

The door opened and she saw him in the doorway. She saw his eyes move down to her bag and its spilled contents, the box with its horrible photograph of the plastic penis – a weapon, it looked like to her, a weapon – still closed, still sealed. She saw him smile, she saw his eyes move to the phone in her hand and he went still.

Sukie stepped back, so she was almost in the fire, she could feel it against the backs of her legs. 'I'm sorry, I . . .' In her hand her phone pulsed, it rang tinily, but she didn't look. At random she pressed, just to stop it. It stopped.

'And what do you think you're doing with that?' he said, in the easy voice of a teacher with something behind his back to hit you with, and then he was there and his hand was on her wrist.

She dropped the phone. He looked at it, face down on the floor, and at her, daring her to pick it up.

Why couldn't she move? He kicked it sideways and took something out of his pocket: a flash of blue latex, a pack of condoms. 'I got some nice pictures of you, the other night,' he said. 'Did you want to see them?'

He was pulling on the gloves, slowly, one finger at a time, peering down at them.

'Pictures?' The words was hardly a whisper. He looked up, satisfied.

'That night when you passed out, and when you woke up the next morning there I was beside you. You just can't hold your drink, can you? And I like pictures, to remember someone by. Or as a – you know – an insurance policy?'

His voice was cold and smooth, it slid and glided, dark under ice.

'What did you do to me?' Her throat closed, her body felt as if it was closing up against him, she was turned to stone.

'Oh, just playing games,' he said. 'I was saving the best till last, you see. Till your *equipment* arrived.' He nodded over at the box on the sofa.

'My . . . that's not *mine*,' she said. 'That thing – I would never—'

But he was laughing at her. 'They'll all have seen it, you know. They look on their screens, the baggage handlers, they're dirty bastards. I wanted to see *your* face, when you opened the bag.' He stuck out his lower lip, pretending to sob. 'And I would have just been all innocence. That's where the fun is, see. Watching you open your bag and see it in there. That *disgusting* thing.' He twisted his face imitating her. 'Wouldn't that have been fun?'

When she didn't answer he went on, and there was a fleck of spit at the corner of his mouth, crusted. 'Only then you had to spoil it all. No mummy and daddy to run to, you said. No friends. So who's been calling you? Missed call from Joey? Who's fucking *Joey*? Missed call from *Mummy*? And emails? Rapist? That's slander, that is. I could sue her, putting that in an email.' He was silent a moment, his mouth set.

Then he looked up. 'But up here, see, there's no one to come after you. They don't interfere, see. They know what side their bread's buttered. Elena at the shop, she didn't say anything, did she? She knows I can hurt her. Nat? Dickless old moneygrabber.'

And then she found her voice. 'What have you done with Betsy?' she said. 'What have you done with her?'

He shrugged. 'Can I help it if she's senile? Can't remember what time of day it is or where you put the rubbish out?' She stared as he admired his hands in the gloves, splaying the fingers. And then he took out the condoms. She stepped back. Betsy, she thought, Betsy, but then Betsy was gone.

'Oh, these aren't all for you, by the way,' he said, frowning down at them. 'I know you saw them. I know you wondered.

That was when I thought this was going to be fun. You think I didn't know you'd been creeping around, looking in drawers, asking questions?' He opened the pack with his teeth and there it was, dull, ugly, innocuous.

'No, they're not all for you. You do flatter yourself. No . . .' and the thing was out, the pale ring, the shrunken pinkish transparent thing, she could smell the rubber and she felt vomit rising in her throat.

'Some of them are for business, you see.' He peered down his nose at her. 'Shipping, I call it. I need a nice innocent girl to carry my product for me. And that's where the insurance policy comes in. Business mixed with pleasure, see?'

His eyes were on her face, roaming it for a reaction. She knew he wanted her to cry or beg, but she just stared. He went on.

'There are places it can go. You can swallow it, for example. Or . . .' His hand reached for her, down between her legs. His finger was hard and she felt her mouth open. 'It can go in there.'

'Pleasenoplease . . .'

Why couldn't she scream?

She felt stiff and dead as wood. She tried to pull back but there was nowhere to go. And then he was on her.

Day Three, Friday: Joey

Listening, holding the phone in clammy fingers, pleading silently in her head, Joey heard the sound of the foreign

281

ringtone, and then it stopped. There was a clatter as if it had been answered then flung or dropped.

And then she heard Sukie's voice, begging.

Chapter Thirty

Day Three, Friday: Heather

Heather tripped almost immediately on the rough cobbles. She fell in the dark and her head struck the wall, crack, above her eye. Something was happening, a wind was rising somewhere, she could hear it roaring in the trees. And as she lay with her hot cheek against dusty stone that smelled of piss, in just those few seconds of pain and disorientation it all played out in her head.

She could hear David's voice, a frightened drone, but she couldn't make out the words.

They'd come here, his parents, who knows where from. Somewhere cold and grey, from joyless places where children were ignored or hurt and grew up to drink themselves to boredom. They thought they could start again, here on the barren hillside with the great blue sea. They had children, pushing them out without care, leaving them to sleep in corners. They began to drink, they strayed, the children left alone on the hill, running barefoot, inflicting pain because it was inflicted on them, out of rage or jealousy or need.

'Heather?' She understood that word. That was her name. She could smell David. Sweat and incense and rough brandy.

'Will you come back with me, David?' she said, trying to sit up, bleary. For a minute she'd thought it was all done, they could go home. She could still feel the heat coming and going at the back of her neck, and the crack on her head made her feel dizzy.

The sound came again, it was far off, but it could have been that animal, lost, cold.

She moved, her hand touched something wrapped in paper, and she remembered. Her fingers curled around it. And then the old man was there, Nat, no more than an outline behind David but she heard his shuffling steps, his voice, high and plaintive.

'That was her,' he was saying. 'That was my Betsy, I'd know her anywhere.' He came around them, disregarding her, walking on in a strange zig-zag, bumping from side to side of the narrow street.

There was something else, another sound, but Heather didn't know if it was her ears still ringing, a sound that came and went, a warning, air-raid warning. She struggled, ungainly, knees splayed, to her feet – where was her bag? She didn't know where she'd left it. She'd come here on her own with just that and now it had gone too and she had nothing left.

There was something wet on her face and Heather

touched it, thinking it was blood, thinking, *Mum*. She almost laughed when she realised she was crying.

David's hand was under her elbow. 'You hit your head,' he said and she felt him tremble. 'Stay here,' a sudden sob in his voice, 'stay still. Can you see my fingers? How many fingers?'

She rested a second on the rough wall. 'David, it's pitch bloody dark,' she said, making herself sound reasonable. Sane. She felt him steady against her.

'Where's he gone?' she said. 'Where's Nathan gone?'

'I don't know,' said David. 'Look . . . let's get you back—'

And then they heard her. Not an old woman, not an animal moan, not far off as the last echoing cry had been, but a long low stream of pleading, *pleasenopleasenoplease* that was so familiar to Heather that it might have run in her bloodstream, the sound of that night, her back against the stones.

Above them there was a sharp burst of Greek and a window banged, a shutter, and she saw David look towards the sound, a remote gleam illuminating the flat planes of his upturned face, his pale hopeless eyes.

'He lives here, doesn't he?' she said. 'In this village. Jacob. Jake. Him. He lives here. Where?'

David said nothing; he lowered his face, hung his head. 'Up there?' she said, pointing up at the window that had banged, pinching his arm. He seemed to come round, his head lifted. 'We've got to stop him,' she said. And then, slowly, slowly, he raised his arm and pointed, along the narrow alley.

They were at a crossroads where the dark shape of a fig tree spread its last leaves like hands when it came. A woman's voice, from the other side of the tree raised in a terrible shout, loud, shockingly loud; a sound of outrage, unleashed, of horror. She roared.

NO

Day Three, Friday: Sukie

Who would hear? No one.

His elbow had gone back, swift, she hadn't recognised the movement until the last moment as the candle sputtered and flared, then his fist connected with her soft belly, unprepared, defenceless. She bent over the pain, the shocking violence of it, and she had not had breath to shout then, she was silenced as she staggered and fell back against the mantelpiece. Her eyes leaked tears as she looked up, she still couldn't breathe.

There was no one to hear, anyway, out here.

Her breath would not come back. Sukie fought for it, silently, she felt her mouth move but no air.

He seized her by her collar and pulled her against him. Sukie thought she would die of this, of suffocation, and her head pounded with the blood. 'You think I brought you here for the pleasure of your company?' he hissed in her ear.

Again her mouth moved but no sound came out. *No, I* . . .

What had she thought? Had she thought they would settle down back home with a little house with a dinner service and grass to be cut, and his little business – wholesome, inspiring, olive oil, supporting local people – bringing money in? Her head moved from side to side and he wrenched her tighter.

She couldn't stand against him, the savage violent hard force of him bearing against her, his knee between hers forcing them apart. Reaching behind her Sukie scrabbled for something, anything, her hand on the mantelpiece grabbing and then it seemed to tip and fall into her hand of its own volition and in the same moment, and in the same moment in a great rushing surge her breath returned to her, and she shouted.

NO

Day Three, Friday: Joey

It was only playing it back, long afterwards, that Joey heard the siren, in the background.

Then, she'd been too frantic. Joey had no way of knowing, then, if she'd got all of it, or enough of it. Fumbling, she'd even opened her voice memo app and tried to record it, aware all of the time that it was just a distraction, because she couldn't hang up, the microphone might not get it, she had to stay on the line. She felt Anastasia move softly in the dark, heard her own name. Anastasia was beside her, and she was listening too.

Because listening was unbearable but they had to listen. The phone clenched between her hands. Someone had to listen.

Chapter Thirty-One

Day Three, Friday: Heather

The silence glittered, hung, as if the single word had brought a shockwave with it and for a moment his face, Jake's face, was blank. And then Sukie brought the thing round and smashed it on the side of his head, the wooden sculpture, old olive wood as hard as rock, she swung it.

He staggered back and she swung it again and it connected with his nose, she saw astonishment, his hand up to his mouth to feel the blood, and then he lunged for her, she stepped back, but they collided and she was knocked off balance and then he was on her again, his hands reaching for her throat. Then he stopped. They both turned.

Because whoever was behind the door was battering it, it bulged inwards, it splintered and broke and a dusty figure fell into the room, a skinny man, a ghost in rags, and behind him in the doorway she saw a girl. The girl.

The girl whose picture had been on her email, the girl who had looked up at her in the coffee shop at the airport oh, so long ago and then had stood and turned and followed Jake as he walked away with Sukie's bag.

'You,' said Jake.

The girl had a knife in her hand.

'Me,' she said.

There were people behind her but the girl moved too fast for them, and Sukie's knees went, then. From where she fell, the smell of ash and smoke in her nostrils, she couldn't see what was happening, and then he was on the sofa.

Someone shouted her name, from outside, *Sukie!* but she stayed where she was, stayed down, she thought she must have hit her head or something, because the voice she heard was her mother's.

Day Three, Friday: Marsha

Marsha Alexander had sat bolt upright in the police car, the rude little policeman not moderating his speed, the dust in choking clouds around the car. He hadn't given Marsha a glance all the way up. If she spoke, she thought he might change his mind. She had to shout, in the end.

Bloody man. Bloody men. Malcolm at home choosing this moment to become decisive.

'Oh no, dear. Greece, at this time of year? I don't think so.'

But then Malcolm hadn't known anything about those kind of people, he'd never had friends who came back from Goa or Greece with their stories. Marsha had met Malcolm when she'd grown out of that phase, the hippy trail and the swingers' clubs she had never been very good at, too fat, too straight.

Her mouth had been open to tell him all sorts of things, but she'd just closed it again and bought her ticket and picked up her passport and left a note.

She didn't know if she was in time. Still alive though, little Sukie, stupid dear little Sukie, alive and tears streaking her cheeks, dirty with soot or something and wearing the most appalling lumpy garment and then Marsha seemed to be on the floor with her and holding her in her arms.

The policeman got in through the door last, typical. Late enough that the knife – the knife Marsha had seen as clear as day in the girl's hand, the girl who'd run in ahead of them as if she was on fire – had fallen to the ground and got kicked quickly under the sofa.

He wasn't dead. He lay on the sofa, very pale, breathing fast, but the blood was coming from his arm, not his chest.

'You'd better tourniquet that,' said Marsha over Sukie's head but no one seemed to hear. They were all shouting together, about someone called Betsy, and all the time the man on the sofa stared at them, at her and Sukie, and Marsha stared back.

And then finally the policeman got in between them, and called someone.

In Deep Water

Day Four, Saturday, early: Heather and Sukie

The two girls – women – ran abreast, in the dark.

She'd tried to explain. Sukie Alexander, struggling to her feet, while the woman whose arms had been around her there in the strange cone-shaped fireplace – the woman Heather had seen stepping haughtily off the large boat in the harbour – had stepped back, staring, as if she didn't recognise her suddenly.

She had tried to explain, to the policeman, to Nat, to David.

'He had told Betsy she needed to take the rubbish out,' darting a glance at him, on the sofa where Heather had let him fall, Jacob Littlejohn mumbling now, unintelligibly.

'I saw the bags of rubbish on her doorstep. Jake must have waited till Nat wasn't there then he took her tracking device. She was afraid of him. He took it down to the town and gave it to someone else, I saw him do that.' Perhaps the squat policeman had no English because he stared back blankly.

'So Nat wouldn't know where to look for her, so he'd go straight down to the town.' The short policeman was looking round at them all now.

But all the time her eyes had been fixed on Heather. 'Where they throw the rubbish into the sea,' Sukie said. 'That's where she's gone.' And still no one moved. David's torch was on the floor and Sukie Alexander had picked it up.

'You,' she said then, reaching out her hand. 'You. Come with me.'

And they ran.

The others far behind, they smelled the garbage dump before they got round the steep slope, slowing as they went, the hillside uncertain and friable under their feet. As the gleam of the moon came into view, they heard the sound, the same sound Heather had heard, the low animal moan but so faint now, it was almost gone. She reached for Sukie's hand.

Betsy was alive, when they found her, but very cold. Scrambling down the mountain in the tumbled garbage towards the sound, Sukie saw her first, lying flat on her back where she had fallen, staring at the moon. They lay either side of her while they waited for the helicopter ambulance to arrive from the next island, to preserve what warmth there was between them.

Epilogue

After two weeks in an induced coma, Betsy regained consciousness. Her memory wandered, unreliable, but she insisted that Jacob had told her Nathan wanted her to take the rubbish to the old dump. She didn't want to see him, she told the police. *Please*, she said, becoming so distressed they had to stop their questioning for two days. *Not Jacob*.

Nat's testimony, combined with Sukie's, Emily's and David's, examination of the books of the nail bar in Streatham and almost half a million pornographic images found on Jacob Littlejohn's various devices, led to his arrest on a list of charges including customs offences, drug smuggling and dealing, rape and child abuse. No mention was made of the knife wound to his arm that caused considerable loss of blood, despite his accusations of attempted murder and police corruption. He is in a prison on the edge of Athens, awaiting extradition.

David has not told anyone but the police what Jake Littlejohn did to him when he was six and Jake was fourteen, but he is living with Nat and Betsy, for the moment. Nathan's children in the United States do not approve, but he is making himself useful, taking Betsy for slow careful walks.

Kit and Heather have moved in together, to a rented flat in an old thirties block in the suburbs from whose balcony you can see hills and woods and a bit of a river, where they go for walks. They aren't going to get married, ever, because they don't believe in it. Or maybe they are, because maybe they do.

Joey and Sukie are taking it slowly, but they're fairly sure they're in love.

And Marsha has asked Malcolm for a divorce, because he made a stupid comment about lesbians.

Acknowledgements

This book was written in the first lockdown. Writing is not being down the mines but it is surprisingly draining, and the lack of a world to run out into hugging and chattering and spying put a lot of pressure on the home front.

So I thank first my patient kind family, my husband and children, for providing entertainment, coffee, warmth, inspiration, coffee, love, interesting conversation, thoughtfulness and coffee.

And then I thank my dear good hardworking insightful editor Darcy Nicholson, my supportive and astute agent Phil Patterson, the clockwork-smooth efficient sales and marketing teams at Sphere and as always the unfailingly fabulous Thalia Proctor.

And I thank the friends who were still there when the plague-curtain lifted, ready to dive in again.